About the author

The author was born in Newquay, Cornwall and spent his first 18 years growing up with Lusty Glaze Beach as his playground and summer season work place, whilst he hired deck chairs and later became a beach lifeguard. Having worked in London for a year as a volunteer working with the disabled, he returned to Cornwall and became a Special Constable in Newquay, and later Launceston, before finally joining the Devon and Cornwall Police as a regular officer in 1990.

Having worked the beat for a few years attending everything and anything, he later joined the Armed Response Unit dual rolled with the Traffic department. As a Sergeant, he was an Operational Firearms Commander, a Firearms Tactics Advisor, a VIP protection officer and Pursuit Tactics advisor along with investigating many a fatal road traffic collision being regarded as an expert in his field.

Harry has 10's of thousands of followers on his award-winning Police Twitter account @ex_arv_sgt and Youtube channels 'Harry Tangye' and 'Frontline Chat'

Also by Harry Tangye

#1 Best Selling autobiography, 'Firearms and Fatals' which led him to use his experiences to write this novel, gaining much of his ideas from very real events.

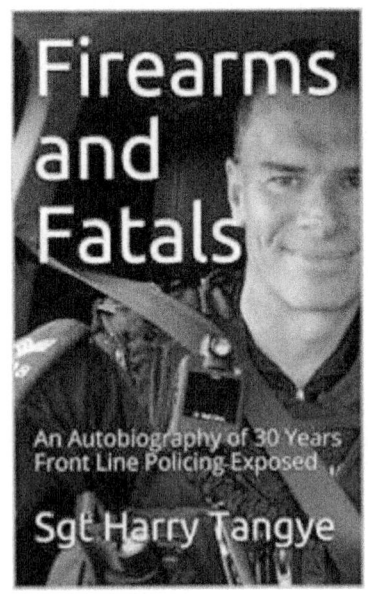

The Cornish Scoop

Based on true crime events
witnessed by former police sergeant

Harry Tangye

To 4338 Olly Tayler. My wingman

for nearly 3 decades.

ACKNOWLEDGEMENTS

Thank you to Tanja Conway-Grim for helping me out to get most of my poor grammar corrected!

... and to my brother's Gerran and Charlie for their advice and support.

CONTENTS

1. New boy in town   11
2. A taste of things to come   28
3. Porn and pasties   43
4. The saddest day   60
5. Educating the young   76
6. The storm   93
7. Where's the back-up   110
8. Ice-creams and death messages   127
9. Snogs and burglars   141
10. Car pursuits and lifeboats   156
11. Death and defendants   176
12. It's just too much   193
13. The Cornish shipwreck   213
14. Crossed wires   229
15. You're nicked   245
16. Crash, crash, crash   261

Chapter 1

New boy in town

It was late at night after a hot August weekend in 1994 and a young Police Constable, Michael Treave, Treavey to his friends, was planting the accelerator of his marked police Ford Escort to the floor. He forced the diesel engine to scream as much as it could, and threw it down the dark narrow Cornish lanes just outside the north coastal seaside town of Perranporth. Treavey was twenty metres behind the car he was pursuing, when he saw it drive up the side of the solid natural stone and earth Cornish hedge. The rear end of the little red car in front of him kicked out violently, but there was no room to spin, so it bounced its rear off the opposite hedge and rebounded once more. It then proceeded to disappear in a cloud of dust and clumps of grass from the hedge. The whirling spinning beast was now vertical, pirouetting like a drunken ballerina, the lights flashed through the earth cloud as if it were a lighthouse beam searching through a thick fog.

Treavey managed to skid the car to a halt, his mouth wide open, his eyes even wider as he watched the dust begin to settle. A part of the exhaust lay on the road immediately in front of him. He surveyed the scene through his car's headlights for what seemed like an eternity before he reached for his door handle and opened it slowly. He grabbed his heavy Maglite torch, purposefully wedged between the passenger seat and the centre console, and pulled himself out of the car.

He paused and listened in the silence, the dust in the light cast from his headlights thinning quickly and he could see the skeleton of what was a Ford Fiesta XR2 car on its roof. It had come down hard and had partially collapsed at the front leaving shattered glass like diamonds glistening in the headlights scattered across the road.

He briskly walked forward to assess the injuries of those inside, or indeed, if there was any life at all. He noticed a sweet smell. He knew what it was as he'd smelt it several times before at fatal road traffic accidents. Differential oil. It was very distinctive in its sweetness and comes from the axle of the car. He realised if he could smell it, it would have been a massive impact and had never filled his nostrils in the past without it signifying death.

This moment seemed an age from just a couple of months earlier when Treavey had joined the Policing team at Perranporth having just completed his 2-year probationary period at Newquay Police Station. Back then, he had felt like he was the new boy in school again, parked in the small car park at the rear of the station which, he thought, resembled a subsiding chicken shack on its last legs.

He was standing in his newly purchased faded jeans and plain baggy white T-shirt at the side door just about to start his first day. He had his whole career ahead of him. He was only 24 years old, which seemed far too young to take on the world's pressures on behalf of others, but he was keen to give it a go. He had been miserable in the last couple of years whilst completing his probationary period in Newquay. He had suffered the scourge of severe acne which had taken over his face and back, and which had wiped all his confidence from him with every morning he'd woken up and looked in the mirror to assess the inevitable devastation before him. He had finally relented and visited a dermatologist who cured him within a few months leaving him with no pitting, to his utter relief.

It felt like he'd been given a new lease of life. He was now quite a handsome young man which gave him certain confidence, but he was still quite nervous though excited too. He looked at the ramshackle door to the station, its wooden frame showing signs of rot and in need of replacement. He gripped his large uniform black canvas bag tightly in his right hand, his collar number, 3908, proudly emblazoned across it, daubed in 'Tipex' correction fluid.

He was a slim and healthy young man, standing with his shoulders held back and enjoying breathing in the fresh salt air deep into his lungs. He knew there was a lot expected of him, a lot of unknowns, and many adventures ahead, good and bad. He wondered how he was going to cope; indeed, would he be able to cope without the backing of a larger station with all his experienced friends and colleagues behind him? Was he going to be exposed for the fraud he'd often felt himself to be?

He slipped his silver fob through the security sensor and pulled the door open with a noisy judder, and stepped forward as if unsure whether he should knock and wait, or just walk straight on in. This was his police station now, although he was currently a stranger to it. How he introduced himself to his new colleagues would be everything. He knew they would be looking him up and down taking instant impressions of him, and he knew he would be making similar decisions about them. He walked past a room labelled the 'Sgt's Office' on his left, and just

13

as he was stepping towards the door of the main report room, and taking a deep breath, his momentum was disturbed by someone striding through the door towards him.

"Hello!", came the soft, melodic but confident, voice from a very tall, and somewhat thick-set, chap with dark thinning hair and a bushy moustache. The latter seemed to make up for the lack of hair elsewhere. He was in his forties and looked quite a sensible chap on first impressions and he was incredibly well-spoken.

"Nearly knocked into you there, sorry, who are you? Are you the new addition?".

"Yes, I am," replied Treavey with a row of white pearly teeth under a mop of blond hair, rather relieved at being thrown into the introduction without having time to become even more nervous. This chap seemed pretty friendly too.

"Good, well, I'm Micky, PC Mick Lenin to those I arrest! I wasn't about to do anything special, so I'll introduce you to the others; most of them are in there. Sorry, I have no idea who I'm going to be introducing." He laughed, presenting a broad, friendly smile. Treavey was already feeling a lot more comfortable.

"Treavey, Michael Treave to those I arrest!" Treavey replied without hesitation, already feeling more confident with his new colleague. He was beginning to realise cops were cops wherever you went.

"Let's hope there'll be quite a few who hear that name, hey Treavey?" Micky retorted with a friendly wink under a dark bushy eyebrow, whilst turning to lead him into the main report room.

Treavey could see it was a small, rather prefab-looking station. A single-storey building put up at minimal expense. He was less concerned about the quality of the building he was going to be working in, rather more about the type of person he was going to be working with.

Several officers were sitting around some tables pushed together to form an island, completing paperwork and chatting amongst themselves. The wall behind the officers hid them from the front door for the public and the counter. He assumed the toilet must have been the door opposite or perhaps it was the kitchen?

"Listen up", snapped Micky, announcing to the room, "This is our new member Micheal Treave, otherwise known as Treavey."

"Hi everyone!", proclaimed Treavey, dropping his bag on the floor and confidently, making his way towards the table, still not feeling entirely comfortable about sitting down yet.

"Hi, Treavey", came the reply from all around with various levels of interest. Micky began to introduce the characters around the table one by one.

There was PC Greg Baddock, known as 'Bomber'. He was a stocky man in his early fifties, thick-set, with a rather gravelly voice and he wore a well-groomed short white beard and had a doorman style shaved head. He had a swagger about him as if he had been there and had seen it all.

Treavey felt there was a certain Cornish Pirate theme going on in this section, in particular with Micky and Bomber. A feeling emphasised even more, as he was sure he could detect the hole for an ear stud in each man's left ear.

The next man was Peter Gordon, known as 'Gordy'. A red-haired chap, with an unsurprising milky complexion and with a muscular frame reflecting the time he'd, quite obviously, spent in the gym. He gave a formal and monotoned; "Hello PC Treave", and promptly looked back down on the desk to continue with a rather dense file he was working on. He wasn't showing himself to be much of a significant character at this stage, but Treavey would work on him.

Micky guided the attention on to a ray of sunshine at the other end of the table who Micky was introducing as if she were the 'pièce de resistance'. A tall, slim woman, who got up from her seat on her introduction and with a wonderful smile, introduced herself as Felicity. Her blond hair was tied up in some sort of fashion, but much of it spilt out of the very bun it was supposed to be captured within. She giggled, giving the impression to Treavey she was just as nervous as him. He watched her right hand lower onto the desk and unconsciously play with the paperwork she'd been working on, all the time looking straight at him and smiling awkwardly as if she were a member of the girls' hockey team meeting the handsome football captain for the first time.

Having started to appreciate his rather rustic surroundings, and wishing to break the ice further, Treavey enquired half-jokingly, "Is there a station cat then?".

There was a slight pause before Gordy replied in his rather deep, masculine voice; "Well yes and no mate, but we sort of adopted the neighbour's cat. He's called Wolfy and he visits regularly. He tends to know the shift meal times pretty well to come in for food." He paused, shuffling his stocky body rather uncomfortably, feeling perhaps he had given a little too much away about his feelings towards Wolfy, and clearly wishing to preserve the impression of his rather hard exterior.

A silence descended on the room, so Felicity took over the awkwardness with; "Fancy a cup of tea, Treavey? We are about ready for one, aren't we boys, it's been about 10 minutes now". Treavey could see she was a kind person, willing everyone to get on together and to fit in. She was very much the attractive yet also mother-like figure, a character who was always so badly needed in any station to cut through the brash macho atmosphere with a bit of warmth and tenderness.

"Love one," Treavey replied, already happy he seemed to have made an ally. He'd get to know the others later, but for now, having initially hesitated, he followed Felicity into what he had initially thought had been the toilet. "That must have been the room near the back door then," he thought to himself, trying to get his bearings.

The standard kitchen laid before him with a concoction of mugs and cups, most with dark tea stains and personal designs, which he suspected belonged to officers from past times. The discussions those mugs must have heard. He noticed the obligatory 'Wash up your own mugs' sign which was in every force kitchen. He'd noticed on his visits to stations that many of these notices have different tones and some were written with threats and comments such as, 'Your mother isn't here, so wash your mugs up', but the one on this wall displayed some imagination. It had a silver milk bottle top stuck to a piece of cardboard on the wall with the words; '*To turn dishwasher on, press button for 3 seconds. If machine fails to start, please wash by hand.*'

They returned for a chat around the table. Treavey wanted to get a flavour of the place. He scanned the mug shots of the local miscreants on the wall and took in a few names; names no doubt he would get to know very well in the near future.

The conversation turned to the town. Perranporth was a bustling summer holiday destination that sported a large, sprawling beach with golden sands and wispy dunes to which holidaymakers flocked to from all over the country. It was a place where young families could make sandcastles, swim or learn to surf in the warm crystal clear turquoise Atlantic waters, fed by the heat of the Gulf Stream lazily meandering up from the far south. When the sun cooled down near the end of the day, they would head back on foot up the sandy paths to their static caravans where they could enjoy a refreshingly cool dip in the campsite pool. Then finally, after a quick shower, they would set off smartly dressed for their evening meal and a night's entertainment.

It was the most picturesque place where one wouldn't expect to see very much crime, and people often made the mistake of dropping their guard completely, which was how the Perranporth officers were kept busy. He was worried he may be a bit bored, but having worked in Newquay for two years, he knew the summer seasons were particularly busy. Time would tell. By the looks of the number of files on the table, the officers were working on, however, Treavey suspected he wouldn't be short of work.

He sipped some more tea and shuffled in his seat to make himself more comfortable. He felt himself settling into his new environment. He would enjoy a trip around the area later, hopefully with Felicity, but he was not too bothered, to be honest. There would be plenty of time to crew up with everyone in the next couple of years. Eventually, he would move on to a larger, more exciting place; maybe Plymouth, Torquay, or even Exeter.

"You will need to fill in the details of any of your private vehicles you come to work in, so we can get a pass for you to park in the police station car park." Bomber suggested, helpfully. He seemed to be a man of some experience. His slightly unkempt white beard showed he probably set his own rules. Treavey had the impression he'd stopped jumping through hoops to please, many years ago.

"Right okay, I can do that now." Treavey jumped up and walked over to join Bomber who was selecting a rather old tatty, covered index book from the shelf. He opened it and inside it was a long list of names scribbled in biro with vehicle types and registration numbers next to them. Bomber ran his finger down the list and paused by his name. He had a few vehicles down there, about five, but one stood out in particular.

"Goodness!", Treavey exclaimed in admiration, "A Rolls Royce. Nice car!"

There was a snigger from the rest of the room, a slight pause followed by Gordy retorting, "Well nobody's seen it, but he drives to work in a crappy Ford Escort"

They chortled amongst themselves and a rather embarrassed Bomber attempted to recover some credibility with, "I'll have you know it's my brother's car and I may well have to borrow it one day."

Treavey noticed Bomber's colleagues had chosen not to ridicule him any further. He could see they had overall respect for Bomber, even though they recognised he was a flawed character.

A bell sounded and Micky got up from the table and sauntered over to the public front desk at the far side of the room. Treavey could hear what was being said, but couldn't see who'd come to the station because of the dividing wall, and this offered the opportunity to eavesdrop on the conversation.

"Good morning sir, how may I be of assistance on this fine and beautiful day?", Micky had some style about him with his calm dulcet tones. The other officers in the room pricked their ears up, but when they realised it was someone coming in to produce their driving documents, they immediately lost interest.

A week passed and Treavey felt he'd settled in quite quickly. He'd introduced himself to the local scallywags driving around like idiots in their cars, with the odd loud exhaust and running the usual timed circuits around the town. It was June and things were warming up nicely with holidaymakers. "This place was going to be a wonderful place to work," Treavey thought to himself. "Lucky me."

A few days later, he'd crewed up with someone who had been on leave until recently, so Treavey hadn't got to know him yet. This shift would be a good way for them to get to know each other. His name was Ken Ford, but the section fondly knew him as 'Rambo'.

"I'll form my own opinions about him," Treavey thought to himself. The others had been hinting he was a little bit of a loose cannon, was slightly crazy and had a love interest somewhere in St Agnes, the next little village south along the coast. No one quite knew who it was, but he would quite often disappear for a couple of hours at a time. There was a suspicion he was suffering a bit of stress, but there was nothing anyone could say to him without fearing a sharp response.

Treavey sat in the front passenger seat, and observed Rambo's rather gaunt figure climbing in behind the wheel of the Panda car. He flicked his rather long, scraggly, auburn hair to the side as he reached for the seatbelt over his shoulder. Treavey noticed Rambo hadn't had a shave for a couple of days and his greying stubble was glistening like dew on his, otherwise, sallow cheeks.

As Rambo drove Treavey around the town and the outlying areas, Rambo began chatting about his suspicions on the problem of drugs within the town.

Perranporth police had been attending a lot of deaths by overdose recently. More so than other towns, so they'd been trying to figure it out. It was like class A drugs were too easily available in the town or were cheap enough to buy a lot of it. No one really knew but they did know there had been a lot of deaths. All of a sudden, this little seaside town had a more sinister background to it.

"I reckon they are being given cheap drugs to keep quiet," Rambo proclaimed with some confidence.

"Something is going on in this town and we need to find out what it is. People don't just get cheap drugs in a localised area for nothing. They get greedy of course, and more addicted. Win, win."

"Golf 31!", the atmosphere was suddenly broken.

"Who's that?" Treavey asked Bomber. "Jesus, that's us!", Treavey realised and scrabbled for the radio handset sitting in the cradle attached to the side of the passenger footwell.

The controller came on again, "Golf 31, thank you, can you make your way to 23 Sandway Close, Perranporth where the caller is reporting a liquid coming through her ceiling and she thinks it's rather suspicious?".

Treavey and Rambo were making their way through the streets, not too fast because it wasn't exactly life-threatening but what was this liquid and how much of it was coming through the ceiling and why was it pouring through the ceiling? What had happened above? Not exactly the crime of the century or any crime at all. Was it always going to be like this?

The officers arrived within five minutes and walked up the path towards several flats, and they soon located number 23. The door was opened by a rather dumpy woman in her 60's. Her uncontrolled hair was barely contained in a particularly dirty looking hair net.

"Hello, Mrs Regent is it? What's the problem exactly?" Treavey enquired politely. Thirty seconds of verbal onslaught was the unexpected response.

"Where have you been? I called you half an hour ago. What do you think I pay my taxes for? I've been waiting here for ages and you two can't be bothered to do your jobs. You police are bloody useless."

The three walked into a sparsely furnished flat on the ground level and the two officers gazed around the worn and dirty furnishings, Treavey concluded she'd probably not been paying any tax for some time contrary to what her accusation had implied.

"It's been pouring through the ceiling and I don't know what to do."

The officers paced quickly behind the lady to get to the source of the problem and hopefully, the probable cause. Once in the lounge, they scanned the location wondering why they had stopped. Time was of the essence surely.

"Quickly now, Mrs Regent, where is it?", Treavey requested expectantly.

The rather short and rotund lady was dressed in, what looked, the same item of black stretchy clothing she had been wearing daily for a considerable period of time. It had, unfortunately, become rather transparent with age, along with sporting a tie-dye of stains. She looked up, squinting slightly, pointing to the ceiling.

All three were now looking at the tiniest of drips of innocent-looking water coming from the ceiling making the carpet a little damp perhaps, but not quite the body fluids from a rotting corpse Treavey and Rambo had been suspecting, but not admitting to each other.

Rambo took charge, and walking over to Mrs Regent's front window, said,

"Madam, would you like to come to the window here, I want to show you something."

"Yes, why, what do you want?" She looked annoyed but wandered over to join Rambo who was now gazing outside towards the police car parked on the road outside. They both strained their eyes to look outside.

"Yes?" The lady inquired impatiently.

Treavey was rather confused too, and impatient to see what Rambo had up his sleeve. He looked a little annoyed to say the very least.

"You see that car over there?" He asked Mrs Regent,

"Yes, that's your police car, I see it."

"Okay, that's good, and can you see what it says on the side of that car?"

"Yes, of course, it says Police," Mrs Regent could see that perhaps she had walked herself into a trap, as Treavey certainly felt she had too.

"Well Mrs Regent, you will notice it says Police... not PLUMBER!" Rambo spun around on his heels and briskly walked straight past Treavey, not even waiting for a reply and out of the front door, and, Treavey, having given a last slightly embarrassed glance towards Mrs Regent, who was now standing at the window with her jaw on the floor, followed Rambo. Halfway down the path, he wondered whether he would be able to get to the car before bursting into laughter. Yes, Rambo was eccentric, but a lot of fun too.

Just five minutes later, Rambo and Treavey were patrolling along the coastline between Perranporth and St Agnes, past the old Airfield on the edge of the cliff which used to have Spitfires stationed in the Second World War, and into the quaint village of St Agnes. Having negotiated the panda car around the delicate little lanes along the coast they eventually arrived at Chapel Porth Beach, and further south onto Porthtowan, another popular beach along the stunning rugged coastline.

Treavey was astonished by the beauty of the place. Even the main roads were stunningly beautiful on this summer's day. He opened the window to smell the hedgerows and freshly mown grass from the roadside. The heads of buttercups and daisies bobbed in the turbulence from the cars passing by, and hungry little birds darted about, filling their beaks with the plentiful insects available.

The two officers chatted about nothing in particular. It wasn't the time in their relationship for Treavey to delve into the private life of Rambo. Perhaps that would come later. They wound their way through the narrow green country lanes and back onto the main road for a quick return to base to have a tea break.

The panda car eventually wound its way down the steep hill back in towards Perranporth. They slowed as they came up behind holiday traffic. These were cars full of families, excited for their upcoming beach holiday and their stay on the local campsites. Everyone would have already forgotten their stresses and concerns in their everyday lives back home.

Perranporth had everything you needed for a wonderfully relaxing holiday, with family time in buckets, as long as it didn't rain for too many days in a row, of course.

Rambo stopped the car near a small junction at the bottom of the hill, which led down to some houses adjacent to the Caravan park.

"Down there," Rambo said in a stern voice and lowered tones as if saying something which shouldn't be overheard. "Down there is where Gary Dawson lives. He's into it up to his eyeballs. Drugs. Lots of it but no one knows how he gets it here. We've searched his cars, his house, we've done everything. We'll get him one day. The word is that he's the main supplier for the drugs in this town and surrounding area and loads of people are dying through overdoses because of him."

The two officers continued on the main road towards the beach, and they approached a pub called the 'Come On Inn'.

Bomber commented, "You'll be coming here quite often. Many a pub fight in there when the sun and the alcohol do its magic, but to be honest more so when the young yobs from the town get drunk and bored."

"Golf 31", blurted out on the radio.

Treavey was straight on to it this time, grabbing the receiver and replying, "Go ahead."

"Golf 31, can you attend a sudden death of a male at Flat 3, number 45 Merrybrook, Perranporth. The landlord has just found the body of his tenant in the flat."

"There's another one." Rambo retorted. They made their way to the location and met the landlord at the front door. He took them one floor up through a rather pungent stale stink through the communal stairway until they reached the flat concerned where the door had been left ajar.

Rambo asked the landlord to wait behind with Treavey at the front door; "No offence Treavey, but the less cross-contamination the better, you know, just in case."

The instructions from those rather boring training courses came flooding back to Treavey. He realised Rambo was bang on and they would get brownie points when CID arrived. A couple of paramedics, who had arrived before them, left the scene shortly afterwards, having found nothing for them to do.

A couple of moments later, Rambo returned and said in a rather sombre voice, "Yes, looks like another overdose I'm afraid. Needles and paraphernalia." He looked at the landlord, "We'll need some details off you. How old was he?"

"Twenty-one." Replied the landlord. Treavey took a momentary pause and thought about the gravity of the situation.

"Twenty-one, blimey," he thought to himself. "That's crazy. In little Perranporth too. Here's something to get our teeth into."

He got on the radio. "Victor, we suspect death caused by accidental overdose, no suicide note, can you confirm CID is en route?"

CID soon arrived from Newquay, and indeed, they were impressed that only Rambo had walked into the flat, minimising the forensic cross-contamination. The less DNA, the fewer footprints, fibres or fingerprints in the flat the better, even though it was clearly an overdose, it still needed confirming it wasn't set up to look like that. Or had someone injected him with the drug with no intention of killing him? That would have meant serious offences for the person involved too.

The issue here was that this was the 15th overdose this year in the area and there just didn't seem rhyme nor reason for it. Treavey realised Rambo was a wise officer, with a no-nonsense approach but professional, and he seemed to have a genuine interest in policing and was motivated to do his best to solve the crime in the area. In other words, a good person to be around.

Both officers made their way back to the station in the panda. As Rambo turned in up the narrow driveway towards the rear car park, he turned to glance at Treavey.

"I know what they say about me, Treavey. Yeah, I may disappear off sometimes, but where I go on my lunch break is up to me. It's my business and not theirs in there. I'll kick you out here as I want to go and see someone now, no offence."

Treavey didn't feel impressed. He didn't want to say it, as they had got on so well on their first day, but where he went in a police car in his lunch hour and how available he was, was very much the business of those officers 'in there'.

He walked into the station which he found to be empty. The door clanged shut behind him. He sat down at the large table and stared into the distance. He planned to have a good chat with CID in the next couple of days, just to see what they had on the drugs deaths in the town. Something needed to be done about that and fast. Rambo's personal issues could wait.

Chapter 2

A taste of things to come

Treavey was settling in now. A couple of weeks had gone by and it was already well into July. It was a night turn which meant he was on his own for the shift. He had the backup of nearby Newquay, some nine miles away, where there was a section of approximately eight officers to assist him if needed, but it would take time for them to travel to help him if he should need it. It was still, very much, a sobering thought for Treavey to know he was so alone.

He knew the local oiks were aware he was working alone, but they also knew that Treavey could identify each and every one of them.

It was 10.00 pm and Treavey waved off the last two late turns, Felicity and Gordy.

"Straight home now!" Treavey quipped as they left the parade room to go home, "Night Felicity, night Gordy!"

His cheesy grin showed he was confident in his domain, and now wondering what would come his way during the night shift. It was something the Met wouldn't understand.

"Single crewed? No chance," Treavey thought to himself. "They may have had the jobs, but they also would have had the backup."

There was a bit of a nip in the air that night, so Treavey was wearing his woollen blue knitted NATO jumper over his crisp white shirt with clip-on black tie. He had his black leather gloves in his back pocket with the fingers hanging over and he grabbed his six-cell Maglite torch to put in the car with him. He added the bag of paperwork he may need during the evening.

His Magnum heavy boots were gleaming on the toe cap. It was important to look the part. He was keen to find how these drugs had been getting into Perranporth so if it was a quiet night, he'd have a little dig around and check some vehicles passing through. You never knew what that might flush out.

Having had a good chat with CID in Newquay, he knew it wasn't an extra pure batch of drugs which was the problem. Yet someone was bringing in heroin by the bucket load, and people were dying because of it. They must have had it at a special rate, surely. Maybe to keep them quiet? More reason for them to keep it quiet and to not dob the supplier in.

The first call for Treavey was not very exciting.

"Can you go to an address in Perrancoombe and inform the women there her ninety-five-year-old uncle has died in Kent in his care home? They can't get hold of her."

Details were passed on and Treavey duly made his way to the edge of Perranporth which had a line of rather upmarket houses running up through the valley.

"This shouldn't be too bad," he thought. "I mean it was hardly a sudden death, was it? He's taken 95 years to die for Christ's sake. Why do they still call it a sudden death? It was not going to be a shock for her, she should be okay about it with luck."

Five minutes later, Treavey pulled up outside the address. The street lights were still on, so he left his torch in the car. He walked up to the detached house which had a rather neat front garden. He paused to ensure he had all the details; the name of the house owner, the uncle's name, the name of the care home and the phone number for her to ring to find out more information for herself and to make the arrangements. He didn't want to look ill-prepared.

"Ding Dong!" sounded the door chime and after a considerable wait, there was no answer. "Ding Dong!" the door chime went again, and still nothing happened.

In frustration, Treavey bent down and opened the flap of the letterbox to get a look inside the hallway to see if there was any sign of life. At this exact point, the light was switched on and he momentarily saw a woman in her late 60's approaching the door.

He jumped back and almost fell over backwards in the process. It was not quite accurate to say he saw the woman, but he had seen part of the woman, who just one minute earlier, had been stark naked in bed and had just been in the process of wrapping her dressing gown around herself.

This wouldn't have been a problem either, but for the fact the dressing gown had not been fully closed at the time of the light switch being turned on. She, no doubt, didn't expect a police officer to be looking through the letter box at the time, so Treavey got full sight of her pubic area, with a rather generous amount of busy, grey pubic hair moving towards him; not two foot away from his horrified face.

At the time the door opened, Treavey had had about 3 seconds to stand himself up, compose himself and try an attempt at a normal conversation with a woman who may or may not be aware he had just seen the most intimate part of her body. In any case, he quickly decided he was just going to try to forget what he'd just seen, but it kept flashing into his mind as the woman stood before him in her dressing gown with a puzzled and rather concerned expression on her face.

The message was passed and Treavey made a getaway as quickly as he could. He was going to grab a bite to eat, but perhaps he'd leave it for a little while longer now.

He decided to drive back into Perranporth again, just a mile away.

"Let's see what the pubs are doing," he wondered. Something to help the night go faster with luck. He drove slowly past the 'Come On Inn' and saw it was looking busy. He noticed a couple of the usual local teenagers hanging around the front. They could get into mischief and liked to bait the police a little just to pass the time, so Treavey was very keen not to get drawn into that game. He slowly cruised past the group who turned and looked at him, noticing his presence, but no comment was made.

He drove on to take a look down the road which Rambo had pointed out to him earlier where Gary Dawson, the Perran chief scrote lived. He drove out of the town slightly and turned left into it.

"Might as well have a good look. You never know," he thought to himself. "Sometimes we give these criminals far too much credit."

As he made his way down the side road, he realised it was a bit more populated than he'd expected. It was a small estate made up of approximately 20 very small and rather run-down houses. He continued down the row until he found the address of Dawson, the notorious drug dealer.

His house was showing off a brand-new white UPVC door, clearly from the last warrant which had destroyed it. He scanned the house, mid-terraced with an unkempt front garden.

"Why is it that these dealers still live in such grotty houses?" Treavey pondered before he slowly drove towards the rear of the house to find a better view, but found no clear view of it apart from a narrow alleyway too small to get a car down.

He was turning the panda car around when he received a call.

"Fight outside the 'Come On Inn', can you attend Golf 31? We have other units coming from Newquay to back up."

Treavey put his blue light on, a single rotating dome light which always gave him an adrenaline surge, and he quickly made for the pub, although he was wondering what he was going to do when he got there.

"Let's hope they've finished, otherwise it could get messy for me," he pondered as he threw the Escort panda along the road leading into town towards the pub.

He immediately saw a melee in the distance as he approached, which spilt out onto the street. There were a couple of scuffles going on in different areas and others were standing back watching.

On his approach, taking it all in, he had an idea. There was a big space in the middle of the group; he'd been practising in the country lanes and car parks during night shifts, so should he make an entrance here? After all, it would probably stop the fights enough for him to gain the upper hand. His youthful exuberance got the better of him and as he approached the clear area within the group, he gently rocked the car by the steering wheel and pulled hard on the handbrake as the steering was thrown to one side. The car responded by slewing to the right in the centre of the disturbance and rotated on the spot almost one hundred and eighty degrees.

The screeching sound of the tyres on the tarmac surface seemed a lot louder than he remembered it would do. When Treavey had a moment's pause, he opened the door and got out, feeling as if he was a cowboy in a Clint Eastwood film who'd just jumped off his horse.

"Now that was an entrance," he muttered, feeling very proud of himself. He glanced around at, what had been, scrapping groups of youths, but who were now standing around transfixed for a second, not quite believing what they had just seen, and Treavey suspected, were ever so slightly impressed.

Treavey was blessed with a loud voice and used it to good effect even though he was of only a medium stature.

"Right gentlemen, I hope you have had your fun for the night. I suspect it is now time to go home unless you wish me to call the van from Newquay."

The audience began to vanish into the darkness, except for one, who seemed to be with some of the more active members of the group. He was extremely tall and gaunt. His fingers seemed to go on forever, thin and spider-like, crawling out of his grey hoodie sleeves. His red hair, of which he seemed very proud, and certainly wasn't going to hide it within the hood, was displayed in full splendour in a ponytail which fell between his shoulder blades.

He sauntered over to Treavey, trying to ensure he gave the impression of not being in the least bit impressed with the officer's grand entrance. Both men faced each other for a moment, until the lad broke the silence between them.

"Who are you then? You from Newquay?" It was clear he was sussing out the opposition.

Treavey replied in a calm and controlled tone.

"I'm new to the area, so I have the pleasure of looking after you locals."

The man paused, and seemed to be taking in what was standing before him, then smirked as he turned to walk away, "We don't need no looking after copper!" he said.

"What's the name?" Treavey shouted after him.

The lad ignored him pretending he hadn't heard, but an idea suddenly came to Treavey.

"Victor, can you give a description of Gary Dawson, please. No offences here but I just need to confirm whether he was here amongst it all."

The reply came back quickly from the female operator,

"He's white European, 21 years old and of a very skinny build. He's 6'4" tall and has a very long ginger ponytail. He drives a white Suzuki Vitara with fat tyres, do you want details, Oscar 31?"

Treavey wanted to have a bit of fun because this was probably going to be the last job he got that night, so he asked, "No, don't worry about the registration Victor, but was there anything distinctive about him?"

There was a momentary pause and then, "No, that's all we've got."

The joke of this man, clearly being one of the most distinctive descriptions, had gone over the head of the operator, but Treavey was happy anyway. He'd now met Dawson and he had the measure of him, and Dawson had decided not to take him on in front of his own friends, probably in case he had been made to look stupid by Treavey. It had been a good start, but Treavey knew he couldn't afford to drop his guard.

It was nearly midnight and the town was reasonably quiet. Any holiday makers were either in bed, tired from looking after their small children on the beach all day, or were enjoying the campsite entertainment put on for them until the late hours. Things had quietened down and Treavey found himself patrolling around empty roads, with the odd shadow of a fox, or a cat, scuttling away through a hedge or over a garden wall.

He eventually found himself turning his panda car onto the beach car park to see how clear the view may be that late at night. He switched his engine off and paused, listening for a moment.

He swung the door open and stepped out of the car with his heavy Magnum boots crunching on the soft sand carried up on the on-shore winds which swirled around the dunes before depositing their gift on the car park and nearby roads.

He jumped onto the beach from the carpark, landing with both feet together before stumbling forward slightly to regain his balance. He strolled across the soft sand which had the consistency of deep snow crunching under his feet. The smell of the day's beach of family fun was still in the air. He could still smell the sun lotion, the salt from the sea lapping the shore and he could feel the warmth from the baked sand absorbed from the day, slowly being released into the night.

He paused a moment listening to the gentle waves building up, releasing their energy as they built into a peak before gently collapsing into a white foam which rolled onto the wet sand where they descended into nothingness.

There was no energy in the waves tonight, they just gently caressed the shoreline as if coming in for a rest. The moon had lit up the area, bathing it in a warm light, making every detail of the cliffs visible. He could see the outlines of white sea birds along the rocks speckled in the blackness, their bodies nestled in for the night, their heads tucked into their inflated feathery duvets. A storm shouldn't wake them up tonight.

How different this place was at night compared to day time. The noise and excitement were now long forgotten like ghosts from a past time. The screams of excitement were replaced with a gentle breeze and the rhythmic ripples of water on the sand. Treavey knew how lucky he was. It was a beautiful place many spent their annual savings to come to every year, yet he was able to work in the same environment, and he was fortunate enough to live in nearby Newquay where he had a decent nightlife with everything he could possibly need.

"The girls aren't bad either!" He reminded himself as he chuckled at his good fortune, remembering the absolute determination to get where he was today, with the initial police application, the failures and further attempts, the interviews and the training. But he was happy, very happy. "Well done Treavey," he said to himself. "Well done indeed mate, you did it."

On the following night shift, Treavey had been fortunate enough to be crewed with Felicity. It had felt so much better being double crewed for a night shift as naturally many topics would come up and the night would go a lot quicker, especially if it was a quiet shift. It soon became clear that even though Felicity gave the impression of being a bit ditsy, he was surprised to hear she had been an ex-Met Police officer and had transferred down to Devon and Cornwall because of her family who lived in the area.

"What's the scariest thing you experienced in London, Felicity?" Treavey enquired.

He suddenly felt rather a long way down the pecking order of experience in both a professional aspect and life in general.

"I remember searching a house for drugs once in a warrant, and when I went into the bedroom, I opened a wardrobe and a body fell out of it. That was pretty unexpected and, I admit, scared the shit out of me," she replied.

Treavey turned his head sharply towards Felicity, "Way, what, say that again? Are you saying there was a murdered body hidden in the wardrobe?"

"Exactly that…", replied Felicity, "…and it pretty much just fell out on top of me."

There were so many questions to ask her, but because there were so many, Treavey found he couldn't decide which one to ask first. So there was just silence instead.

During the previous week of shifts, and having worked on his own, he had been patrolling around the area a lot to get to know the patrol area, the roads, and lanes which linked each area. Building up this local knowledge would be especially useful in any pursuit and, for him, becoming more familiar with the hamlets and villages nestling along the coast, was a priority.

He always hoped for pursuit of course, which would be made much easier if he knew where he was. If you couldn't orient yourself then each green country lane looked very much like any other, and the control room could only do so much for you. And if they didn't know where you were, there would be little that could be done. The helicopter was stationed at Exeter so it would be 40 minutes before it was on scene to help in any way. He had been pleased to get the latest model of patrol car, the Ford Escort, which had updated rounded styling in contrast to the previously dated square-edged Escorts. It was diesel, but it was a good car, and when he practised his hand brake turns in it, it spun on a penny and he got very proficient at it. He was now turning it in lanes which were only just big enough to spin the car around in. It made for a quicker turnaround to go after cars or attend jobs, but he always made sure there were no witnesses when he practised.

During one of these patrols, Treavey's foot had caught a lever in the footwell under the dashboard. He noticed it was moveable by either pushing it with the toe of his left boot or pulling it back up with the top of his boot and as a direct result, the heater dial on the dashboard would move around from red to blue and back again. Driving with Felicity in the car next to him, he had an idea.

Treavey nonchalantly declared, "Heater hot" and he pulled the lever up and the dial moved around from cold to hot. He said nothing further. The fishing line had been cast and there was now a pause.

Felicity remained silent for a second or two and then replied, "What was that, what did you do then?"

"Oh," replied Treavey without a second thought, "Did you not know the heater in this new model car is voice-activated?"

There was now a short period of time when Treavey wondered whether the fish had been caught on the end of his hook, or whether it was going to break free. So just to ensure it was well and truly biting, he repeated, "Heater cool." He pushed the lever down with his foot and the dial swung around to the opposite side to a comfortable compromise between hot and cold.

"Wow, that's incredible!" shouted Felicity and the next couple of minutes were spent with Treavey matching the vocal demands of Felicity by moving the dial accordingly. It was one of the many tricks to make the night pass.

Once the initial novelty with regards this new supposed technology had worn off somewhat, Treavey pulled up so they could look at the view of the moonlight shimmering on the sea below from their clifftop vantage point. There was a lone ship in the distance making its way with its cargo which looked like a piece of dirt on the windscreen. Nothing else was moving.

He thoughtfully glanced across to Felicity, "Tell me about Dawson. What's he up to, Felicity?"

She was knocked out of her relaxed trance, and it took a couple of seconds for her to take in the question fully.

"Oh, well, he's up to no good but no one knows how he's doing it at the moment. We think he gets hold of the main supply of drugs down here in Perranporth. He has a very loyal close-knit group of people around here, so it's hard to get any information from them. CID have done jobs on him, fishing exercises really, managing to get a warrant a couple of times but they've never found anything in his house or his car apart from a bit of personal use. I'm not really sure how the drugs are getting in but there's definitely a network where it is feeding from Perran, and we think he's supplying cocaine and heroin to his loyal workers to keep their silence. A way to guarantee their loyalty, I guess, which is why we have had so many drug overdoses. Sixteen since the year began, which is unheard of really. Thing is, they don't turn up on the crime figures and strangely enough, the crime figures may even go down around here this year because those involved in petty crime are dropping like flies."

They both watched a light aircraft breaking their line of sight, its green navigation lights flashing as it made its way north up the coast.

"Lucky sods," remarked Treavey, "Wouldn't you love to have that freedom and what this place must look like from the air on a night as clear as tonight. Maybe one day, eh Felicity? Just imagine there are cops having fridge freezers dropped on them off blocks of flats in Toxteth and we get to work in a place like this and look at views like that."

They both sat there in silence for a few moments watching the plane disappear, before the diesel clattered back into life and they made their way back towards the town of Perran once more.

As the panda car drove through the lanes, they saw headlights approaching them. It was 3.00 am now so it was a little unusual to see people about, but often you would get someone on shift-work either going to or coming back from work.

Treavey slowed the panda car and allowed the approaching headlights to pass at a slow speed, pulling in his door mirror ensuring it didn't get clipped by the oncoming vehicle. That would be far too much paperwork if that got broken. They could see it was a four-by-four car of sorts as the headlights were high, and then they saw him. Both Felicity and Treavey shouted, "It's Dawson!"

The white Suzuki Vitara sped away from them in the opposite direction.

Treavey hesitated, "Shit!" he shouted as he realised, he was facing in completely the wrong direction and had nowhere to turn the car around to give chase. He floored the accelerator hoping to find a gateway or junction to turn around in, but it was no good. He approached a part of the road which widened slightly and thought, "This is where I see if my practising has paid off. Can I do it under pressure?"

He pointed the car slightly towards the near side, then threw the steering to the right and yanked on the handbrake. The panda car slewed around perfectly, Treavey held his breath to see if the back end cleared the hedge which it successfully did. The car was now firmly pointing in the direction of where Dawson had gone. He floored the accelerator and with front wheels spinning, they began to hunt their quarry.

Felicity was recovering in the passenger seat, "Shit Treavey, what just happened there?!"

She didn't expect an answer, the diesel engine was straining to reach the next gear as Treavey's eyes were locked onto the road ahead, desperately waiting for the rear lights of a car in front to appear. "Come on, where is he?"

He drove as fast as he could until he reached the outskirts of Perran. "Remember the rules of pursuit," he thought to himself, "Left and left again."

It was highly likely when someone being pursued wanted to find a way to get away if they turned right, there was more time for the officer to see the offside of the car across the road, however, the overriding urge was to turn left. If they turned left, they were soon gone from sight, exposing themselves for far less period of time. If they turned left again at the next junction, they'd think this adds to their chances of getting away further, unless the pursuer was already aware of this human behaviour, of course.

So, as he approached the next junction Treavey turned left, and then turned the next available left again, into a cul-de-sac. He scanned his eyes around but he found nothing. "Damned!" He says in frustration. It did not pay off this time.

"What the fuck was he doing out and about at this time Treavey?" Felicity surprised Treavey with her rather forthright language.

He giggled to himself and smiled at her. "Okay Felicity, calm down, what would your mother say?!"

She stared directly at his face, "Fuck, fuck and fucking hell once more. You should have done that turny thing earlier than you did."

She looked quite sternly at him, and Treavey stared back, the incident still running back through his mind. He thought he couldn't possibly have acted more quickly, but then he saw Felicity's expression change. Her stern expression began to break slightly, then completely into a most wonderful cheesy grin before bursting into laughter. Both were belly laughing as they sat in the panda in a cul-de-sac. They should have been angry and frustrated, but instead they just kept laughing.

There was little point in waiting too long outside Dawson's address for him to return. He would have got rid of whatever contraband he may have had, so they both returned to the station and Treavey submitted the night's events onto an intelligence slip which would be put on the police intelligence systems later to hopefully add to the jigsaw on Dawson.

Felicity made them both a cup of tea. They looked at each other, trying to come up with reasons why he had been there at that time of night, and why he had made off if he had had nothing to hide. He'd certainly been up to something, that was certain and Treavey was determined to get to the bottom of it.

Chapter 3

Porn and pasties

He was a fit young man lying naked on a king-sized bed with an expression of pure ecstasy across his face. He showed off his strong, masculine arms whilst he cupped his hands behind his head, as if he were in submission to whoever was before him. He tensed his athletic, bronzed, six pack stomach muscles which glistened with oil before a woman who was kneeling between his granite like legs, and he flexed every sinew of muscle as he moved. The just as naked woman was paying particular interest to his rather large and erect penis which stood proud before her. She, herself, had a model-like body, bronzed and slender like a statue, and she wore a shock of glossy brunette hair, which swayed as if in a shampoo advertisement. Her emerald-green eyes glinted and dazzled as she glanced up at the gladiator of a man whilst she continued to pleasure him.

Treavey watched for another second or two, and then, feeling rather awkward, shook his head and looked back down at his paperwork which he was trying to concentrate on.

"For God's sake Bomber, do you need to bring this into work?" Micky said in desperation. Bomber had brought in a VHS recording from his newly-installed SKY package.

Bomber looked at Micky with some surprise and retorted in his deep gravelly voice, "What do you mean, I

43

thought you'd like it. The job gives us a VHS cassette monitor to view their crap fortnightly briefings, I think this is a much better use it's been put to, no? Better than listening to the Chief Constable spouting on about the latest targets and initiatives."

Treavey shuffled the final papers of his shoplifting file which he needed to get rid of, as he'd had it for a month already. He had two more months to submit it if he needed to. He had quickly learned that if he kept a priority list of paperwork in his tray, the lower priority work never got completed. It would just sit in his skippet for weeks on end and soon be forgotten, as there was always fresh, higher priority paperwork being generated in the meantime. That was a way to get into trouble, so he had tried to have a 'when it comes in, it goes out' policy which seemed to work well and certainly reduced his stress levels.

"Come on Treavey, we're leaving the car behind today," Micky announced, showing great enthusiasm for the shift ahead.

"Sure, okay Micky. Where are we going?"

Micky was already collecting his stuff and walking out of the side door. Treavey grabbed his custodian hat and followed. It was a beautiful day again on that July afternoon. After an early turn of tea, a briefing amongst themselves, and a perusal through the intelligence reports, it was always good to have a chat and catch-up with the rest of the gang, but then to clear the paperwork too. After all, all the bad guys were still fast asleep in bed at that time. They don't usually have the discipline for early mornings if they were up to no good late the night before.

Treavey did as much as he could with his mini typewriter he'd brought into work. It was so much quicker than handwriting all the forms and it was small enough to pop into the back of his car. It also impressed quite a few of his witnesses when he touch-typed their statements, a skill he learned when he was brought up in Newquay. where he had completed a touch-typing course alongside his commerce diploma. The eighteen girls and only one other boy in the class probably had something to do with the attraction to the course for him.

This morning the typewriter was left at the station and Micky and Treavey started walking towards the town centre. There wasn't an awful lot of foot patrol time available, but it was a good excuse to unwind, get a bit of exercise, and generally have a chat with the public. They were dressed in white short-sleeved shirts, clip-on black ties, heavy black trousers which got very hot in the sun, and helmets of course. A few of the guys including Treavey preferred the flat caps; far more like the TV show, 'The Bill', with the Met running around in their Metro cars, but Micky was a stickler for his helmet, hence Treavey followed suit so their uniforms matched.

Micky had a very old-fashioned traditional helmet which he'd managed to find and keep. Treavey was more than happy to reciprocate with his more standard, but very smart-looking helmet. He felt his helmet looked awkwardly large on him and, indeed, it was a necessary large size due to the length of his head rather than the width, so it could look as if his helmet was too large for him.

Treavey felt extremely exposed when on foot patrol, even though he had been in the job for over 2 years now. He had the feeling that everyone was looking at him. Everyone assumed he knew all the answers and he was the instant expert and could sort everyone's ills.

What he did know was there must have been a lot of orchards in Britain in the past, as all he heard on his meanderings was, "Well officer, things have changed now haven't they? I remember in my day, officer, when I went scrumping, and I was caught by the local bobby, he'd give me a clip round the ear, and I'd go home, tell my father and I'd get another one from him."

It was an account he'd heard numerous times. Either scrumping was at pandemic levels or it was a convenient story that made a point about how respect for the law had diminished over the years. A point that if any child or teenager brought a police officer to the door, it was a moment of shame on the whole family. Now unfortunately with how things were, it was more likely to lead to the officer facing a complaint from the teenager and the parents.

As they walked towards the town, Treavey and Micky chatted about nothing in particular, except the rather inappropriate use of police video equipment by Bomber perhaps.

Micky looked thoughtful, "Can you imagine if a member of the public had entered the front office unnoticed, and had sat there listening to all that groaning?"

Treavey gave a knowing nod, "Amazing what you can get on Sky, mind, not sure I'd leave the house if I had it at home!"

They both laughed, releasing the rather awkward tension of the elephant in the room. It may have been quite fascinating to watch, but for their own integrity, they would have to detach themselves from it and try to show little interest in what they were seeing in front of them.

They were soon onto the main street which ran near to the entrance to the beach. It was like walking down the beach version of a cowboy town with quite ramshackle buildings, just two storeys high. The higher level of the building, a basic flat being the living accommodation, and the lower, the space to sell wares. The main road was the coastal road, with a series of shops on either side. It was narrow and covered with a dusting of sand blown up from the nearby beach. Half-dressed tourists bustled amongst the parked cars, and display racks showing off their seasonal items for excited and happy visitors.

The smell of warm sand, and salt wafted through the air and filled the officer's nostrils. Treavey felt relaxed and happy to be there. He breathed in the seaside atmosphere and gazed over the kiss-me-quick style shops which lined the main street, each selling much the same thing as the others. Colourful inflatable airbeds and beach balls, postcards with topless cartoon figures with rather cheesy innuendos printed on them. Then there were flip-flops, yes, lots of colourful flip flops; and quite randomly, Allen's picture framing shop which must be serving the needs of the local population, as well as the tourists. Something was required to frame the beautiful scenery outside, so it could be painted and photographed, taken home, and placed inside.

He chuckled, picking up a pen from a display rack on the pavement, noticing a figure of a woman printed on the side wearing a black bikini, however, when the pen was flipped upside down, the black ink disappeared revealing her nakedness underneath. He blushed, remembering he was in uniform, and replaced it amongst its companions. Probably not for his pocket notebook at this time.

They wandered on slowly, in that 'two coppers walking along the street' type wander. Nobody teaches them how to do it, maybe police officers learn it from cop shows on TV, but their pace had to be slow enough to not cover the whole patch in 10 minutes, be slow enough to be approachable to the public but to not look as if they were lost either.

Once Treavey was aware of this awkwardness in being on foot patrol, he felt conscious of where his hands were and where he was putting them. What was he supposed to do with them? He certainly couldn't place them casually in his pockets, good God no, but then they looked awkward just down the side of his body too. Photos of police on foot patrol usually had them pointing out to the distance as if showing a member of the public some directions. How very awkward all of a sudden. He discussed this with Micky who laughed in recognition. "Or you can just think of something else," he replied, "how about that?"

They made their way to their favourite bakery which baked the absolute best Cornish pasties and carrot cake. It made a lovely change from the cheddar cheese and Branston pickle on granary bread sandwiches he usually made himself. But the early turn was the shift to have a treat.

They seemed to fill the shop with their tall helmets as they made their purchases. Micky bought the same as Treavey as it was the best selection the shop was known for. Homemade Cornish pasties and then carrot cake for dessert; nothing was considered better.

Half-naked tourists in swimming trunks and bikinis filled the shop making it even tighter, scattering sand from their bare feet and flip flops around the slate floor and they looked on at the two officers as if they were a couple of aliens.

"Morning!" Treavey exclaimed to break the awkwardness and walked out of the shop to await his colleague. They would usually take their lunch back to the station if they were in the car, but it was too far and their foot patrol had just begun. They were going to have to face eating it in public, with the same sandy tourists looking on at them as if they were in a cage at the zoo. Of course, they couldn't casually sit on the wall and eat it as anyone else might, so they wandered over to a friendly-looking group of pensioners and struck up a conversation with them.

"Ah," exclaimed Micky, "so you are the ones we've been after; up to no good I see!"

The elderly woman was northern and typically very confident, which was to Treavey's initial regret, and soon turned into absolute pleasure as they both attempted to skilfully dodge their unlikely outrageous flirting and innuendo between them.

A rather rotund woman in her seventies, wearing a loose, brightly coloured blouse with black nylon trousers, took the lead; "They do look very young, don't they, Agatha? What would you have done with them in your day, eh duck?!"

Agatha, a very skinny woman of similar age in a long summer dress, was happy to take on the challenge and replied instantly, "Oh no, Deirdre, you know you were the one who was good at all that, darling, I was far too shy!"

Her glowing rosy cheeks on a pale complexion awaited the next return serve by Deirdre, and it soon arrived.

"Me, my sweet, no, no, no, I was shy and retiring my love, don't you remember, you were the one who introduced me to all those gentlemen at the dance hall remember, one, in particular, I may mention?"

"Oh shush, Deirdre, the officers don't want to hear about that one, but goodness, I enjoyed his foxtrot that weekend!"

Now Treavey completely understood where the author of those cartoon postcards got his material from. It was here, being played out for real. The tennis match of innuendos continued for a while longer until the pasties were finished, and the officers decided to move on whilst they still had some integrity intact.

"Any unit in Perranporth town centre?"

Micky was already on to it, "PC 442, go ahead Victor."

Both officers paused and placed their hands on their radios, the main body of the radio firmly attached to their utility belt and the head of the radio clipped on their shirt tab on their chest with a long thick grey wire running between. Treavey adjusted the volume button up as he didn't want to miss any detail. It was a sense of pride to not have to ask Micky to repeat what the operator had just said, and it could sometimes be difficult to understand, especially as the reception could be a little poor at sea level.

"Could you go to number 24 Parkwood lane in Perranporth? There's a regular caller, Mrs Sarah Irons who lives there who says she has intruders. This is the 54th time we've had a call from her about this issue this year. She does have known mental health issues."

Micky had worked the beat in Perran for a while now so knew the street names well. Without looking at a map he opened his stride and Treavey hurried his pace to keep up with him.

"It's a problem, isn't it Micky? We don't go, she gets hurt and it's the Police's fault, we don't go and she's being burgled, we would clearly be at fault, but we know we do go and we are completely wasting our time. We just have to play the game, don't we?"

Micky didn't even glance in Treavey's direction, but continued striding forward for a moment and then, after a few paces, answered directly, "Ours is not to reason why, Treavey, yes, we have to play the game and then at least we know we've done our bit right. I mean, if she is a nuisance caller then there is a list they could put her on, but mental health, that's a tricky one. That's care in the community, my friend, basically, chucking them out into the streets and getting the lovely community to look after them, or not. How sweet... and disastrous." Micky was being sarcastic and he showed he was quite angry at how society was treating these people.

Treavey replied, "The alternative, of course, is the mental homes where I'm not so sure many improved their condition either. They were all just hidden from society. Some quite cruelly."

They were both trying to subtly stuff the rest of their carrot cake into their mouths which was proving almost impossible. The eating was possible, but scoffing it subtly was not quite so easy. Treavey laughed through the crumbs, and commented, "It certainly isn't like the TV cop shows where they get a job and throw their food away or leave it where it is. We'll make damned sure we don't waste any, that's a guarantee!"

Micky nodded in agreement, unable to hide his rather red face as he was already half choking on the last piece of cake, whilst still walking at a fast pace, "That's why we tend to have a massive bladder and a cast-iron stomach mate, after a few years of doing this!"

They got to Parkwood Lane and walked along quite a tidy and affluent road. Large Victorian semi-detached houses framed each side of the road, with each resident in their front garden seemingly attempting to outdo their neighbour.

Treavey was counting aloud, "That's 16, 18, nothing on that one, 22 and, well, we could have guessed really."

The house was a ramshackle property in need of much attention which it clearly had not received for some time.

The front garden was completely overgrown with an old enamelled cast iron bath hidden within the brambles. It was obvious the front door wasn't the one being regularly used, so they walked to the side door, through where a wooden side gate would once have been, but where now just a half rotten frame remained.

Micky took the lead and the officers were invited in by the woman who confirmed she was called Sarah. She looked as though she was in her 60's but she was probably 20 years younger. She looked like a scarecrow with her straw-like but dark matted hair, and a leathered face with pain and fear painted across it. Treavey felt immediate empathy for the poor woman standing before him. What a miserable way to live. She was gaunt and crouched forward, hunching her shoulders, as if she was in extreme fear. She glanced around her and then over the officer's shoulders into the sky as if looking for intruders, the enemy, aliens, whatever, or whoever it was she feared so much.

Treavey filled his nostrils with the fresh air outside before he entered the dank interior as if it were a smoke-filled room. The place was filled from top to bottom with rubbish and books, with items which should have been skipped a long time ago but would probably remain there until the day she died. She led the officers to the front of the house into the lounge area. There was a stained makeshift bed with a form of a sofa frame underneath. She was living between the kitchen and the lounge. They saw silver foil on the windows which darkened the whole room. There was a 40-watt bulb doing its best to light the room but doing it badly. Even Treavey felt spooked in this room.

"I'll be back in a minute, Treavey," and with that, Micky's large frame was walking purposefully out of the lounge with his moustache high in the air leaving him alone with the woman.

"So... what seems to be the problem, Mrs Irons?" Treavey asked hesitantly.

She stared at him through dull, mat eyes, but finally broke into a warm smile. Treavey could see the woman she possibly could have been, given different circumstances. Her messy dark scruffy hair now looked more flowing, and chestnut than it had done previously.

"Oh, call me Sarah," she replied.

Treavey realised it was probably the only human contact she'd had in weeks, or at least since the last police visit, she'd had. It was probably one of the main reasons she called the police so much. Her face resorted back to the fearful, panicked expression he'd seen when they'd first met her at the door.

"They are everywhere, officers. They come in through the windows and are here amongst us now. Can you hear them?" Her eyes jumped from one spot in the room to another, then another and she crouched down in fear.

Treavey pondered, "Christ, what it must be like to be in this constant fear, poor love.", he thought to himself.

"Begone, thou evil demon, begone I tell you," Micky made the most extraordinary entrance waving what looked like to be a huge silver wand around his head. With great theatrics, he pranced and jumped around the room, jabbing the wand out in front of him, "Die thou evil spirit, die, I tell you, for you are not welcome in this house."

Treavey was taken aback wondering if Micky was the one who was off his trolley and perhaps it wasn't Rambo on the section who was the crazy one after all. Micky ripped the foil off the windows letting the light flood in. Sarah staggered back as Micky ran past her and out into the hall. His shouting continued, up the stairs and back down again. "And another, you evil spirit, I see you and you will be gone and never return to these hallowed grounds again, for there is only good which will remain here. Be gone and never come back thou devilish hound."

He dramatically entered the room once again, throwing the silver wand down onto the carpet in front of him. He arched his back, throwing his head even further back with arms reaching far behind him as if his chest was drawn towards the heavens. He let a huge sigh out, then after a short pause, relaxed, looking shattered. Silence.

Sarah fell at the feet of Micky, weeping. "Thank you, thank you so much. I can't believe they have gone. Thank you so, so much."

Micky gazed into the woman's eyes and spoke softly, "You are very welcome, my love."

He carefully picked up the wand, turned around, and slowly walked out of the room. Treavey followed and watched Micky remove a silver foil sleeve from his wooden truncheon, crunch it up and throw it into the depths of the rubbish in the kitchen.

Walking back into town slowly, and after some considerable silence, Treavey quietly asked, "Micky?"

Another pause as he attempted to find the words, "What the actual fuck happened back there?"

"I got rid of her demons for a bit," Micky replied as if answering a question about the weather. Nothing more was said. Nothing more needed to be.

As they approached the police station, Treavey was looking forward to taking his helmet off when he got in and maybe even risk taking his boots off under the desk to give his feet an airing.

The hot sun was taking its toll, but Micky had other ideas. "I just want to nip down here for about half an hour."

Treavey dutifully followed down a narrow alleyway between two houses almost directly opposite the station. Micky abruptly stopped by a large window which, unsurprisingly in the heat, was slightly ajar. He crouched down underneath it with his back to the wall and Treavey, feeling rather confused, did the same. Both stared at the wall opposite sitting there in silence.

Treavey turned his head towards his colleague, but Micky already had his finger to his lips for him to hush. They waited for a few more seconds and heard voices coming from the room behind them.

The penny dropped for Treavey, "Oh," he thought, "that will be the Bradford brothers address, I wonder what we are doing here?"

The answer soon became clear. "(inaudible) shipment was coming soon, so don't fuck it up. (inaudible) will fucking kill you if we mess this one up."

Another person then said something but it just could not be heard, and then, "It's going to be late, and we have to be there (inaudible) going to make a lot of money."

The other voice then says, "We gonna be rich bruv!", followed by two men laughing.

The two men in the house seemed quite excited but there were too many gaps in the information. Questions were spinning around their heads. What was the shipment? It must be drugs as it was going to make them a lot of money, and they only earn a lot of money if it was illegal right? And when is the shipment going to happen? Late one night, but which one and where was it going to happen, and who's gonna be mad if it goes wrong, who's running this thing?"

The officers waited for a few moments more, hoping for a convenient recap and maybe, for a hand-drawn map and itinerary to flutter out of the open window, but even they thought that may be hoping for a bit too much, so they straightened their aching limbs and silently walked back up the alley and across the road to the station.

PC Baddock, 'Bomber', was still in the parade room taking another VHS cassette out of the player, and Gordy was elbow deep in a file.

"Isn't all that wearing you out, Bomber?" Micky asked, sounding rather annoyed at Bomber's latest interest. "It probably isn't the best thing to do in a police station, to be honest mate. You get caught, we all get in the shit and I won't thank you for that."

Bomber purposefully ignored him and carefully placed the cassette back into a cardboard sleeve and released the catches to his brown leather briefcase.

"Another attempt to look more executive no doubt" Treavey suspected, watching Bomber replace the cassette in his case.

"We've had an interesting day today," Treavey announced, feeling rather proud of their accomplishments. He was always happy to share his adventures as a police officer with the others and the rest of his new colleagues were usually happy to listen, but he caught Micky looking towards him with a stern expression. A stare that was telling Treavey to shut up.

Micky replied, slightly annoyed, "Oh yes, we walked down the town, we ate pasty and cake and got chatted up by a couple of grandmothers!"

PC Gordan, Gordy, breathed in deeply expanding his gym-built chest and running his fingers through his wispy red hair and smiled, "Got to say they all need loving, oh yes, they all need loving."

Micky laughed and grabbed Treavey's arm, "Come on, old chap, let's make a round of tea!" and pulled him towards the kitchen. Once out of sight he spoke in very quiet, but rich tones, "This one's ours mate, we let them know what intel we've got and someone's going to step in with two size twelve boots and ruin the whole lot. If we don't get anything else over the next few days, then we can tell the others, but let's just keep this to ourselves for now."

"What if it's the final bit of the jigsaw for someone else?" Treavey enquired with some nervousness.

Micky gazed at him in a manner of a wise professor looking upon an over-keen student, "Yes, like who? Who else will know what's going on in this place other than us?"

The door chime rang signalling someone had entered the front office. Treavey took the opportunity to break the awkwardness, and it would prevent him from having to make the tea as well, so he marched over to the front desk to speak to the caller.

He saw a rather dirty matted grey-haired woman standing there looking rather out of place. She was the vagrant who wandered around the town. She was wearing numerous layers of clothes over what probably was already a rather large figure underneath it all, quite strange on such a hot day. She had a kind face, but a weathered complexion from being beaten by the storms and the sun over repeated years. Treavey noticed a pink plastic bracelet on her wrist, which no doubt told a story. She smelled strongly too, and it was not a good smell. One which mixed a cocktail of sweat, urine, and alcohol and lingered around the front desk area which wasn't helped by not having any windows to open.

"Good afternoon madam, how can I help you?" Treavey purposefully put on the same voice he'd have used for a pinstripe-suited man coming into the office.

"Grace," she replied in a soft, sweet voice.

"Hello Grace, how can I help you?"

"PC Treave. Lovely to meet you at last. Now Treavey, I want to make a complaint."

He was surprised, not only did she know his name but his nickname at that, and yet he had never needed to speak to her before.

She continued, "Those young Bradford boys, you know, Tom and Billy, you know, the ones that live opposite you, they think it's funny to take my drink you see when I'm a kip. I find my bottle broken and they are always laughing when I find out. It helps me sleep, you see, and they keep doing it. I want it stopped before I take the matter into my own hands. Now they've got that Red Fiesta XR2 car, I have the registration if you want it."

Treavey was even more impressed, not only did she know his name but also the names of the two brothers, first and second names and where they lived, and the make model and registration of their car.

"Goodness, Grace, we could do with someone like you in the force, you know. You are quite in the know, aren't you?"

He took a liking to her and quickly wrote down some details from her. He probably wouldn't be taking a formal complaint of theft or damage over a vagrant's bottle of whisky, but she deserved to sleep safely at night and to have this nipped in the bud. Anyway, it would be a good reason to knock on the Bradford's door, to introduce himself so to speak, in the presence of their mother who lived in the same house and was known to be very pro-police. It was believed by the local police, she had lost control over Tommy and Billy when their father had left soon after Tommy's birth.

It was better to wait until she arrived home, however. Especially when dealing with two young men in the house together. Any bravado tended to disappear when a mother was present. She knew all their vulnerabilities and wouldn't hesitate to expose them if she felt they were being cheeky to the police.

Just then, he heard something on the radio, and all the officers in the room sat up straight and took immediate notice. This sounded big.

Chapter 4

The saddest day

"All units, can you attend a road traffic collision in the high street urgently, please. We are getting reports of a vehicle which has lost control, mounted the pavement and there are casualties reported."

Treavey popped his head around the corner and saw Bomber and Micky had already gone with the door swinging behind them. He grabbed another set of car keys and followed them out of the door and as he jumped into the spare panda, he could see the other two were already driving away towards the town. There was no waiting around for politeness here; lives could be at risk and it could take an age to get an ambulance to a place like Perranporth especially if there was holiday traffic clogging up the lanes.

Five minutes later and Treavey was on the scene as well. He quickly attempted to make sense of the scene, but it was complicated and quite overwhelming at first. There was a red Volkswagen Golf with damage to the front off-side corner in the centre of the road at an unusual angle and a young man was sitting on the kerb next to it with his head in his hands. Much further on he could see a commotion. As he got closer, he could see the shoulders of Micky rhythmically moving up and down gently whilst he knelt on the ground, his shoulders were arched as if pushing repeatedly on something in front of him, but he was facing away from him so it was not very clear what he was doing. He noticed Bomber was kneeling on the opposite side to Micky, facing the same item in front of them.

As Treavey quickened his pace, he saw it was not an item they were working on after all, but a person. He could see some little feet with shoes on. The body was lying down with his bare shins and knobbly knees on the hot tarmac, then as Treavey got a little closer he could see it was a child wearing little red shorts, and a yellow and blue T-shirt with a cartoon print of Goofy on it. Micky had started chest compressions on the boy with one hand, to not put too much pressure on the tiny torso. Bomber was supplying gentle breaths. Treavey saw there was nothing else he could do at the moment but to update the control room and ask for an ambulance, even though he knew it would probably already be on the way. He was staring at what was in front of him for a moment. He gazed at the boy's face between breaths. He must have been six or so. He was pale; his petite face had a frame of dark wavy hair falling around it, a face of such innocence. What on earth had happened?

He felt himself coming back into the moment, noticing the sound of weeping around him and looking around to see holidaymakers of all ages in shock. One was shouting at the man next to the red VW car who remained with his head in his hands, others were pointing at a silver people carrier, what looked like a Renault Espace. It was on the same side of the road but a considerable distance ahead. What on earth had gone wrong? He couldn't see any other casualties, it looked like just the two vehicles had been involved, but there were a lot of people crying and shouting in a fog of noise around him. He had to make some sense of it. He was a police officer for goodness sake, but he kept looking at the little boy and his tiny body, then at his two colleagues sweating as they worked on him.

61

Treavey moved his gaze across to a young boy holding hands with his parents watching Micky and Bomber. All three were looking intently at the casualty. He studied the three; a woman staring with eyes filled with tears, her blond hair tied back in a short pony-tail, her light green blouse draped over her slim frame with a colourful floral skirt. She must have been 30 years old, and she was holding her husband's hand who was of similar age and build. He was dressed in beach attire and was transfixed with a look of utter horror on his face. His other hand cradled that of the boy standing motionless next to him, about 11 years old. The boy dropped a plastic shovel he had been holding in his free hand. It was not important anymore.

These three were the family of the little boy. They were the parents and his older brother. Micky threw Treavey a glance and got back to work. Treavey could see their effort of CPR was just for show. They had to do something for this boy, but it was obvious to Micky it was a waste of time, except to offer a little hope, perhaps, to the family, to show them the officers did care and were doing all they could to save their son's precious life.

Sirens were heard in the distance.

"Come on ambulance, where are you?" he thought to himself.

He stepped a little closer and offered to take over from one of his two colleagues but he was quickly dismissed; they wanted to continue. The boy was being pummelled to try to push some life back into him, and then with some horror, Treavey saw what Micky had been hiding from the parents with his thigh. He was trying to cover the gaping wound in the boy's skull and the sight was not a good one. He could sense Micky looking at him and the message was clear. Move this family now. Treavey realised he needed to ensure no valuable witnesses disappeared and he knew a team of horses wouldn't get the family away from their dying son, and where would they have gone anyway? Sitting them in the back of a hot panda car? Wound or no wound, they were going nowhere and Treavey knew he needed to establish what had gone on, before all his witnesses had wandered off.

The ambulance was threading its way through the crowd of tourists. Treavey was updating the control room and asking for more units to help with transport and witnesses. He saw the young man by the VW and having waved the ambulance onto Micky and Bomber, Treavey quickly paced over to speak to him.

"You okay mate?" He asked.

He came to the very quick decision he was a 'mate' and not a 'sir.' The man pulled his head out of his hands; it was evident he'd been sobbing.

"I just pulled out and it hit me, that's all. I didn't mean for it to all go wrong like this."

He spat out his name to Treavey who confirmed it fitted with the registered keeper of the VW. Some people were hovering around them so Treavey took the opportunity to grab some independent witnesses to the carnage.

"Did you guys see what happened?"

A middle-aged man, looking rather shocked, but clearly in control of himself spoke in low tones.

"Officer, I was walking along the pavement here, on the way to the beach with my family. It's a much nicer day today and we hadn't made it down in the past week so we thought we would come down to the beach."

Treavey was impatient for the man to get to the point, but didn't want to disturb his flow. He was willing the man on, thinking, "For God's sake man, just get to the

63

point here, I don't care about your fucking family holiday, what did you see?"

"I see sir, and what did you see?" Treavey translated his thoughts into a far more composed question for him.

"Well yes, and then I heard a crash behind me so turned around and saw the Espace had hit the side of this car here. I think this car had just pulled out from the side, maybe he didn't see the Espace coming up from behind, I don't know."

"All very useful," Treavey thought, but he was keen to see what the man actually saw, not what he thought happened. He knew the brain could fill in gaps and give the impression to the person they saw something they were merely presuming. He often got completely contrary witness reports to an event, that people were convinced they saw with their own eyes, but was shown later to not have been possible. They'd have sworn on the bible at the time. Treavey snapped out of his thoughts and encouraged the man to continue.

"Well anyway," the man continued, "I'm looking at this thing, that there Espace expecting it to stop and does it? No, it doesn't, it just keeps piling on, revving like a mad thing it was, and then, all I see is it driving past me. I thought it must have robbed a bank or something. No idea why it didn't stop, but it eventually did over there."

Treavey grabbed the details of where the man was staying and importantly, how long he had left of his holiday. The trouble with witnesses in these parts, he knew that they tended to disappear very quickly by returning home. It was never a surprise how many witnesses were on the last day of their holiday and their home force would not have thanked him for asking them to take important, long, and complicated statements for him, especially for just a seaside town like Perranporth.

He thanked him for his time, explained he'd be in touch for a statement, and paced past the now huddle of officers and paramedics around the casualty still showing no signs of life and onto the Espace people carrier. Expecting to find some teenagers he was surprised to see a man in his 50's standing in front of him. He was with a child who was about six years old and they were standing next to the Espace together. He was staring into space and it seemed he was aware of the other child's condition. Treavey gently spoke to him to get some idea as to what had gone on. He knew he'd have to be careful as he didn't want to carry out an unlawful interview, but he also badly needed to find out some basic details of what had occurred.

"What's happened?" Treavey asked with the simplest of questions to start with. An open question where now, hopefully, metaphorically having pulled the plug from the obstruction, he could now just sit back and listen to the man talk; and he did.

"I've driven along with my grandson in the car, we are on holiday, coming to meet his parents on the beach, we had to stay behind and... well, anyway, I'm driving along the road with no problems at all and suddenly this car, the red car over there, pulled out in front of me. I was understandably shocked and so slammed on the brake but my car didn't stop. It just kept on going and I couldn't stop it. It was going faster; I panic and stamp on the brake but it just goes faster and faster. I'm trying to avoid hitting people but there's someone in the road so I swerve to avoid them and then, and then..." He falls silent as if he couldn't bring himself to say the words and resorts back to the stare again. His grandson next to him was holding the man's hand and looking increasingly impatient, as if he'd just wanted to go to the beach, oblivious to the whole tragic affair. That was enough for Treavey for now. He didn't need any more quite yet.

"Have you contacted his parents yet? Are they collecting your grandson?"

"Yes, my son is coming for him."

Treavey collected the most urgent basic details he could and found, to his relief, the details of both cars matched the driver's details and they both had insurance. That made things a lot simpler. He was also thinking about any drink-driving suspicions on both drivers, but he'd got his hands full at this stage. He didn't think they'd been drinking, but he knew he couldn't let them go until Traffic got there. "Traffic, yes Traffic, shit have they been called?" he thought. He got on the radio.

"Yes, Traffic's on their way," confirmed the police control room.

Treavey was reassured and thought, "Oh brilliant, they'll know what to do. They'll take the whole thing over." He felt the stress lift from his shoulders and he felt motivated to do the best job for them he could before they got there, so he went looking for other witnesses.

The beast of a traffic car with its full strobe bar of flickering blue and red, coasted its way through the hot summer's day like a shark patrolling its territory and pulled up next to the scene. Although the Traffic car had coasted in so slowly, it was obvious it had been on a cross country rant, with the sound of the engine cooling down, the fans, and the 'pinking' of the hot metals beginning to contract once again. The ambulance was driving off in the opposite direction with its sirens on. Micky and Bomber were speaking to the parents, so the Traffic officers, looking splendid in their impeccable uniforms and their dazzling white flat caps with shiny black piques, unfold themselves out of their sleek vehicle. The yellow stripe and chequered markings on their Cosworth car brought the full attention of the tourist crowd onto them.

Treavey recognised them but not enough to know them by name. One was a sergeant. "We have the big guns here now, that's good." Treavey thought to himself as he hurried over to them and introduced himself. They answered with a confident smile and welcome.

"Okay Treavey," the sergeant said as if just about to make an announcement, "I'm Sgt Olly Tayler, where's our scene then? It looks a bit busy around here."

Treavey felt put at ease, yet also a little foolish that the cordoned-off area wasn't as much as he'd have, but he recovered it well. "There were only the three of us here, so Bomber and Micky were working on the little chap..." he paused as the severity of the situation dawned on him and he stuttered a little, "...and it was only me left, so I managed to confirm details of the drivers with their vehicles, that they were insured, and have tax so we know who they all are and everyone is accounted for, and I've got three witnesses which I thought the time was better spent doing just to make sure we didn't lose them."

"Okay, good job, well done. We need more people here to cordon this off but for now, we can get some breath tests done between us, let's make sure the cars are safe and the area between them and where the boy ended up is secured for forensics. We'll have to divert traffic around at the junctions on either side. Let's call the accident investigator please, Jim," he glances around at his colleague, "...and Scenes of crime, oh and let's get the council to help with these diversions. Jim, can you get on to Comms and sort that out?"

His colleague answered without fuss, "Sure sarg", and immediately turned to get on his radio.

The sergeant continued talking to Treavey, "Right, take me to the very beginning of everything, Treavey. So, what do we think happened?

Treavey explained as clearly as he could, walking together from the beginning of the scene to the end. Sgt Tayler knelt to road level, explaining he was looking for skid marks or 'striation marks' which was when a car slewed to one side usually with harsh steering. He explained he wanted to know whether the Espace was out of control before the collision with the car or as a result of it.

Treavey was organising some tape and ensuring the scene was kept as clear as it could be, 30 metres on either side of the scene. There was a large group of onlookers peering over the tape looking fascinated, with some, also looking quite bored at what was going on too. Treavey was keen to get as much as he could from this scene as it had just dawned on him what department he wanted to join. He realised the feeling of relief he had when the traffic car turned up and he wanted to be the person to exude confidence in situations of chaos such as this.

"So how come we have SOCO coming?" Treavey asked in a vain attempt to not look like he was interfering?

"We use Scenes of Crime for the photos really, the accident investigator will be doing most of the work here, but I've also called a vehicle examiner, a VEX, 'cos that Espace hasn't stopped for some reason and I need to see if the accelerator was stuck open, or whether it was bad mechanics from a garage or indeed if there's foul play. Got to check the lot you see."

Treavey listened intently. He realised he may be pushing his luck, but he felt like he was getting a good reception from the sergeant. "So, the family is currently with their son in the hospital, what will happen with them?"

"I've sent another traffic officer up to the hospital," the traffic sergeant replied, "they will be there to get any updates on the child, be with the family and if the little man dies, well then, not that the parents will be in the frame of mind to understand, but the Traffic officers will be there to explain what happens next. We'll get a statement from them sometime later of course. That's going to be a difficult one, no doubt." He looked over to Bomber and Micky who were with the two drivers before his thoughts were disrupted by his radio.

"Tango one, from Victor", the control room female voice sounded solemn.

The Traffic sergeant, Sgt Tayler pressed his transmit button, paused for a second, and replied, "Go ahead."

He knew what the next words were going to be.

"Your colleagues have updated us over the phone. This is now a fatality."

"A fatality, received." The sergeant slowly faced Treavey and said quietly, noticing some holidaymakers making their way past nearby, "Now that gives me my power of arrest for 'death by dangerous' if we need it. Okay, when my other unit gets here, I'll get them to take both the drivers in for a quick interview voluntarily. If they don't want to come with us voluntarily, well then, they'll leave us no choice, we'll have to nick 'em. We can't have them wandering off without us having spoken to them formally."

A few hours later, with SOCO, and the accident investigators still on the scene, Treavey, Micky, and Bomber retreated to the sanctuary of the police station and were going over the day's events. They sat at the table together with a mug of tea each in their hands, poured from a rather stained, stainless-steel teapot placed in the middle of the table. They'd just had a 30 minute debrief with the traffic officers in town and Treavey had been comforted with how empathetic they had been. Not quite the 'stick their own mother's on' types he'd thought them to have been, after all.

Sgt Tayler explained how the team had ensured evidence had been captured from the two cars and that full examinations would take place later on, along with in-depth interviews and statements. They'd put a media request out for more witnesses as so many people in a situation like this assumed the police had sufficient witnesses already, and would proceed to continue to carry on with their daily business, feeling they were not required.

The sergeant had said they had noticed the driver's side door mirror of the VW was shattered which may have led to the car pulling out in front of the Espace causing the initial collision. The big question was why had the Espace driver not stopped? Sgt Tayler had replied to that question,

"A number of reasons, but the driver swore the brakes didn't work and the car just revved, so we have to prove whether the throttle was sticky or whether it was a mistake in panic by the driver. The vehicle examiner has exposed the throttle in the Espace and they have videoed it moving freely and not sticking at all. We'll get SOCO to take a lot of photographs of the scene, the cars, and the mechanical workings before recovering the cars for a further more detailed examination."

He went on to say, "The first thing we did, even before the vehicle examiner had arrived, was to take the tyre pressures from each car. We need to establish whether any tyres were under pressure before the collision and this evidence could be lost if there had been a slow puncture caused by the collision and the tyre had completely deflated just before they were formally examined. It could complicate matters, so just as well to catch their condition early on. We'll see how much sleep the driver has had in the past few days too. Lack of sleep can cause little errors which can add up to huge repercussions."

Something the other Traffic officer, Jim, had said, stayed in Treavey's thoughts. "The driver of the Espace had a 6-year-old grandson with him, didn't he? Well, it was his birthday. Whatever happened, I doubt he meant to kill another 6-year-old child today, but he'll have that reminder on his grandson's birthday, now, for the rest of his life. The reminder every year he killed a child on his grandson's birthday and he'd even have been the same age. Poor bastard, no one wishes that on anyone." Jim had had a tear in his eyes as he reflected on what he had been saying.

Treavey was surprised. How did he ever think these people were just robots giving speeding tickets out walking about like the Gestapo? He ticked himself off; he'd assumed, like many of the public do about himself and about the job he does, something which simply wasn't true. He assumed he was the only person who gave a shit about people, but no, here was a hardened Traffic officer almost shedding a tear, even putting himself in the position of a suspect, showing empathy, and then going out to face the same thing again, day after day.

He knew it was something he wanted to do in the future. Perhaps he could speak to the sergeant later and try to get an attachment with them one day, but this was not the time to discuss careers. A six-year-old boy had lost his life today. The local officers were deep in thought as they sipped their tea. There was no messing about, no laughing, just a reflection on the day they had all had.

Micky sat straight and proud. His duty had been done and to him, it was just part of the job. A proud and professional man. Like a soldier in the trenches in the first world war, he flicked a piece of dirt from his uniform but avoided some blood on his woolen nato jumper sleeve before taking another gulp of tea. Bomber and he did their utmost to make this whole torrid affair have a different ending, but real life was different from the films.

That family, how on earth do they go back to their family home minus one important member of it, to miss that mischievous, cheeky grin, that endless energy powering around the house being told to "slow down." For the mother to walk upstairs to see the crumpled pile of clothes in the corner of his bedroom, his bed having been slept in with the duvet tossed aside by an excited boy rushing to go on holiday, and looking at the toys thrown about the floor she'd have told him off for not tidying up. How guilty must she feel now? Just how on earth does the older brother get over missing the brother he found a total pain on all those occasions before that fatal day. All that didn't matter anymore.

He was gone and was never coming back. Just when do you clear the room, or would it be some sort of morbid shrine, who knew? This was a problem every parent hoped they would never have to worry about. The wrong place at the wrong time; it could have all been so different.

Bomber unexpectedly broke the silence but only just, as he muttered to himself, forgetting where he was for a moment maybe, "Regrets and what if's, there will be so many, poor bastards."

He had some blood at the tip of his white beard where he'd touched it with his bloodied hands. He had a weathered face of experience and stout shoulders to support the pride that man carried. He wanted to impress so much but often struggled by trying to impress them too much. They all knew he was a good man though, and the others knew he didn't need to try so much to show it.

The others all knew what Bomber meant. It was natural to play back time if you were a parent and to be able to change the scenario in a million different ways; to have left five minutes earlier if his older brother hadn't dragged his heels, if his father hadn't insisted on going to the shop for a new lighter first, as he'd lost his old one in the sand the day before. They would have already been on the beach if they had. All things to tear a family apart in the following years.

Their family had been devastated. A feeling that families have felt over past centuries for many different reasons, be it war, accident or illness, but that same feeling, all the same, ripping the soul apart in grief. A sudden traumatic change no one could alter, and, of course, they had an investigation to deal with to find out exactly why that car hadn't been able to stop and spare the life of their son.

"His name. I don't even know his name," exclaimed Treavey.

"Steven. His name is Steven," replied Bomber forlornly.

Felicity came bounding into the room for the next shift closely followed by Rambo, laughing about a private joke they had just enjoyed. "Hi, guys!" Felicity shouted at the top of her voice.

Rambo joined in, "Yes you bunch, what's the matter, someone died?!"

Their happy faces waited for a reaction from within the room but the expected one was not forthcoming. As they realised something was amiss, their demeanour changed to fit the solemn mood within the group, and the others tried to explain what had happened.

"Jesus, I'm so sorry," Rambo said softly, "you okay you two? How do you feel after doing CPR on a child, you okay?"

It was unusual to hear this very straight-talking, slightly wacky man speaking with such care.

Bomber nodded in recognition. No one had been more up close and personal than Bomber with the little lad taking air from Bomber's lungs into his and being so close to his ghastly injury too.

"Yes, I think we are okay, aren't we Micky," Bomber replied, "just a shame we couldn't get a result on this one."

There was a pause for a few seconds before Rambo continued, "What's happening with the driver then?"

Treavey had had a fascinating conversation with Sgt Olly Tayler, almost shadowing him whilst on the scene and so he felt as though he could speak with some knowledge. "They are going to get short interviews from the drivers first, then bail them, then once they get the statements from the witnesses, get the reports from the vehicle examiners and accident investigators, they will interview the drivers again and put the file over to CPS to decide what to do. Was it causing death by dangerous driving, or was it just a tragic accident? Who knows right now, but the coroner will want answers. All we know right now is if the VW driver had replaced his door mirror, that 6-year-old, Steven, may well be alive today."

"Shit!" Bomber exclaimed, shaking slightly, "It could come down to that couldn't it, I mean, a stupid door mirror? Woe betides anyone drives past me now with a broken door mirror!"

Micky purposefully stood up behind Bomber and placed each of his hands on his shoulders. "Right, I've had enough of today. It has officially been a very crap day. I'm going home, and I suggest you do too, Bomber and Treavey."

They stood up and began collecting their things leaving Felicity and Rambo behind, Rambo lifting the teapot and shaking it to see if there was one more cup in there.

Rambo shouted after them as they left the station to head home, "Just another day at the office. Well done guys. We are proud of you, aren't we Felicity?

Chapter 5

Educating the young

Felicity and Treavey were attending to a shoplifter in town just a few days later. The premises were a local clothes shop called Riley's and the suspect was Tommy Bradford again. The shop sold high-quality Helly Hanson sailing clothing and it had become very fashionable to steal by local youths. The shop staff were very aware of Tommy in particular, as they knew him as the local shoplifter, so he had to go in unseen and be out quickly with his ill-gotten gains. In order not to be recognised, he had to ply his trade in Newquay or Truro, but sometimes he took his chances and went local again.

It, perhaps, wasn't too surprising because once someone had a conviction, there was little deterrent from carrying on. He was 17 years old and knew he could either work for two weeks to buy a jacket or he could steal one and immediately own it or, at worst, suffer a ticking off in Juvenile court if he was caught.

Treavey and Felicity knew they were wasting their time. That was the whole shift gone now. Processing Tommy, collecting statements, taking him to custody, and sorting out the file was all going to take hours, and for what?

The officers walked into the shop which displayed beautiful and very expensive nautical wear, with little enthusiasm and were invited into the staff room. The shop assistant knew the script. He waited for Felicity to say what the accusation was to Tommy and caution him. Tommy was sitting on a chair wearing a T-shirt and a

Helly Hanson baseball cap. There was a large empty navy-blue backpack lying next to him on the floor.

The shop assistant explained he had been at the counter bending down behind it, sorting out some spare till rolls when he saw Tommy enter the shop, spotted through the glass on the front of the counter. He suspected Tommy believed the shop was empty of staff as he saw him 'select an item,' and nonchalantly walk out of the shop. He followed Tommy, who he had recognised from the beginning and detained him outside.

"Right, was the cap stolen too?" Treavey asked the shop assistant, pointing to the Helly Hansen cap sitting on Tommy's head.

"I imagine so," the staff member replied with a rather despondent sigh, "He definitely hasn't bought it from us, and that cap is our latest style we sell, but I can't prove it, so it's only this jacket, valued at £250, we can say is stolen."

"Right, thanks, are you able to write a proforma statement for us?" Treavey asked, which was soon confirmed when he saw the assistant was already pulling a blank statement from a metal cabinet drawer.

"Yes, I'll be fine. I can fax it to you later if you like."

The two officers led Tommy out of the shop, exposing him to the disapproving passers-by, making the walk as long and painful for him as they could. It was probably the only punishment he would get. "£250?" Treavey said under his breath. "No wonder he does it. He'll put his poor puppy eyes face on, and that youth court will fall for it yet again."

Treavey placed Tommy into the back of the car. He had not cuffed him as there was no way he'd be able to run away from the pair of them. They knew it was just not his style and where was he going to go exactly? He lived opposite the station, for crying out loud.

Felicity sat into the driver's seat and waited for Treavey to get himself in beside Tommy. Tommy was put behind the passenger's seat so he couldn't grab the driver from behind if he felt the urge.

"Right, which station?" asked Felicity. "Truro is about 3 miles nearer and 5 minutes quicker. Where do you fancy Treavey old boy?"

"Whichever," Treavey replied, but then had second thoughts. He had not eaten yet. "Let's go for Newquay, they have a better canteen there!"

The panda car began its slow drive up the hill out of a wonderfully sunny Perranporth on its thirty-minute journey in amongst the holiday traffic. Treavey smiled when he saw the shocked faces of holiday makers in their swimsuits staring at the police car, as a realisation occurred that crime actually did happen in a heavenly place such as this.

Treavey left no time before he was straight on to it. "Right Tommy. I have a very good friend in Perranporth, do you know who that is?"

"Uh? No, and I don't care either," came the disinterested reply from Tommy, who was forlornly sitting hunched over, staring straight ahead at the back of the seat in front.

"Well, I will tell you. Her name is Grace, and she lives in the town, and I understand you and that brother of yours have been causing her a little trouble. It has to stop."

"That fucking tramp. Prove it," he replied with a smirk which every sinew in Treavey's body wanted to slap off his face. Treavey realised this needed a careful approach.

"That 'Fucking tramp', Tommy, is a person. A person called Grace, Tommy, and the great thing about this is I don't have to prove it. Every time I get to hear you have been bullying her; I will go and tell your mother. I talk to Grace all the time, so I will get to hear about it if it happens again and I will make a note of how many times this goes on, and then I can go to the magistrates to get you bound over to keep the peace and guess what, I will then go to the Perranporth Gazette and tell them you have been bound over to stop bullying the homeless. That wouldn't go down too well with your mates now, would it? Hardly the most macho of crimes, bullying the homeless."

The car fell silent for a few moments as it rumbled on through the stunning green Cornish scenery of patchwork-like fields and hedges. It was not a day to be tucked up in a police station interviewing suspects. It was a day to enjoy driving to the beauty-spots, to feel the cool breeze on his face whilst taking in the coastal views and the atmosphere of Cornwall at its absolute best. The sky was a wonderful deep blue with idyllic fluffy cumulus clouds as if painted on canvas.

Tommy looked bored with the routine of being arrested too. Treavey knew Tommy was annoyed he had been caught and it would have been a good jacket to get a quick hundred pounds for, if he had managed to get away with it.

The car was small and for a moment the knees of Treavey and Tommy touched slightly.

"Oh my god, you little faggot!" Tommy shouted in a rather theatrical display. Felicity looked up at the internal mirror, and Treavey rolled his eyes. Tommy had his audience so continued, "You touched me up in the back of the car. Like a bit of sweetmeat, do you? Gay boy!"

Treavey remained silent for a second or two and then very purposefully lifted his left arm and placed his hand directly down on Tommy's knee. He looked straight into Tommy's eyes uncomfortably closely, and replied, "Oh, Tommy darling, you've guessed right, sweetheart, but you know it is perfectly natural to have feelings for men, don't you?"

He gave his knee a little squeeze with his hand, and removed it, before looking straight ahead and carrying on as if nothing had happened. Tommy sat motionless, with his jaw dropping down silently, but nothing came out. There was a slight quiver on his bottom lip. The point had been made. Felicity could not quite believe what she had just heard, and the car remained in complete silence for the rest of the journey.

The panda car entered Newquay Police Station rear car park and Felicity jolted the car gently to select reverse to park it into a space. Treavey swiped the baseball cap off Tommy's head which Treavey suspected he had been wearing as a trophy to rub their noses in to the fact he could often get away with stealing. "Oy! That's my hat!"

"Yes, I'm keeping it safe for you," Treavey replied, but had already opened the car window and the cap was dropped down beside the car onto the tarmac as Felicity reversed back. He was hoping for an accurate placement of the cap in line with the front tyre as it reversed back.

As the car straightened and pulled up, and with Tommy shouting his grievance, Treavey got out of the car and exclaimed, "Oh no Tommy, I'm so sorry, it blew out of the window and Felicity seems to have driven over it."

Treavey sauntered over to the rather squashed looking cap and kicked it in front of him as he comically mimed the process of bending down to pick it up from its original position. Every time he bent down to pick it up, his foot would kick it a few more metres making sure Tommy could see exactly what was happening to his beloved headwear.

Tommy watched as Treavey finally stepped on the cap with his right foot and ground it into the tarmac. He stood up straight whilst standing directly on the cap and gazed around him as if searching for something. "Nope, I can't find it, Tommy, it seems to have gone."

He spun around on his right heel, grinding the hat further into the dust and tarmac. "Hang on, what's this? Here it is, I've found it!" He looked directly down at his feet and picked the, by now rather bedraggled, cap up, walked over to the rear passenger side of the panda car and opened the door. He threw it on Tommy's lap, dirty and scuffed and not looking like a new hat anymore.

Tommy was angry, "I'm going to tell my solicitor." he protested, enraged at what he had just seen.

"You mean my solicitor, right?" Treavey replied, with a rather forced puzzled expression on his face. Felicity had heard this routine from Treavey before, but it was always fun to listen to.

Tommy was straight at him, "No, no dick head, I'm going to tell my solicitor when we go into the station."

Treavey was in full theatrics now. "No, no, no dear boy, he's my solicitor, I'm lending him to you out of the goodness of my heart, don't worry about it, you can borrow him. I'm just a nice guy."

Confused now, Tommy was struggling for words. "Are you mad? I get my own solicitor, you know, he helps me, not you. He's my own."

Tommy decided to release him from his state of confusion as they were walking towards the custody door.

"No Tommy dear, he's definitely my solicitor, because as you will know, I am working and paying tax. You are not working or paying tax. You are, in fact, a drain on society. I am a contributor to society, paying my tax to pay for your solicitor who you have no hope of paying for as long as you continue nicking stuff and being a complete twat. I, on the other hand, am now happy to pay out of my own tax for you to have a solicitor. Is that clearer for you now? Now all I require is a simple thank you. I don't ask for much, just a thank you. Do you think that's unreasonable?"

Treavey smiled at Tommy to confirm he was joking with him and even Tommy was bright enough to realise he had been led into a trap and made to look a bit of an idiot.

Some hours later and both officers were heading back to Perranporth Station with Treavey behind the wheel driving the panda as if it were a taxi cutting through the busy summer traffic of Newquay. They were happy to get out of the station and were free of Tommy.

"That was my old school," Treavey pointed out on the top of Trenance Hill, before swooping down a frighteningly steep decline towards Trenance Gardens, on their way back. "I remember my old green double decker school bus straining to get up this hill to my primary school at the top. Number 577, I think it was. Oh my god, when driving up it, I remember it had to change down a gear at about this point as it's so steep and it always used to roll back a bit and scare the living daylights out of us 6-year-olds in the back."

He turned right at the bottom of the hill and drove along a straight road adjacent to a beautiful green park area bursting with wonderfully manicured summer flowers. There was a large lake in the centre with islands and foot bridges stretching across at a couple of locations. It was called the Boating Lake, and as Treavey and Felicity passed by, they watched the swans and the ducks on the lake and the carefree tourists taking in the stunning flowers whilst eating Kelly's Cornish ice cream. Other tourists in pretty coloured motorised boats chugged under the little bridges separating the various parts to the lake.

"Someone fell into the lake once. It came up to his knees!" Treavey declared. "It gives the impression of being so much deeper, doesn't it?"

Felicity was relaxing in the passenger seat, enjoying the guided tour. The signs of Newquay began to diminish as they whipped along the Gannal, Felicity's attention being caught by some horse riders riding alongside the river and watching some amateur fishermen along the banks casting their lines.

"How come you give Tommy such a hard time Treavey?" Felicity asked, without turning her head from the view.

He turned his head towards hers slightly, to see Felicity still looking across him at the view to his right. Her face felt very near to him as she leant forwards towards him to achieve a slightly better view, very much in his personal space, but he didn't mind at all. Her skin was bright and fresh. He stared at her loose wisps of blond hair from her fringe fluttering like pieces of cotton on the breeze coming through her open window. He studied her a little more closely, observing her tiny freckles on her cheeks like speckles on a Thrush's egg, he hadn't noticed them before. He could feel himself falling for her. He was being hypnotised by her stunningly radiant blue eyes, so dazzling in the sun. Those same eyes which had just caught him out when she glanced at him, anticipating an answer.

Treavey obliged, "If I didn't tease him a bit, he wouldn't fear us or respect us, and it would be twice as bad next time he gave us some cheek. I'm nobody's mug."

"Fair enough," she replied, flashing him the most electric and flirtatious smile. Treavey felt happy right now. Life was good, but he still felt like a schoolboy from that same school he had just passed and his junior and secondary school after that. Nervous about asking a girl out. Nervous about making the first move. It wasn't any easier the older he got.

As they neared Perran, he asked Felicity whether she minded him taking a small detour into town as he wanted to speak to Grace, the vagrant woman. "You like her, don't you?" Felicity remarked with a warm compassionate tone to her voice.

"Yes, I do, Felicity. There is something about that woman. Something special. There's a story there and I'd love to find out what it's about."

Felicity placed her hand on his which was holding the gear stick. "You're all heart aren't you Treavey. You are a kind soul. I like it."

Treavey pulled up at the bottom of the hill in Perran and stopped the car. He glanced back at Felicity, "You drive it back, Felicity, I'll walk back up and I'll see you later."

He marched up to Grace in a park near to the beach car park. She had all her worldly possessions with her, nothing of any value but a lot of bags full of things you wouldn't want to touch without gloves.

It was 4.00 pm and Grace was sitting on a bench gazing out into the middle distance. "Hello Grace, how are you today?"

"It's bloody hot!" she replied rather robotically, then turned to face Treavey who had hesitantly sat down next to her. She gave him a big smile. "Hello, Treavey, what have you been up to then?"

He was soon finding himself being interrogated by Grace about the day's events, so he took advantage of her chattiness and told her the story of him and Felicity taking Tommy in for theft, minus a few details of course.

"That won't teach him, will it? He'll just be let off and free to do it again." Her voice echoed 70 years of experience and resignation. Her weathered face looked at peace with the world. It felt good to talk to her, Treavey was relaxed, almost feeling like he had been talking to his grandmother. He sighed and looked towards the sea he could just about glimpse from where they were sitting.

"I've warned him off messing about with you. I told him, if he does it again, I will make trouble for him, that I'd tell his mother about him and she wouldn't be happy, I know that. After that, I told him things would have to be taken more officially."

Both chatted and enjoyed the glimpse of a sea view ahead through some buildings. Grace paused for a moment. She was deep in thought. "Those brothers, Billy the older one, you know the one who drives the little red car, and Tommy, well I know they are both up to no good with that Dawson chap. It's funny how invisible I can be when I want to be!"

She was fully expecting Treavey to ask more about it, but he didn't see the invitation and so she didn't hold back.

"Drugs, Treavey, drugs!" she shouted, "as you know, that Gary Dawson is the main player, he scatters a bit of the stuff around to keep the rest of those idiots happy, but Billy and Tommy are his runners. But don't think it just stops in Perranporth, oh no."

Treavey suspected this vagrant with a drink problem was a font of knowledge on what was going on in the town or was it all bravado, perhaps? Did she really know what was going on?

They sat in silence for a moment. Treavey leant forward and turned his head to say something to Grace. He was surprised she was wearing such a heavy Harris-tweed overcoat which enwrapped the numerous layers beneath. The smooth glint of that pink plastic bracelet shining through the layers on her wrist caught his attention once more. She was playing with the surface with her dirty engrained fingers, gently rotating it around her wrist, softly touching the childish printed motif as if it were the value of a thousand king's crowns. Her wrinkles on her face couldn't disguise the tragedy she clearly felt in her heart as she gazed at it, and yet at the same time contradicted her emotions by adding just a little joy for her. He had to ask about it one day.

"I used to be in the Police." Grace confided out of nowhere, and as if talking about something rather mundane.

Treavey nearly fell off the bench and had to settle himself. "You what? You used to be in the police?"

Treavey felt perhaps he had been led down the garden path. How could it be true? How could someone end up like this from being a police officer with a steady wage? How could they go from being a police officer to then being in this state, even though she seemed, well, reasonably content with her lot?

"Yes, dear. West Midlands, I joined after the war and was in there for 10 years. Got onto CID and I was exceptionally good at it too."

85

It dawned on Treavey, she really was quite old, around 70, and not just looking old from the hard life she had had.

"What happened?" Treavey asked, trying not to sound too doubtful, but finding her credibility a little hard to swallow.

"It was a long time ago. I was married, had two children." She faded slightly as the memories seemed to come back raw. "Yes, well, it is all over now."

Treavey had his opportunity sooner than he thought. "What do you mean? What happened?" He knew he sounded direct, but he could not leave without knowing more.

Grace shuffled her body to a more comfortable position and stared at him intently. A bright smile spread across her face and her blue eyes seemed to sparkle. "My parents used to bring me on holiday here, so I came back here to live." She turned away from him again and stared towards the sea once more.

He was feeling he was not going to get any more from Grace today. He had updated her on the Bradford brothers and that he'd warned them off. He had got some information they were working alongside Gary Dawson dealing drugs, even though not confirmed but it added to his suspicions, and he'd realised there may just be quite an interesting side to Grace as he had suspected, after all.

"Right, I'd better get off now Grace. It's been really lovely talking to you..." He hauled himself up from the bench and took a few steps towards the entrance of the park. "...I've still got a statement to do before I go off" he shouted back to Grace. He saw her smile at him and she looked content. Treavey felt it had probably done her some good to talk. There can't be too many times she gets the opportunity.

He began walking towards the park exit getting into his stride and heard Grace shout after him. "James and Bee... Barbara was her name." Treavey spun around a little confused. Grace was trying to say something but was finding it difficult to get the words out. "My children. 7 and 9 years old. A car crash you see; killed the three of them. James, Bee and Ron, my husband. All gone in an instant."

She pulled her tatty handbag tight to her chest with both hands. She looked melancholy, deep in her thoughts. Her sparkle in her eyes had faded slightly as she stared ahead in quiet contemplation.

"Right..." Treavey thought to himself, feeling everything was now falling into place. "No wonder she's ended up like this, the poor woman. That explains her pink bracelet. It must have belonged to her little girl. Poor, poor woman, but she's got a friend in me now"

A couple of days later, Treavey and Micky were sitting at the desk in the report room sorting out some paperwork, including some outdated stop-search forms and driving document producers. The sergeant was in his office.

Sergeant Charlie Sash was a mature man although still good looking; athletic, and smart in appearance with well-groomed salt and pepper hair. He had a rather relaxed attitude perhaps, but he made sure things were done correctly and he was much respected amongst the officers under his command. He had a red Audi car he was very proud of, and being a former Traffic sergeant, he kept it in immaculate condition even though it was now a few years old.

"Those brake pads are the same ones I had put on 40,000 miles ago. And still good as new!" he would boast with pride.

The station video player had just finished playing the fortnightly force briefing, the porn had gone and wouldn't be back although Treavey did see a couple of magazines in the desk at the end of the station which someone had placed there for the benefit of others on those lonely night shifts.

Treavey informed Micky what Grace had said about the Bradfords and Dawson.

Micky sat back and slowly breathed in, taking in what had been said. His dark, bushy moustache quivered as released his breath and began to speak. "Yes, that makes sense," he replied. "We need to get the Bradford brothers mobile numbers so we can send them off for a trace. CID asked us if we could try to get the numbers if we can."

Treavey was out to impress and felt rather brave all of a sudden. "I can get them now if you want?" he declared. "Watch this, I've got an idea, it might just work."

He looked on the wall and gazed down the board for the phone number they'd kept for the Bradford household. It was the home number of course, but Treavey quickly dialled it from the station phone and settled himself. Sergeant Sash who had been listening to their conversation from his office next door, wandered in, leant against the door frame, and folded his arms. Micky raised an eyebrow on his bald head looking rather confused and unaware of what Treavey was just about to do.

Treavey put the receiver to his ear and listened to the ring tone. His heart was beating fast, and he could feel his adrenaline pumping around his body. "Hello, is that the householder, please? I need to speak to the owner of the house."

The others were listening intently. The rather one-sided conversation heard by the sergeant and Micky went on. "Ah, good, thank you, Mrs Bradford, congratulations, you are one of a very few people we have called to put you into our free lucky dip here at Vodafone. You have a very good chance of winning a brand-new Vodafone Contract with our very latest model. You have a free Vodafone lucky dip for every mobile number you have in your household."

There's another pause, the stress and concentration were showing on Treavey's face, but his voice didn't give it away. His face relaxed as now it was clear he had the information he needed. He reached across the table for a pen. "Okay, Mrs Bradford, two numbers you say, your son's first?" His face lit up as the sense of victory rushed through his body. He scribbled two numbers down and repeated them out loud for clarity, and he slammed the phone down in victory.

"Bingo!" he shouted with euphoria, standing up and punching the air. Even he didn't think it would actually work, and as a bonus, as he glanced around, he could see the approving nod of sergeant Sash before he turned around without comment and returned to his office. He could not officially approve what had just been done, but he looked impressed.

Micky was grinning which confirmed the approval which Treavey so dearly wanted. Treavey could not quite believe the victory he had just had and relished in the moment, sitting back looking quite smug.

"You'd better watch out when you speak to her next..." Micky added, chuckling, "...she'll say, 'Hey aren't you the one from the Vodafone competition?!'" He laughed before standing up and declaring, "Time for tea, there's always time for tea isn't there... Sarge?!"

The radio blurted out, "Golf 32, are you receiving?"
Treavey answered after a slurp of tea. He had already thought how typical it was. The radio was always disturbing them just as the tea had been poured.

"32, can you attend number 41, Reeves Road. There should be a Mr Giles Bedford. Are you aware of this gentleman?"

"Yes Victor, he's one of our local scallywags."

"He's the one." The reply came back quickly. "Well, he's breached his police bail by being seen out and about last night breaking his curfew of 2200 hrs to 0600 hours. Officers have written statements in Newquay to confirm this.

"Coming Micky?" Treavey shouted, keen to get going.
Micky remained motionless apart from taking a slow slurp from his tea. He paused, purposefully giving off an air of superiority, and replied, "All in good time, after my tea, all

in good time. He isn't going anywhere, is he? He may not even be there."

Treavey was only too happy to oblige and returned to his seat to enjoy the rest of his tea too. Half an hour later, however, they were trundling along to the address of Bedford to arrest him for breaching his bail conditions.

They pulled up to the semi-detached council house and got out of the panda to make their way to the front door. It was an old wooden door with peeling paint and did not look very strong at all. If they knew he was in there, if he'd refused to come out, then Treavey was certain he had a power of entry. He placed the 'big red key' outside the front door. This was a 20-kilogram doorbuster painted red which would get through almost anything when swung at it. Micky slipped around to the rear leaving Treavey at the front. Both officers stood back from the house looking up at the windows.

Treavey shouted up to what he believed was the bedroom window. Of course, he would still be in bed, it was noon, and he would have been up most of last night breaching his curfew. "Giles. Giles Bedford? It's the police, we need to talk."

A rather bored sounding voice came from the open top window. "How many of you down there?"
Treavey hesitated. There was no point in lying. "Two," he replied.

"Well speak to each other, then," he replied.

"Oh boy," Treavey thought, "a comedian" and stepped forward to press the doorbell. Almost immediately, he heard the same voice again,

"Fuck off copper, you ain't welcome here."

"Giles, you need to come to the station to answer why you have broken your curfew, can you come downstairs please?"

"Fuck off," was the rather abrupt reply once more and the upstairs window slammed shut. Micky returned around to the front and they discussed their options. Treavey was first to share his opinion.

"Well, he's just told the law to fuck off, we have a power of entry, so I think we send a message, don't you?"

Micky stood in quiet contemplation, then very calmly added, "If you are sure, you newer guys probably know the latest I suppose, it sounds right."

"Yes, I promise you, Micky, breach of bail and we can pile on in there, otherwise it would be ridiculous to have to allow someone to put the V's up to the law and not be able to arrest them over it."

Treavey, gingerly hauled the big red key to his waist and slowly swung it back to find momentum. He aimed for the door lock, swinging the metal weight towards it with a firm and accurate swing, but to their surprise, it promptly bounced off with almost no effect. The door was stronger than he suspected so he swung it again, then again.

"Need a hand?" Micky chirped in with a wry smile.

"Nope," came the reply between puffs. In frustration, Treavey smashed the enforcer into the centre of the door which promptly split it in two, down the centre.

"Woah, I wasn't expecting that," exclaimed Treavey, "but I guess that does the job just fine."

They sauntered into the house to meet a rather annoyed and speechless Giles Bedford sitting on the stairs staring at them. In as calm a manner as possible, Treavey said, "Ok Mr Bedford, that was all rather unnecessary, wasn't it?"

The officers took him to Truro and had a good chat with him, mainly about the drugs coming into the town. As with most criminals, once the bravado was over, it was quite a civilised conversation, but he wasn't giving much away. Micky and Treavey did not want to give away what they knew such as who they suspected. They didn't want him to warn the Bradford brothers and Dawson that the police were on to them, so, unfortunately, it was a conversation which danced around somewhat and achieved very little.

The officers returned to the station having dealt with Bedford, feeling rather pleased with themselves.

"Time for that tea I think Treavey," Micky declared on entering the station. "Your round I think!"

Sergeant Sash casually appeared around the corner and stood in the doorway.

Treavey cheerfully asked, "Tea Sarge? We've got one on the go. We got Giles Bedford in."

"Yes, so I hear, well done," the sergeant replied, but he was standing in a manner which hinted more would be coming. He had that look about him. "I've had the landlord of his flat on the phone asking if we are going to pay for the door. Are you absolutely sure we had a power of entry for a breach of bail?"

Treavey confidently responded, "Yes sarge, breach of bail holds a power of entry," and to confirm the fact, he pulled out a photocopy of some legislation he had located earlier. The sergeant took his time reading it. "Court bail. It talks about court bail but doesn't mention police bail."

Treavey felt the blood drain from his face and his mouth ran dry. "Oh, right, bloody hell."

Sergeant Sash looked quite stern. He stared at Treavey, glanced across to Micky who shrugged his shoulders, and as he turned to walk out towards his office, he shouted, "Best we pay for the door then, and with some luck, they'll never even guess the rest."

The subject was never mentioned again, and it grew the respect for their sergeant by the team. He backed them when they did things with good intentions, but which unfortunately may have gone a little wrong. He knew he would have far more problems if his officers were not 'go get them' people, who just sat back and did as little as possible. He far preferred an energised and dynamic team, and his team knew he had their backs. Treavey would never forget that.

Chapter 6

The storm

It was a cold, very wet and windy night shift at the beginning of August which Treavey had just begun. He was on his own tonight and was looking forward to it being quiet as he had not slept well. He stared at the clock in the report room and noticed it was only 2.00 am. Wolfy, the jet-black neighbour's cat had come in and was curled up in his temporary bed. He looked perfectly settled, purring quietly whilst manipulating his body around so his nose met all four paws, and he was blending his rich thick fur into the quilted bedding next to the radiator. Police station radiators were usually blaring hot in the summer and switched off in the winter. Nobody knew why; they just were but Treavey was thankful for it tonight.

There was certainly a nip in the air and not a lot was happening to keep him stimulated. There was no traffic on the road to stop-check, there were no troublesome youths up to no good in the town; he felt it was going to be a long night.

"Golf 31, can you attend 'Range View' on Brecon Road, St Agnes? Reported by the son of an elderly lady who is suffering from Alzheimer's who has disappeared from the house sometime in the last 3 hours. There is currently a great concern for her safety as it's believed she could be just dressed in her nightie."

Treavey felt a pang of adrenaline rush through him when he heard the call. He stood up, catching the notepad on the edge of the desk which flew across the surface of the table clipping the edge of an empty mug and making it clatter loudly. Wolfy was awake, up and in a nanosecond, through the cat flap and out of the police station. He had gone in a flash.

"Ah, sorry mate, didn't mean to startle you," Treavey muttered whilst he stared at the rain pounding against the glass outside, the wind forming the raindrops into swirling patterns on the glass.

He held his breath as if diving underwater and pushed the door open, striding through it purposefully and ensuring it slammed behind shut him. He felt the ice-cold rain on his skin and the wind battering his face as he made his way to the panda car parked at the rear of the station car park. As he trotted towards the car, he noticed the bushes lining the car park being tossed in all directions by the raging whirlwind, so he hastened his pace, ducked his head down to hide his exposed neck from the elements, dragged the car door open and slumped into the driver's seat slamming the door beside him. He settled himself into the seat and checked the back seat for his waterproofs. He was going to need them tonight.

"Okay Victor, I'm en route, I'm not happy about this so can we have whatever units you can get hold of, even from other areas please, she won't survive long out here. Could you ensure we have a dog coming and is Oscar 99, the police helicopter, available? I assume the weather counts that one out?"

"Yes Golf 31, the heli is grounded. We do have a dog coming from Truro. In the meantime, we will update you with any information by the caller. He's still on the line but he's going out again to search for her as she's been known to gravitate towards the cliffs."

Treavey remembered his tutor saying with Alzheimer's patients, they were usually a lot nearer than you expected, and they tended to walk downhill and in a straight line." He remembered his tutor had been a 30-year manual of experience for him, and all that knowledge had been at his disposal whilst being tutored by him. He would be using that knowledge again now.

"Victor, I'm going to go towards the cliffs around St Agnes Head, down to Tubby's Head just in case as she would be around there by now, but can we make absolutely sure she isn't in the spare room at home, or in the garden shed or something?"

Treavey remembered spending hours looking for a small child who had gone missing from a house only to suffer the embarrassment of the owner locating them in the dog kennel outside after much time and resources had been used in searching the area for them. Another missing child had been found under the duvet on the bed playing hide and seek, and generally, unless it was a stormy night at 3.00 am with rain and wind, then someone would have reported an elderly lady wandering the streets in a thin nightie. Of course, there would probably be no witnesses at this time of night at the location she'd gone missing in, unfortunately.

The dog handler came on the air, "Victor from Delta 21, can you just hold that unit, as the son has been walking around, it is going to be tough to distinguish which is his track and which is his mother's? Can you get him to update us where he's been and stop him going any further, he's going to mess up my track?"

Treavey agreed to meet the dog handler at Wheal Coates car park on the coastal footpath and carry out a search on foot up the coast path along the whole clifftop towards St Agnes Head. Hopefully, they would come across her if she had gone in that direction. Otherwise, she should be found in the lanes. If she had gone into a field somehow, then they'll probably never find her unless the dog picked up her scent. The control room had managed to contact the son who had agreed to return to the house to assist a Truro unit to help him search the house and grounds for his mother. It may sound a bit strange, but people could hide themselves away in the tiniest of places if they were suffering from a mental illness. There was another reason to search the house of course. To search for the body in case she had been murdered by the son. It happens.

Twenty-five minutes later and Treavey met up with the dog unit at the RV point. He recognised the dog handler immediately.

Dave was a slim tall man in his 40's, with the weathered looks of someone looking very much his age. He had pointed facial features with wispy blonde hair and a kind face which invited conversation, especially if it was about his dogs. Dogs were very much his priority in life, and it showed with his style of practical clothing and dirty, scuffed boots. Treavey liked him and was always relieved when he turned up as he always put maximum effort into any job he was sent to. He had two dogs, Finchy, the German shepherd, and Lucy, the spaniel for drugs searches and of course he always brought them both along, just in case.

"Hey, Dave, great to see you mate, not looking good this one."

Dave looked up with a cheerful grin through the lashing rain and spoke in a surprisingly soft voice, "Oh I don't know Treavey, it seems the perfect place for a lovely evening walk. But think of the poor buggers in those tents, mind. Wouldn't like to be on those campsites tonight."

Dave released a beautiful beast of a German Shepherd out from the rear of the van. "Come on Finchy, good lad, let's see what you can do for us today, eh boy?"

Before long, the leash was fed out and Finchy had his nose to the ground. He was instantly scanning the gaps in the hedges and over the stone walls with his nose where any scent would waft and scatter in its attempts to escape the path. An experienced dog and handler would recognise a false lead and after a cursory investigation, would be back on to the original path of the scent. Dog and handler were in complete harmony, and whatever Finchy noticed from the point of his incredibly sensitive nose, Dave recognised at the end of the leash some ten or so metres away.

Treavey followed Dave and Finchy at a distance, ensuring the light from his Mag-Lite torch didn't disturb or distract them, but it was as black as the ace of spades and he wondered how the hell Dave managed to guide his way through the uneven ground, with rocks and stones jutting out in the pitch blackness, ready to catch a foot or a shin. Vicious gorse bushes bursting out from either side of the narrow path and thick ferns were randomly blocking the way, ready to trip up the unsuspecting walker and to toss them into a nearby gorse bush.

Treavey glanced across to his left, over the vast expanse of sea but just saw blackness. He squinted his eyes against the stinging rain and attempted to focus on what may be out there, but he could only see dark shapes moving like monsters frolicking through the Cornish surf, which crashed onto the glistening black jagged rocks below letting out howls of pain and anguish before repeating the process over and over again, wave after wave.

How terrified those seamen in wooden ships under sail must have been, and for each generation of shipwrecked seamen to hear the very same sounds, having fallen foul of the enticing perceived security of the Cornish motherland. A motherland which so cruelly drew them onto the hidden rocks set some distance off from the jagged line of the coast. They would surely have known they had met their final hour, heading towards those very same cliffs before the wooden hulls of their ships were smashed to a mass of splinters. Their souls lost forever, their bodies rarely to be found, but, if washed up some days later, would have been buried far from home in local graveyards, which still remain today.

"Mate!" Treavey shouted up to Dave having to cup his hands to form a loud hailer around his mouth, "I'll go back to the car and go around to St Agnes Head to wait for you there, okay?"

Dave put his hand up in acknowledgement and carried on with the track without turning around. Treavey shone his torch again like a lighthouse scanning its beam across the cliffs, lighting up the silver darts of rain coming in from the Atlantic. The sodden jacket being worn by Dave flapped in the howling storm. It was clear Dave was past caring now, he was going to get wet, so he embraced it. This was a man and his dog with a purpose. Dog handlers lived dog handling, it was part of life itself, it was not a department which could be joined one moment and moved on from the next. It was almost majestic to see them in action, one unit of handler and dog working together, each knowing exactly what the other was doing, thinking even, and trusting each other implicitly.

Treavey returned to his car and cleared the back seat. There could well be a very sodden dog handler with his friend sitting on that seat in a moment, so it had to be prepared. He slowly drove to St Agnes Head and listened in to the radio which confirmed the lady was not in the house or nearby.

"We'll soon see," Treavey thought to himself, "many have been found hiding nearby in the past."

As he drove into the small car park, he waited for a moment, enjoying the shelter of his car. He switched the headlights off as they were merely illuminating the granite wall opposite. He sat in silence and listened for a few seconds more, listening to the howling storm and feeling the car rocking gently, being buffeted by the wind before a sudden jerk jolted the car as if the storm giant was throwing its disgust at him for daring to try to combat its efforts.

He watched a creepy moonlight attempt to break through the thunder clouds, so angry were they, they soon shut it out again, and the moon disappeared behind a thicker and even more angry storm front than before.

"Sod it!" Treavey said, holding his breath again as he threw the door open against the wind and strode out into the night towards the footpath to await Dave and Finchy.

He made his way over to a slab of granite protruding out into the Atlantic and sat on his haunches, cupped his hands over his eyes to protect them from the stinging rain and wind, and stared towards where he expected them to come from. He felt a drop of rain running down his neck, down his bare chest and into the warm folds of skin around his stomach forcing an involuntary freezing spasm across his muscles.

"Ah well, it wasn't going to last for long was it?" He resigned himself to the fact, adjusted his position slightly, pulled the hood more tightly around his face and continued to stare into the far distance along the coast. He felt a raindrop run to the end of his nose, hang there for a second or two before another drop pushed it off the end and took up its position.

In the distance, Treavey could faintly hear a humming sound which distracted him, and he attempted to hone in on it to locate its direction. "Surely nothing would be flying tonight, right? It must be a motorbike or a car, maybe a boat, no, don't be silly, no chance. What the hell is that sound?"

The sound got louder, and he realised he was not imagining it. It was as if the engine was struggling against the elements, but he could not see what it was.

"It must be a plane, but surely there is simply no way it can be?"

The sound of the engine changed from a distant buzz to a much louder throbbing motor. It did seem to be a light aircraft, but it simply could not be seen. Treavey listened intently, hearing it getting louder and louder as it made its way very low level up the coast towards his position. The engine managed to beat the sound of the storm for a second or two as the plane passed overhead before disappearing further towards the north hiding any trace it was ever there at all.

"Victor, did you say the Police Heli was not available, I've just heard an aircraft above us?"

"Not a chance on a night like tonight Golf 31, nothing is flying tonight if it knows what's good for it."

He sat there for a moment, wondering if the atmosphere had been playing tricks on him. He gazed towards where the plane had gone. No lights, no sound of engines, nothing. He glanced back expectantly along the cliff looking for Dave and Finchy.

"Is that something? Yes, I see them, a torch, it dims and is flicking around all over the place. Finchy must have got a scent. A fox maybe, you never know but these police dogs are usually pretty good at not being distracted, but these are testing conditions."

He watched the torchlight for a little while longer. He watched it head back slightly in the opposite direction, then turn again towards him once more, and finally head through the gorse towards the edge of the cliff.

"Shit, be careful Dave," Treavey exclaimed.

"Got something here!" exclaimed Dave. "Yes, she's here, stand by..."

There was an unbearable pause whilst everyone listened on the channel. The radio operators in the room were waiting patiently with everyone else.

"Victor from Delta 21, this is the lady we are looking for; confirmed. She is very cold and wet, but she is alive and she's conscious. I am going to cut across to the road at the simplest point I can from here where hopefully we can meet another unit? Can you call an ambulance please?"

"Well done Delta 21, brilliant work," the radio operator announced.

There was a very audible sigh of relief as normality continued for the control room. Treavey was already running back to his car and he eventually met Dave at the most convenient point with his panda car already prepared at 28 degrees set on his heater.

"Hey Dave," Treavey said having shut the frightened lady in the rear of his police car, "you earned your money today mate, well done. A life saved without a doubt."

Dave shrugged his shoulders and replied quite solemnly, "Well yes, maybe, but I wonder if she's thanking me for it, bless her heart. She's in a world of fear in her mind, there for the grace of god mate, there for the grace of God."

Treavey reflected for a second or two. He wondered what this woman used to do for a career when she was in the prime of her life. This awful disease chose anyone at random it seemed. Indeed, that could be himself one day. No one knows. All the more reason to make the best of life now. Now, he had said that to himself before enough times.

"Hey Dave, did you hear that plane fly past?"

Dave looked at him a little confused and smiled as if expecting the punch line. "Plane?"

"No, nothing mate, well done anyway," replied Treavey. Perhaps he had been hearing things after all. It couldn't possibly have landed anywhere in this weather.

Dave queried, "Hey, that plane you spoke about, you don't think it was a late Spitfire returning from a sortie, do you? After all, you do have that old second world war Spitfire base just over there." He did not wait for an answer but continued packing his equipment back in the van.

Treavey didn't reply either. He was feeling a little nauseous now. Could it have possibly been the lost soul of a Spitfire pilot returning to base?

He slowly drove towards the woman's home address having asked to meet the ambulance crew there, and where he was going to meet her son too. Treavey was sweating from the heat and could hardly see through the screen due to the condensation from the damp interior with the car heater being full on. He was rather uncomfortable, but it was the least he could do. The elderly woman was wrapped in a space blanket supplied by Dave which impressed Treavey. He had been prepared to have that blanket with him when he found the casualty. Treavey glanced at her aged face in the mirror. Like the bark of a tree showing decades of experience, and stories behind each wrinkle.

"Enid, isn't it?" enquired Treavey.

He already knew of course, but he wanted to have an in for a conversation.

As bright as a button, she replied, "Yes dear, Enid, and who are you? You aren't Mark. Where is he?"

"I'm taking you back to your son Enid. You walked away from the house in the storm, I think you were a little confused, but you are safe now, we're going home."

The space blanket was falling aside exposing her frail skeleton beneath, her skull barely covered by the thinnest layer of skin, her sodden grey streaks of hair almost transparent. Treavey wondered if he would be like her one day. What did she use to do? The inquisitiveness got the better of him. She probably wouldn't remember but it was worth a go.

"Enid, my darling, what did you used to do for a career?" She continued staring ahead as if the question had passed her by. There was silence as Treavey manoeuvred the panda through a junction around a large collection of gravel washed into the centre of the road and continued towards the house which wasn't far now.

"It's very hot in here," she exclaimed in an authoritative voice.

"I'm sorry Enid, I'll turn it down. I'm glad you aren't cold anyway." Treavey stared through the screen as the car pulled up to the front of the house.

"Headmistress," came the reply, splitting through the atmosphere like a streak of lightning. "I was a headmistress, for 30 years at an all-girls school. From 8 to 18 they were. My subjects were mathematics and English."

Treavey felt sad. Sad that this fine woman, assuming it was true, and he believed so, had been an incredibly intelligent and influential woman for so many young women. She would have shaped their lives and helped them decide on careers, they would have looked upon her as a stable figure of authority as they grew up through the troubling age of youth. They would have no doubt wept if looking at her now. How life had been so cruel. How evil it could be.

The ambulance pulled up behind the patrol car and Enid was coaxed into the back for a check-up. He waited in the porchway of the little house and chatted to Mark, her son. Treavey sparked the conversation off with, "She was telling me she was a headteacher."

"Yes, a bloody good one at that. One of the best. It is such a shame this has happened to Mum. She gets very frustrated. She gets so frustrated in fact; she can get quite angry. It is most unlike how she used to be. We have so many arguments now, I try to keep calm but, oh my god, it can be frustrating for me as well."

He sounded very despondent and at the end of his tether. Treavey didn't say anything in reply, but stared at the ambulance, thinking about the women's torment inside.

The ambulance door opened, and Enid was led out with a warm cotton NHS blanket around her.

"That's better," he thought. Treavey had no faith in those space blankets at all. How on earth could any heat be passed on to a person's flesh and not just waft away on the breeze?

As she shuffled past Treavey, she gave him a casual look and said, "Oh James, when are we going to the school? You are late, you silly boy."

Treavey replied without hesitation, "Yes, don't worry, we'll be leaving in 10 minutes, is that okay?"

"Righto, how lovely," she replied, as she shuffled enthusiastically into the house with the woman paramedic making her way up the stairs with her.

Mark stared at Treavey, his mouth hanging open for a second before saying, "I'm sorry?"

"Oh, I do apologise, sir, I should know my place," Treavey corrected himself and looked rather embarrassed, but continued, "My great aunt suffered from dementia, and I was brought up with her as a child. We used to just agree with her which took the confrontation out of it. Say she'd just had dinner and she then asked when dinner was; if we told her she'd just had it, she would be frustrated and angry because in her mind she was convinced it wasn't true, but she'd forgotten she had just had it. She would be embarrassed and may even think we were deceiving her. So, we'd just agree with her and say dinner was on the way, and 10 minutes later, she may ask again, and we would say it again. Obviously, we'd make sure she wasn't hungry."

Mark chuckled and looked at Treavey with a smile. "I should try that, thanks. It makes sense. I suppose it gets rid of any conflict."

"That's right," confirmed Treavey, "Often you will find they only say something once, you reply to them and you don't hear about it again, rather than having that confrontation which can frustrate both of you. It's worth a try anyway. I'm not an expert, but it worked for us most of the time. Who is James, by the way?"

Mark looked solemn and quietly replied, "He was my brother. He committed suicide 10 years ago."

"I'm so sorry, Mark, really I am."

The paramedic walked out of the house and looked at Mark. "She's fast asleep. Out like a light!"

Mark spun his head around to Treavey. "Oh my god, I think it may just have worked, thank you so much."

Treavey made his way back to his panda car and got in. He pulled his door hard, to close it against the wind and rain and he was back safe in his oasis of shelter and warmth once more.

"This is the best bit about policing," he thought to himself, "It's a cliché maybe, but boy, helping people who need it beats everything. You can keep the shoplifters."

He set off in his car and with a quick flash of blue lights as a farewell, saluted Mark who was waving from his front door, and he headed for the station for a well-earned hot cup of coffee.

As he made his way back, he negotiated the flood water in the lanes, the branches and mud which had collected in the road. There was a flood pouring off a saturated adjacent field cascading water across the road in front of him and bringing debris with it. He manoeuvred his way towards the main road and sighed with relief as the road became a little wider and more forgiving. He saw the dog handler's car draw up behind him some moments later. It seemed Dave was heading back to the nick for a coffee and a dry-off too. Treavey was happy as that would be a good chat for a bit, and it would kill another hour or so.

They drew up to the station car park and Treavey glanced opposite to the Bradfords' house. His attention was drawn to the upstairs lights being on.

"Strange," he thought, "they aren't usually on this late."

He dismissed it and walked into the station pushing himself against the gusts of wind which were still incredibly strong. He pulled the station door open just a little and waited for Dave to get out of his van. Dave trotted towards Treavey, with Finchy shaking himself off behind him and they all headed into the report room.

Wolfy the cat was back resting on his bed by the radiator too, making the most of the peace and quiet that had just been so rudely disturbed. He lifted his head lazily and looked over with quiet indignation, as unconcerned as a cat could possibly be, when looking at a huge beast which had been trained to catch humans and bring them down with its bed of shark-like teeth. Finchy sniffed Wolfy's rump and sneezed, plodded to and fro with his huge bear-like paws and circled, slumping down on the floor next to him. By the time Dave and Treavey return from the kitchen with a coffee, Finchy was lying flat on his side next to Wolfy.

"Like the best of friends," Treavey observed warmly.

"Oh yes," Dave agreed, "He's such a big sop really, and he knows it!"

"Golf 31, we are getting a report of a fire in the trees near Penwartha. Local reports say it looks as if an aircraft has just come down."

Both officers as well as Finchy were instantly en route, with blue lights reflecting shards of dazzling blue lightning 360 degrees around them. After a few hundred metres it became clear the blue lights were a hindrance with no traffic on the road, so they switched them off. It could be incredibly distracting for the driver of the police car in front, especially when reflecting off the raindrops too. They headed off into the storm in the general area of Penwartha, hoping to find something obvious and indeed there was. As they approached a wooded area, they saw some flickering candles in the trees with what looked like a bonfire at the base of them. The officers stopped their cars and tramped across the fields towards them. Dave left Finchy in the van; he probably wouldn't be needed here.

"Fucking hell Dave, have a look at that up there!"

Treavey pointed right above his head into the tops of the trees to point at what looked like a manikin caught up in the branches, its upper limbs hanging down, the low limbs caught up like pieces of rope twisted within the leaves. The scene resembled a horror movie.

The officers updated the control room and moved forward looking for any survivors. It looked like the wreckage of a relatively small aircraft. They saw very thin pieces of fibreglass being blown around in the gale, some large pieces flapping and slapping against a nearby tree trunk.

Treavey flashed his torch along the ground into the woods and found another body laying across the grass, still attached to a seat. A male, he suspected by what was left of the clothing. He rolled the seat over and saw the person had such bad injuries from being catapulted out of the aircraft and tossed through the trees, he decided it was not worth attempting to breathe life into him. Alongside the body, was an engine block from the light aircraft with its propeller still attached, but twisted and bent with the impact of the trees and then plummeting to the ground.

"We've got to push the button on this one, Dave mate. The civil aviation authority or whoever they are will be all over this. I wonder what they are doing out in this weather. I knew I had heard a plane earlier tonight. I thought it was my mind playing tricks on me."

Treavey surveyed the scene with his torch again to see if he had missed any further bodies. He saw the plane had hit an area of trees on the top of a hilltop. It seemed they must have got lost and as the plane had hit the trees, the weight of the engine had tried to pull the very light plane through them with its momentum, but it was just shredded, instead. The place stunk of aviation fuel, but it was raining bucket loads, so they felt relatively safe.

"Shit, you don't think they were delivering drugs, do you?" Treavey said.

"Why do you say that?" Dave inquired.

"We've been getting a lot of drugs into Perranporth recently. We know its cheap stuff and we are well above our average for drug overdoses. We reckon a few of our local scrotes are involved. You never know, it would all make sense. We have a couple of old airfields around here including that Spitfire one just down the road."

"Let's have a quick look to see if there are any drugs amongst this lot before all the fuss starts, Dave. Is yours a drugs dog?" the thought suddenly coming to Treavey.

"Yes, I have a spaniel in the van, he's drugs trained." He looked at Treavey and both were looking mischievous as they knew they should be shutting the scene down for a fingertip search tomorrow in the daylight, but they wanted answers and it would be nice for them if they were the ones to find the drugs.

Ten minutes later and Lucy the spaniel was ignoring the gales and the torrential rain as she was simply happy being at work, wagging her rear end with huge, exaggerated enthusiasm. She ignored the body lying on the ground after a cursory sniff and went to work amongst the foliage at the base of the nightmarish scene which lay above.

She darted off to the right and lay down calmly beside a larger part of the fuselage which had fallen between two tree trunks. Dave dragged his legs over the obstruction to wedge himself into the cavity left by the tree and bushes to get a closer look. He glanced back at Treavey who was standing motionless in the torrential rain, the daybreak beginning to make itself known behind him, now soaked to the skin but not feeling any of its discomfort anymore. He couldn't wait to see what Dave was going to reveal. Lucy was showing all the signs of a drugs find, lying down looking back at her master with an excitable bark.

"Guys, what are you up to?" A voice came from behind making them jump as if caught with their hand in the cookie jar.

"Felicity! Morning! You're early." Treavey replied.

Felicity was marching across the field, the light from the morning very much apparent now, but certainly not enough to cast shadows as the storm was still making itself known with a vengeance.

"Yes, hi guys," Felicity sounded out of breath, perhaps from the excitement from the unusual seriousness of the scene which lay before her. This was one to tick off her bucket list as a police officer. A plane crash. Gruesome enough but not enough to leave a lasting mental scar as a larger plane disaster may do.

"Probably best to just leave it to the experts now," she continued, "don't want to miss anything or step on any evidence. I'd just come away guys, as you probably aren't helping at the moment."

Treavey stumbled over an attempt at a reply to sell his argument to Felicity but he soon realised he was unable to do so convincingly. Forensics was paramount, not settling one's inquisitiveness. Dave, Lucy the drugs dog, and Treavey reluctantly moved out of the scene and Felicity began to put out blue and white police cordon tape around certain obvious access points to the scene.

"How come so early Felicity?" Treavey asked as he tied one end of the tape to a gate post whilst she tied the other end.

"Oh, I was called in early because of this job. You've got a statement to do, still haven't you? I'll wait for CID; you get yourself back and start your statements if you want."

Treavey and Dave gratefully made their way towards the cars, Lucy still wagging her back end enthusiastically.

"Blimey, that was a night, Dave." Treavey declared. "I was expecting it to be a dull one and dear old Edna, that missing lady, seems ages ago now."

Dave paused in thought for a moment and replied, "Certainly does mate, let's hope they find some drugs in that bit of fuselage. Wish I had just opened it now. Lucy must have wondered why I didn't. There just isn't any other reason for the plane to be here at night and especially with the weather like tonight."

Treavey nodded in agreement. "Shame Felicity turned up when she did, or maybe we are just missing the obvious innocent reason why it was flying around here. I'm going to call in when I wake up this afternoon to find out what it was all about. I can't wait until tonight to find out."

Chapter 7

Where's the back-up?

"Nothing?" Treavey exclaimed as he walked in for his final night shift the following day. "Bloody nothing?"

He was gutted quite frankly and slammed his bag onto the report room desk with a smack. Wolfy sprung off from his bed and made a beeline for the cat flap and he was gone. He knew it was likely to get louder.

"Who put that fucking cat flap in the door anyway? It's not even our cat!" shouted Treavey, not waiting for an answer. Bomber was beginning to stand up with his finger raised but soon sat back down again, having realised it was a rhetorical question and that it was probably best not to upset Treavey any further.

Treavey stomped off into the kitchen and began making a cup of tea for himself.

"Yes please!" Rambo shouted, looking at Bomber wearing a wide grin and very much enjoying the moment.

"Fuck you! Fuck you all!" shouted back Treavey to which Bomber and Rambo burst into laughter. Treavey looked around the corner with pure rage on his face but soon saw the ridiculousness of the situation and joined them. Wolfy returned through the cat flap as he felt it was finally safe to come back. Peace had been restored.

"Who's on nights with me?" Treavey enquired. "You both look knackered, to be honest, so I hope it's not either of you two," he quipped. "I'll take my chances with the cat."

Rambo replied, "Your cheeky twat," with a chuckle.

Treavey carefully placed a fresh cup of tea next to him and returned to the tray he'd brought in, to hand one to

Bomber too. They were both grateful and normality had been restored.

"So, I now know they found no drugs, but have any further details come through yet?" enquired Treavey.

"No, nothing," answered Bomber, "Except they think they were bloody stupid flying around last night and were probably flying under the radar. They aren't entirely sure where it came from but think it flew down from a private airfield in the midlands somewhere. They think maybe they got rid of their stash already if they were delivering drugs, or perhaps it was to do with something completely different we don't know about yet. The crew are well known, one ex-forces pilot. Incidentally, did you hear about the guy who killed that wee lad in the high street with his car the other day?"

Treavey snapped from one interesting topic to one he found just as fascinating. "No, what about him?" he asked, looking intense.

Bomber continued, more solemnly now. "He only went and bloody killed himself."

"Fuck off he didn't," replied Treavey genuinely shocked.

Bomber tried to show he didn't care too much, and it was just one of those things.

Treavey continued, "But, but seriously? I mean, he had a grandson of the same age." Treavey was struggling to know what to say.

Bomber looked thoughtful, "You just don't know what is too much for someone to bear. He found out it was his fault the car ran away with him. The brakes were fine, the car was mechanically sound, he simply slammed his foot on the accelerator thinking it was the brake and panic did the rest. We made comments at the time he would be reminded every year of the lad he killed, as he was the same age as his grandson. He would have learned to cope in time. It wasn't really his fault at the end of the day."

Rambo cut in, "I know you guys were there, it can't be easy. Some people just want out. They think people are better off without them; how many times have you heard someone say that on the top of a multi-storey car park? They are always grateful if they get through the bad times. Life just isn't fair, is it? Like Bomber said, it was just a bad reaction to a car coming out in front of him. He couldn't control his reflexes, but it's a lifelong reminder, feeling pain every time he sees his grandson."

Treavey sipped his tea and stared at an area of blank wall in front of him. "I wonder what the other chap feels now, the one who started it all? Ultimately it all started with him, coming out into the road thinking it was clear. A series of events starting from something as insignificant as a broken door mirror leading to the deaths of two people. Who'd have believed it?"

They finished their tea in silence. Policing wasn't all that great sometimes. Treavey got up off his seat and meandered over to Wolfy who was snoozing. He bent down on his haunches and gently stroked him listening to him purring contentedly. He reflected on things for a moment, thinking about how fragile life was, and although things may have seemed good being on holiday for example, or retiring by the coast having had a fulfilling life as a headmistress, life could change so quickly.

He gives himself some advice, "Just make the most of life Treavey, don't waste it mate."

The other two were packing up after their shift. It looked like Treavey was on his own again tonight. He did not mind too much especially if he had a few jobs to attend to keep him busy. He knew the control room was fully aware he was single crewed with back up some time off so they looked after him and made sure he had others on the way if they thought he may be needing it.

"Good luck with the rave, Treavey," said Bomber as he followed Rambo out of the door.

"Rave?" Treavey enquired, suspected they were winding him up.

"Yes, of course, you won't have heard," Bomber continued, "It's probably all about nothing. Shame it wasn't last night, to be honest, but as you see the weather is decidedly lovely out there tonight. There has been a lot of cars meeting up in St Austell, Truro, Bodmin and of course Newquay, but no one knows exactly where the meet is happening. I suggest it won't be anywhere around here. It's not like we have two large airfields near here is it?!" Bomber laughed louder than he had intended, "Sorry mate, I'm sure you'll be fine!"

The door slammed behind them and Treavey sat in silence. He stared at Wolfy, watching his ever so soft little belly moving up and down with the sleepy breaths he took. "How comforting it must be to be a cat," he thought. "Just blissful, prancing about as if you owned the place, grabbing some rare mammal out of nature and playing with it until it gives up its will to live. Or of course, he can just wander over to one of several sources of ready-made meals set out for him in several houses in his neighbourhood. What a life, now sleeping by a radiator on a comfy bed. What mugs we are."

Treavey was bored already. He was examining the lifecycle of a cat whilst watching Wolfy doing nothing but enjoying the warmth and security of his bed next to the radiator. It could still get a little bit nippy on night shifts though so he was no doubt very happy to accept it's warmth.

He was distracted by the radio which was reporting a convoy of cars leaving Newquay along with others having just left Truro in a convoy. Local police have already lost them, so the control room was eager to receive any updates.

"Best I go to high ground then," Treavey decided. "Can't be too hard to find a whole convoy of headlights driving through the pitch-black countryside."

He drove the panda car out of Perranporth driving to the top of the hill but found nothing as he scanned the countryside around him. He drove to Rejerrah Hill on the way to Newquay, a hill very much like a big dipper on a fairground. It was a very long straight road which crossed a very extreme valley. Cyclists loved going down it, but they were not so keen on pedalling up the other side. Treavey remembered doing just that when he was a teenager cycling from Newquay to Truro just because it was something to do but it was also where the nearest Halfords was available to buy new bike parts from. He'd had to attend quite a few collisions along there too when drivers got a little too enthusiastic, thinking they could overtake more cars than were physically possible with the speeds and distances involved.

There was no sign of any convoy of cars when he got there. They seemed to have disappeared so, having stood on a nearby hedge to get a better view, Treavey returned to his panda. It was now just after midnight, so he decided to go on a general patrol and perhaps check the airfield out. The radio was silent, and he thought perhaps they'd just had their meet and have now all gone home.

"Shame really," he thought to himself, he'd have enjoyed a bit of excitement to help the night pass.

He pulled off the main road and headed down the lanes towards the airfield. There were two near this place, but Perranporth Airfield would be the place to go as it had better areas to congregate. Of course, they could have gone anywhere else in Cornwall, or Devon for that matter, but he thought he had better check his patch out. It would have been a bit embarrassing if he hadn't noticed several thousand people raving with drugs and music on his patch when he had no one else to blame but himself.

He noticed how much easier it was to drive through these same lanes when compared with last night's drive through the storms. He trundled along the lanes, wondering what else he that night could do if it became clear the rave was not going to materialise. He saw nothing but darkness in the distance but continued nonetheless for good measure. It would be good to see who was about anyway. He drove around a bend and saw a few cars parked on one side of the country Cornish lane, half on the verge, but mostly in the road leaving just enough room to get by.

It felt strange, and he wondered what they could be there for but gradually realised there were more and more, and now there were a lot of people standing around. It seemed rather hostile once they saw his car, so he looked for somewhere to turn the car around as there was no point in going any further. He slowed the car down to try a three-point turn but he realised there just wasn't the space to do so.

Treavey came to a stop because there were now a lot of young and rather spaced-out revellers blocking his way. He realised he could be in for a lot of trouble. This wasn't a Sunday afternoon drive in a busy car park with holidaymakers; these people were bucking against authority, and he was that lone authority figure, turning up without backup available for a considerable period of time.

Before he knew it, he couldn't see further than the bonnet of his car, as bodies of revellers pressed up against it making it impossible to see outside. He selected reverse and revved the engine, slightly creeping backwards but the human gate had already closed behind him. He was trapped and had no way to get out of the crowd. He could hear the cheering outside, and the car began to rock.

"Victor, Golf 31 here, I seem to be in a little bit of trouble. I'm at the airfield in Perranporth and that rave is here in large numbers and I seem to have driven directly into it."

He heard a couple of impacts on his roof and then a smash, the rear windscreen collapsed, in an explosion of shattered glass diamonds, each one razor-sharp. The

115

crescendo of the dangerously unpredictable crowd became louder as the shouting and heckling burst through the broken window.

Treavey tried to stay cool. "Right, I need to just make use of this confusion and darkness," he nervously told himself, "I need to get out and run for the trees, they are going to eat me alive here and probably throw my body over the cliff with the way they are acting."

He remembered he'd had this feeling only once before when he was at the bottom of a large number of people fighting. He knew they could do whatever they wanted, and they would never have been identified, and what was worse was that they knew it too. All their frustrations about authority could come to a head and they could take it out on Treavey. He wasn't a human after all, he was the enemy, he was the oppression.

He had to think fast. Amongst the crushing bodies around the car, one stepped back from the driver's window and faced him head-on, his eyes showing he'd been enjoying some hallucinogens of sorts. A mature looking man in his early 30's, with a mop of dark hair and an air of authority about him. He looked relatively composed so Treavey opened the window, trying to give the impression of calm.

"You didn't want to come here on your own did you copper?" He declared in a monotone voice with his arms folded across his chest.

The other revellers around him seemed to calm down a little, he seemed to be a leader.

Treavey decided to use his tactic of being a country bumpkin, carrot cruncher or whatever would give them the impression he was harmless to them, that he wasn't like 'the rest.' At least until he could get some assistance.

"I heard there was a party going on here, I was a bit bored so thought I'd come for a dance!" Treavey said.

The man smirked and paused before saying, "Okay, you want a race between our cars whilst you are here? See what you have under this bonnet, or is it just a gutless standard Escort?"

"Na, they like to put a punchy engine in these things, as we are stuck out in the sticks a bit, I reckon I could thrash your pants in this thing." Treavey challenged in as convincing a way as possible, to at least change the subject of him being so vulnerable.

"Come on then, let's do it, down the main straight, I'll race you." said the man. The tide of humans parted as if by magic and there, revealed in front of him was a jet-black Escort XR3i spotlessly gleaming with the full race kit. Treavey was thinking fast, but he had few options. He couldn't just tell them all to go home; they would laugh in his face. No, he needed to recover the situation, get out safely if he could and then go for plan 'B', and that would be for someone else to deal with.

The XR3i roared off to the beginning of the runway. Treavey knew he was going to be exposed for the fraud he was, and he would be back where he started, with no way of getting out of the situation.

"Victor, any update? Things are developing here a little." He remained as calm as he could on the radio, always talking as if he were a captain of an airliner, showing calm and composure so everyone could think straight.

He drew up alongside the black XR3Ii and looked forwards into the darkness ahead; the cool breeze flowing through his broken rear screen reminded him of the lawlessness threatening him right now. This didn't look good. And if someone had a camcorder, it was not going to look good at all. He looked across to the man in the other car, the crowd were lining up either side of the runway and Treavey had a quick look in his rear-view mirror and saw… he saw a gap.

It was narrow but half a chance, and if he got it wrong, he could seriously crash his panda car into the scenery. Then he may as well jump off the cliff himself. He took another look around him, he heard the revving of the car next to him and decided. The XR3i flew off the line and Treavey planted his foot on the accelerator at the same time and went... backwards. He reversed and reversed on full acceleration and as he did so, he could see the bystanders buzzing by him on either side. It was still clear behind but he was entering the lane soon and he needed to face forwards so he could get better control and momentum.

He grabbed the bottom of the steering wheel with his right hand, slipped the car into neutral, felt the weight of the car swap to the rear and spun the steering wheel as hard as he could a full 360 degrees and let go of the wheel. The car spun around on its axis, Treavey not having to care where it ended up facing, as his practising in car parks and later country lanes showed him it would always face 180 degrees if done assertively. He slipped the gear into second as the car was straightening and planted the accelerator once more. It worked perfectly and the car was heading for the exit without any deviation. A glance in the rear-view mirror and he saw the crowd applauding above their heads. He may just have got away with it.

He flew down the road hoping not to meet any other cars head-on and turned off at a few junctions to shake off any tail. The police were being pursued, and it didn't feel good. He pulled over beside the main road so he could watch the glow of lights in the distance behind. He was shaking. The adrenaline was surging through his body and he felt he'd overdosed on it. He picked up the Bakelite receiver noticing his hand shaking uncontrollably. He was feeling euphoric. His training had worked, unofficial as it was. The repeated practising of his driving skills in car parks on night shifts and his assertiveness had managed to get him out of a whole host of trouble tonight.

He listened to the radio and could hear they were trying to contact him. "Golf 31, welfare check, Golf 31, what's your situation please?"

He paused to collect his thoughts. He couldn't exactly say what he'd done, could he? "Victor from Golf 31. I've managed to make my way out of there."

He carried on with the update having taken another breath. "There are about 1000 people there I suspect. A lot of people, quite out of control, and many are off their faces on drugs. I have sustained some damage to the car so I will review that when I get back to the station."

The control room operator was audibly relieved. "Very glad to hear that Golf 31. We do have the heli en route to the location and we have put out a call for public order units."

Treavey realised the only thing that could be done was to prevent any other partygoers from getting to it once the other backup units arrived, but that would take time. They didn't have the resources to clear the scene and there would no doubt be violence if they attempted to, which the police would be criticised for, of course. Criticised by those who never have to put up with the drug driving, the noise keeping whole villages awake, the disgusting mess left behind for the poor landowner to clear up and undoubtedly the distress to farm animals nearby. Not to mention the odd drug death of a teenager.

"Same old, same old. Why don't the nasty police let the little darlings have some fun with a little party?" Treavey mockingly thought to himself.

Time had gone on, and he'd decided to leave the scene to the bosses now. Let them decide how they were going to handle it. As he set off for the station, he saw the lights of the police helicopter flying low from the mainland having just made its way from Exeter, the other side of the two counties of the force. It was rare to see the helicopter in these parts as it was so far away from its base.

The aircraft was flying flat out and was low, it flew over Treavey's head and banked sharply to the left to introduce its presence to the revellers above the music. It then rotated back to the right in a large arc gaining height as it did so, its navigation lights flashing. Having come to a hover, it introduced a 30 million candle watt power torch blasting down onto the surface of the rave like some alien UFO hovering above looking to select its first victim to teleport up its cone of light for dissection.

Treavey trundled on, feeling a little jaded and battered. He was running over the experience in his mind and was beginning to pop up with a few rather unsavoury options of what could have happened to him. It was obvious he couldn't have just driven out with all those people there. If this had been upcountry, he wondered if the reaction from the revellers would have been the same against him? After all, policing in Devon and Cornwall was rather laid back and there was little conflict with the locals. Just the usual youth versus authority friction but nothing to the extent of in London or other major cities. They could have attacked his car and dragged him out, drug-fuelled or even hallucinating, beaten him to death, and who would have been able to identify who had done what? Not that it would have made any difference to him as he would by then be lying at the base of the cliff on those same jagged rocks which so many sailors had ended up on in previous centuries.

It was not long before he was driving up the driveway into the rear of the police station yard and reversing the panda into the parking space. He paused for a moment, noticing the orange glow of dawn through his windscreen, beginning to make an appearance over the house roofs far in the distance to the east. The beautiful orange glow was stunning and forced Treavey to stop and stare for a moment. It was hinting of a sunny day to come, but one Treavey would be missing out on whilst he slept after his night shift.

He sighed heavily and pushed the driver's door open stepping out into the cool, crisp morning. He collected his belongings from the back seat which they had been covered in a layer of sparkling diamonds shattered from the window, and with the door still open, stepped back to survey the damage.

"Jesus Christ!" he exclaimed out loud. He had no idea it was so bad. The car looked wrecked. Shame, as it was one of the newer ones too. The blue lens and bulb were missing from the roof of the car, kicked off by someone who must have been trampling on the now dented roof, a crease running down the full length of it. The rear window was smashed, and only now did he notice the side window was broken too. Two of the door panels were displaying large dents in them. The car resembled a write-off.

He pushed the rear door shut and listened to the broken glass falling through the inside of the door, sounding like ball bearings in a pinball machine striking the plungers and flippers on the way down. He slowly walked to the door of the station carrying his belongings scooped in his arms.

He was shattered and was finding it difficult to establish why, as he'd not done anything particularly physical. The night shift had just flown by which was nice. He assumed it was the huge adrenaline dump he had experienced which was making him feel so tired, and now he was feeling the after-effects of it. He'd made it through safely though. He was fine, and he was glad to see this job he had joined was very much no ordinary job. He wasn't going to have a dull life, that was very apparent.

He made himself a coffee in the kitchen and sauntered out into the report room where he sat down. He was startled momentarily by the cat flap swinging open, but quickly calmed as Wolfy jumped up onto the desk and made his way over to him next to his coffee and settled down to be fussed over, which he was more than happy to oblige with. Treavey sat there in silence feeling the incredibly warm soft fur, beautifully kept, immaculate in appearance and touch, and so wonderfully glossy.

He heard a tap at the door, and he looked up but saw nothing. He heard it again. He glanced at Wolfy, his brain engaging the cat was already in the station so it couldn't be him, so he got up and walked over to the door.

"SFQ no doubt," he thought to himself. A well-known term for 'Silly fucking question' usually created by someone who was either rather bored and had seen a police officer so they felt they had to ask something to strike up a conversation, or in this case, someone who couldn't sleep, maybe. He identified the outline of the figure on the other side of the glass panel, and he felt warm as he opened it.

He was pleased to see her. "Grace my lovely. Come in," and he led her into the report room. "You pop yourself down there, Grace. Ignore the photos on the wall won't you, you shouldn't be in this area, you know, but it's just between you and me, right? I think we are safe from the early turn shift arriving for another hour."

Grace sat down awkwardly on the seat at the corner of the table, the same one Treavey remembered sitting at on his first day at the station. It seemed to be the perfect seat to aim for when someone felt they were intruding a little.

He made a cup of tea for Grace and plonked the mug in front of her. "I chose the mug especially, Grace," he said, whilst winking and making his way over to his original seat with Wolfy again.

Grace read the mug out loud, "'Best used when sharing with friends.' Oh, that is nice Treavey, thank you." She had a warm glow on her cheeks and an infectious smile across those 70-year-old wrinkles. Treavey felt good. Grace took a sip of tea and put the mug down on the table. Her pink plastic bracelet rattled on the table.

"You were in the West Mids for 10 years, you said? You are as sharp as a knife with your observations, I've noticed that, so I completely believe you."

Treavey felt he may have needed to fill any awkward spaces with chat, but he needn't have worried. When she fell silent, it felt okay. It was like having his grandmother in the room.

"Look, Grace, it's entirely up to you, but I reckon we have about 45 minutes before the early turn are here. You are more than welcome to grab a shower here. There is a spare towel there someone left behind. You don't have to, of course."

No sooner had he finished the last syllable had Grace replied, "Thank you, that would be just lovely," and she was standing up to follow Treavey to the toilet which had a shower cubicle in.

"It's nothing much I'm afraid, but it will have to do," commented Treavey feeling rather embarrassed at the mould around the edges of the tired standard white tiles which had lost their sparkle a long time ago.

Grace replied as dead pan as a politician, "Oh well Treavey, I am used to so much better, as you can imagine."

He stared at her for a moment, and he was confused until he noticed her grinning.

He saw this rather dumpy elderly lady, hardened by the rigors of life, standing in front of him. He felt deep empathy for her, and wanted to help just a little, if he could. He noticed there were some wildflowers in a jam jar on the windowsill next to the shower. They were fresh, bright, and colourful; Felicity's little touch no doubt, and it took the sterility out of the situation.

"Take your time Grace. As long as you aren't too long about it!" Treavey said, as he shut the door to give her some privacy. "Don't you dare tell anyone you came here, Grace. They'll kill me, you know!" Treavey was already walking back into the parade room.

He trusted her emphatically already, but he could see there were no other officer's personal belongings in that area anyway. He was been breaking a lot of rules with his actions, though.

He waited in the parade room thinking about the poor woman inside the shower room. "Sod it, who cares, she's had a rough life, a very rough life, lost her husband and two young children in a car crash and had to leave the force after 10 years because of her alcohol problem, I suspect. Now she's ended up on the streets where she used to go on holiday as a child. Yes, the least I can do is to allow her to take a shower."

Within 10 minutes the shower stopped and after a short pause, Grace was back in her layers of dirty clothes. Treavey felt so sorry she had to put them back on again.

"That's better darling," Grace announced with a warm smile. "I enjoyed that. It has been a while you know. Oh, I don't want to get you into trouble, so I thought I'd be quick."

"Bless you," he replied, "Hey Grace, did you come up for anything specific, or just to say hello?"

"Oh, I saw you drive into the town again, and I wanted to tell you those two Bradford boys, especially Billy, are well at it with Gary Dawson. He's got them up to something and it is big. I know that because they are usually up to stuff, but they are looking incredibly stressed at the moment. Plenty of meetups in town. Lots of serious discussions. Something about a drop-off, a big one and Gary said to Billy, clear as you like, 'This one will give you a massive payout Billy, ten grands if you get it right.' You see Treavey, they don't see me, they don't see me at all, even if I'm sitting right next to them whilst they are talking. I'm invisible to them, you see."

"That's huge Grace, thank you. Will you keep an eye out for me and let me know what you hear?" he asked, knowing he was perhaps putting her at some risk.

"Yes love, of course. Anything for you my love." She waddled over to the door and pushed it open, and in a flash, with a warm morning sun rise making its efforts, and a dawn chorus singing in the background, she was gone.

"Right better get on with that damage report." It was criminal damage after all, not that he was going to find an offender for it. The taxpayer was going to have to take this hit. He grabbed the pad and started to write.

Without warning, the door burst open, and Felicity strode in with Micky behind her, who asked in a rather mundane tone, "Morning Treavey, how was it last night?"

Treavey was initially distracted by Felicity who was staring at him. She looked extremely attractive in her civilian clothes which he didn't get to see often. She was wearing a delicate low cut, white lace top which exposed her peach skin cleavage on her otherwise slim torso. The lace top was framed by an elegantly styled and quite expensive open black leather jacket, the contrast of which Treavey felt was quite exciting. As she walked past him, he couldn't help taking a sideways glance and appreciating her perfectly rounded bottom in tight pale blue jeans.

He was driving himself mad. For that time of the morning, he was surprised she looked so damned good. If she looked like that then, goodness knows how she would look at a more civilised time of the day. He'd found himself checking her shift to see when she was working with him next, and he was very much looking forward to it. He was counting down the days, in fact.

He didn't want to embarrass himself by exposing his childish crush on her, so he answered Micky's question, "Oh, pretty quiet really, Micky. Boring to be honest."

He paused for a few seconds and continued, "Oh, can you have a look at the car, I did a bit of damage to it; think I may have scuffed it a little. Wondered if it showed in the daylight."

Micky raised his eyebrows, slightly and his bushy moustache quivered. His large sturdy frame and Victorian features turned towards the door he'd just entered from. "Oh, okay, come on then Felicity, let's go and see how much we can paint over with some Tippex shall we?"

Felicity glanced back at Treavey and fired him the cheesiest of grins. He was sure there was a glint of something special there, or was he just imagining it? The door clicked shut as the two left to survey the damage and he waited in anticipation, waiting for the trap to be sprung, and it soon was.

The door swung open again and Felicity marched in, "Holy Christ Treavey, what the fuck happened to that car? It's been destroyed!"

She cackled with laughter and Micky and Treavey laughed along with her. They were desperate to find out what happened to him. It was probably the fourth scenario of how the damage occurred which Treavey gave, that he finally came clean with.

"Well done, Treavey, there wasn't a lot you could have done, so there shouldn't be any problems," Felicity said encouragingly.

Treavey already knew that, but it was always nice to hear someone else say it, especially from her. Right. Time to go home. He was suddenly very tired, and he needed his bed.

Chapter 8

Ice-creams and death messages

It was a lovely sunny early Sunday afternoon a couple of days later at the beginning of August and Treavey was making his way over to a house near the town centre to deliver a death message to a woman who didn't presently know what was going to hit her.   He had a large plastic bag in the back of the car, a present for Grace so he was going to track her down later, but he had a fair idea she'd be near the beach on a day like today. He had just been to an isolated field where a horse rider, fully kitted out in jodhpurs, blazer and whip attached to his wrist, had been found having had, according to the paramedics, a massive heart attack. They had managed to keep his heart going for 20 minutes or so, but the ambulance blue lights were switched off halfway to Truro. The last flame of hope had been extinguished, and that was one life no more.

Being in his early 50's, the gent, a Mr Robert Mitchell, had been otherwise very fit and well, apart from the fact he was now considerably dead and Treavey knew these death messages were always going to be the tricky ones. He had confirmed Mr Mitchell's identity with the driving licence he had had with him in his blazer pocket and as he had his golf membership with him as well, which fortunately had a photo attached, it confirmed it was the same man. Now, how to pass the message.

Treavey went over it in his head. "Hello, Mrs Mitchell, I'm afraid your husband fell off his horse, and he's had a heart attack, not the horse, your husband, and he's dead, again, not the horse, but your husband." Treavey paused and contemplated for a moment, "Oh dear, this isn't going well at all."

He remembered what his tutor had told him when he'd first joined the police and was just about to give his first death message. He said," Get to the point and make it clear and short." ‛

He prepared himself again, "Right," he cleared his throat as he steered the panda car into the road of the Mitchell's address.

The road gave a lovely impression of opulence, the houses weren't huge, but they were expensive and well maintained. You clearly would have earned the disapproving eye of the other residents if your grass was considered too long. With the wealth being shown in the area, with more than a few Range Rovers on driveways, it was no wonder this man rode horses. It just showed you could have all the wealth a man could wish for but then something like this could happen to anyone.

Right, time to practise the death message again. "Mrs Mitchell? Hello, my name is PC Treave. I am a police officer from your local station, I'm afraid he's dead. You know, your husband. He died on a horse. Well not on a horse, oh for god's sake, this is a disaster, I'm just going to have to blag it."

He pulled up opposite the house number at the entrance to the gateway and slowly drove up the short gravel driveway, with expensive wooden fencing running the length of one side. He stopped outside the large studded oak front door of a large redbrick house with opulent white pillars standing outside.

"Right, cap or no cap? Yes, walk up wearing the cap, then hold the cap as she opens the door."

He grabbed his cap, stepped out of the car, and stood next to it for a second, placing his cap on his head and straightening it using the reflection of the car window to assist him. He could see the beautiful blue sky behind his image in the reflection and wondered, what a terrible day it was to die, although, rather premature, at least he died 'doing what he liked doing most' he imagined. He spun around and having reminded himself of the gent's name, walked up the path to the front door.

"Oh hell," he thought to himself. "My throat is dry; it always goes dry when I'm about to give a death message."

His mind flashed back to him standing in the doorway of a hospital relatives' room for his first death message, facing the family of a man who had just been brought in from a road traffic collision. He had prepared his speech which was direct and to the point so there would be no misunderstanding by the man's wife. He remembered opening his mouth and absolutely nothing coming out. Panic set in as he heard a squeal come forth and not much else. He had to physically stop, find some moisture to swallow from his mouth and try again. From then on, he swore he'd always have some water nearby for just prior to giving any message like that again.

He pushed the doorbell and waited. It was going to be all in the timing with when he would take his cap off at the time of the door opening. He saw a shadowy form approach the door through the glass and after a second of hesitation, the latch was turned and the door opened inwards revealing a rather well-dressed, middle-aged woman with immaculately groomed platinum hair. Either she had just had her hair done or she most likely got it done every week, looking at her wealthy lifestyle. He gazed at her for a moment, taken in by her beauty even though she was nearly twice his age. He found her quite striking.

She was smiling at him, which then faded slightly as she registered who Treavey was. She was no doubt hoping for a rather mundane reason for his presence. She invited him in not giving him a chance to talk and so he followed her, instantly smelling the Sunday roast cooking in the

129

kitchen; chicken and the wondrous smell of roast potatoes wafting through the hallway.

She sensed Treavey had come to pass some terrible news and Treavey followed her into the spotlessly kept lounge where she sat down in a floral Laura Ashley style wingback chair and he did, likewise, perching on the end of a brown leather wingback armchair and swallowing hard in preparation. He should be okay, but he would not know until he attempted to speak and, unfortunately, he did not have any water to hand. After everything he told himself, he was ill-prepared.

"Mrs Mitchell, my name is PC Treave. I am here to ask if your husband is Mr Robert Mitchell, and whether could you tell me if he went horse riding this morning?"

She sat up nervously with her back bolt upright and her knees touching, whilst she grasped her hands tightly together exposing her white knuckles. Treavey noticed her impeccably polished slip-on shoes. Her legs were slender, and her slacks had a crease as sharp as a knife running down them. This wasn't usually his sort of clientele.

A short silence and a hesitant, "Yes, why, what's the problem officer?"

This was the time to come out with it. No messing with 'passed away, passed on' or other rather soft descriptions to describe someone dying. He knew from his tutor that if he wasn't straight, then relatives often hung on to every little hope and, 20 minutes later say something such as, "So will he be alright?" They needed to hear the words 'dead' or 'died', and 'his body is in the mortuary,' not, 'he's at the hospital.'

"I'm very sorry to tell you, Mrs Mitchell, that a man we firmly believe to be your husband, has died from what paramedics think was a heart attack whilst riding his horse this morning. I'm afraid there was nothing the paramedics could do to save him."

"Right, stop," he tells himself. "Let the words sink in and wait for the reaction."

She looked rather dazed at first as if she was coming out of a dream and then asked a rather strange question.

"But I've made his Sunday dinner. Who's going to eat that now?"

Treavey stood in front of her, looking rather stunned at her first words. He had expected her to either throw herself at him beating his chest whilst wailing, or to quietly sit there and weep, but this was a new one on him.

After a pause, he felt he could risk breaking the silence and said in rather a comforting but authoritative tone, "Shall I make you a cup of tea Mrs Mitchell?"

"Oh, that would be lovely," she replied, and so Treavey walked into the kitchen where the aroma of the fatty chicken spitting in the oven, the roasting potatoes with herbs and vegetables sizzling in the roasting tin all smelled so heavenly.

She shouted through from the lounge, "Officer, you can stay for lunch if you want."

It flashed through his mind for a second, but no, all his integrity instincts had to override his hunger instincts, but it wasn't easy doing it. He had to walk away from the sensory overload screaming at him to say, 'yes'.

He left the house about an hour later once a friendly neighbour had come to offer her support. That was his get out. It wasn't the time to give too many details as she was in no state to listen. Nothing was going in. He had one last thought as he started the car up and began making his way to the town centre to find Grace. "I wonder if that neighbour ends up having the dinner. I bet he does."

It wasn't long before Treavey located Grace sitting on the same bench she usually sat on near the beach. Slightly off from the throngs of public but near enough to smell the salt air being blown in from the Atlantic. He wasn't sure whether she would be offended by his gift, but it was worth a go.

As he approached her on foot, she smiled as if she'd just met a good friend for the first time in weeks. "Hello, my lovely," she said.

She was down to her rather grubby and stained T-shirt as it was now extremely hot with the sun beating down. The summer was in full swing. "Hello Grace, are you well?"

"Yes, my darling, I'm enjoying this wonderful weather and remembering those summer holidays I used to have here with my parents. Such good times they were too."

He hesitated for a second but decided to just go for it. He could feel the sweat dripping off his forehead into his eyes and so didn't want to hang around for too long. He wanted to have a quick walk around the beach car park before he drove off again, just to feel that breeze on his face and take in the holiday smells of suntan lotion and salt air. All those heavenly Cornish smells he had come to appreciate so much.

He handed her the plastic bag and said, "I hope you are not offended, Grace, but I know how difficult it is to get new clothes around here if you don't have a car."

He dropped the bag at her feet and turned without waiting for an answer from her. As he walked towards the car park, he heard Grace shout after him. "Oh lovely, thank you Treavey!"

"Well, that's a good sign," he thought, "but I'm not waiting around in case she changes her mind."

He could feel the sweat seeping through on his back through his white shirt. He could get away without wearing the clip-on tie, and he could roll his sleeves up to above the elbow. It had officially been decreed 'short sleeve order' by the Chief Constable, a welcome relief; however, the summer was well in progress by the time the order usually came through. The heavy black trousers felt like they were made from a hessian potato sack material, but at least they were wide enough to let the airflow up the legs. The cap stayed however, but it was important to look smart and official so Treavey was happy to keep it. He had tried talking to motorists whilst wearing the hat and without it, and he was sure he received more respect, more 'Yes, officer' whilst wearing the hat than when he hadn't. 'Yes, officer' tended to change into 'okay, mate', and it definitely felt like the person he was talking to believed there was more chance to argue himself out of a ticket if the cap was not being worn. The Custodian Helmet was for foot patrol. Woe betides anyone on foot patrol wearing a cap.

"Oh, what absolute heaven!" Treavey exclaimed out loud as he felt the grind of the sand on the tarmac under his heavy Magnum leather boots, and he inhaled the addictive sea air with the sweet smell of suntan oil and Kelly's ice cream. Kelly's had always been the best Cornish ice cream he had ever tasted and which his taste buds were now screaming out for. He wandered over to the ice cream van, which was doing a roaring trade; however, there was a rather long queue, and it wouldn't have looked good if he'd pushed in, so he politely turned away the first offer to jump the queue.

"Oh, come on officer, you are a busy man!" insisted a rather pot-bellied man who was wearing rather unflattering mustard-coloured speedos which had been engulfed into the folds of his belly, and to top the look off, he wore a cheap straw hat.

"That's very kind of you, I have to get back to preventing all those bank robberies on the high street after all," Treavey replied, grinning broadly. The rest of the queue was in an equally good holiday mood and insisted he should move in front of them.

Treavey walked away with a Kelly's 99 ice cream which he had insisted on paying for, but he was sure he'd received an extra flake. Jumping the queue was enough liberty taken for one day; he wouldn't have felt comfortable having it free as well. Whilst starting to make his way to the panda, he observed a mother struggling

133

with a small child who was in the process of having a tantrum and was demanding an ice cream, it seemed, slightly too soon after the last one he had consumed. The woman was running out of patience. Treavey leaned forward to the child who promptly shut up and stared at him with huge wet eyes and red face.

"Hello, young man. I'm afraid I seem to have taken the last ice cream, so I'm sorry about that."

The woman gazed at Treavey with a look of slight shock at the situation of a police officer in full uniform telling her child they'd run out of ice cream. She couldn't help but give out a muffled snigger.

"Thank you, officer, that makes things easier, now come on David. Let's go back to the beach." They started to turn and walk towards the beach again, but she hesitated slightly and added, "It's like he's addicted to ice cream. Every time he hears the ice cream van at home he kicks off until I give in."

"I know someone who said that if the ice cream van is playing its music, it meant it had run out of ice cream!" Treavey offered, as a rather cruel solution but his grin gave away the fun behind it.

"That, officer, is genius!" She spun on her heels and trotted off after her son who was halfway down onto the beach by now.

"Happy to be of service ma'am, happy to be of service!" he replied under his breath. It's come to having to advise on child-rearing now, has it, and yet he hadn't even got his own?

He began walking back towards his car again when a slim woman, with golden, bronzed sun-tanned skin wearing a rather small bright yellow bikini caught his eye walking towards him. She was walking from the ice cream van towards the beach and was getting closer. She completely caught his attention.

"Blimey," he thought, "How do I look at her more closely as she passes, with everyone looking at me, without her thinking I'm ogling her, and everyone else thinking I'm ogling her, when in fact I am ogling her?"

He was transfixed at her loose flowing blonde locks of hair pouring over her shoulders like liquid sun, and he observed a scattering of freckles he thought were extremely cute; she had freckles just like…

"Hi Treavey!" she exclaimed in a bright, chirpy voice, smiling at him with a glint in her eye, sending him a flirtatious glance as she proceeded to pass him.

"Uh, oh, hi Felicity!" He stuttered over his words like an embarrassed schoolboy and just had time to break into a coy smile. He quickly glanced a last look over her bronzed bosoms peeping out over the top of her bikini as she passed, which was when her familiar perfume filled his nostrils sending his senses wild. He watched her walking as she made her way towards the beach, admiring how she moved, and admiring her perfectly rounded bottom in the bikini which left little for his imagination, until he was suddenly shaken out of his trance. He was standing in the middle of the car park, holding a melting ice cream, staring at a beautiful female body dressed in no more than what could otherwise have been her underwear, but had been renamed a bikini for societal acceptance.

"Afternoon officer!" a voice announced to him and he turned around to see a rather elderly gentleman grinning from ear to ear having completely busted him.

"Yes, afternoon sir," Treavey replied, feeling rather embarrassed at being caught so red-handed, and headed off towards his car.

As he drove out, he saw an older lady waving at him from the side of the road. "Goodness, that's Grace, she's looking amazing," he said out loud. Amazing for a vagrant woman perhaps, but he was surprised at the transformation she had made. Those clothes from the charity shop in Newquay had been accepted, and she seemed to be very happy with them.

He pulled up beside her. "You look lovely Grace, I'm so glad you like them. I thought that no matter how beautiful you are, Grace, you still deserved a fresh change of clothes!"

He began to move off again and then out of the blue decided to say just one more thing, so abruptly stopped.

"Hey, Grace!" She looked at him in expectation, waiting for his next comment. "I may see you on my next night shift. I'm on my tod next Thursday okay?"

Grace reached into the plastic bag Treavey had given her earlier and pulled out a clean blue towel, and she waved it at him, her face like a beacon, shining in the Cornish sun. She looked so happy.

"I love this job," he thought to himself. He knew he was crossing a line by letting her have the odd shower, but to hell with it, he knew it was the right thing to do.

He carried on towards the police station, turning across the busy main road with holidaymakers walking around in various forms of scant swimming attire. He chuckled to himself as he realised, they wouldn't be doing that on a hot day in Manchester or Liverpool. No, when they were on holiday, they were very much on holiday.

He slowed the car for a moment at the spot where little Steven had been killed. A moment of melancholy took over him and a tear arrived in the corner of his eye. He pulled the car over to the side, not caring if anyone was looking at him, no doubt criticising him for the inconvenient place in which he had parked. He looked around and saw a shop with some flowers for sale outside. He wandered over to it and looked at the selection. They were pretty. He had no idea what they were, but he had a strong urge to buy some. A tall bunch and another smaller bunch seemed to catch his eye. They seemed to go together in some strange way.

He took them up to the shopkeeper who looked at him for a second. He was an older man with thinning grey hair and a matching well-groomed beard who had run the shop for several years and had managed to survive by selling a bit of everything. He had to make hay whilst the sun shone to get him over the much quieter winter months. He studied Treavey's face but didn't say a word. He just remained respectfully silent. He seemed to know exactly what Treavey was about to do.

Treavey stepped out of the shop with the two bunches of brightly coloured flowers, one bunch taller than the other. He crossed over the road and walked to the spot where he had seen the driver of the car who had crashed into the little boy, standing with his grandson, waiting for the police. He remembered the man's face perfectly. He had been shocked to hear so candidly how he had since committed suicide even though it could be argued it hadn't been his fault at all. The other car had crashed into him sending him into the little boy, but it was more than he could bear. He had been willing to give up his own life and depart from his own family and his little grandson forever to rid himself of the guilt. How his grandson was going to recover from the whole experience he'd never know. It was all such a mess. All because of a sodding door mirror being broken.

He slowly bent down and placed the taller bunch of flowers at the point he remembered seeing the man standing with his grandson. He stood back with his head bowed. He could sense there was movement around him, a busyness of people who he couldn't see, as he was paying little attention to them. He didn't care what they thought. He just needed to do this.

After a couple of minutes, he continued to the pavement area where little Steven had met his end. He distinctly remembered Bomber and Micky carrying out CPR on him right there on this spot. This rather dull piece of tarmac which showed nothing of the importance of that date, that incident, or the utter despair the location had brought to the family.

He placed the flowers at the base of the wall and paused a little. A tear forming in his eye again. He brought his two fingers to the top of his right eye in a mini salute and took a deep breath. He looked up feeling a little self-conscious now and saw a group of elderly pensioners congregating around him, all standing in respect.

"Is that where the little lad lost his life, Officer?"

"Yes," Treavey replied to a rather stout looking rosy-cheeked lady. "Yes, that's where, God bless him."

Treavey returned to his car and sat there for a moment, pausing. The heat of the day overwhelmed him, so he sat there with the windows wide open for a bit, and with his car fan blowing warm air over him at full speed, waiting for the heat to dissipate a little.

"Right," he thought, "Time for a cuppa." He turned the engine on, but a sound caught his attention. A sound like the snorting of a pig. It was quite short and at first, he wasn't entirely sure whether it was directed at him, but yes, it was completely distinguishable from the background hustle and bustle. He looked across the road from where his car was. There were three larger lads with a group of younger ones. Treavey suspected they were from Newquay and thought he recognised one from a public order he'd arrested him in some time ago. "Yes," he thought to himself," it was coming back to him now, "Mark, his name is, I'm sure of it."

The boys were smirking to themselves looking at him with sideways glances whilst they continued talking amongst their group.

Treavey was in no mood for this. If he let it go, the youngsters would learn their insulting behaviour was acceptable and the older boys would be placed on a pedestal by the younger ones. He had to knock them off that. Very slowly, and with controlled definite movements, he opened his driver's door again, and stepped out of the car, placing his cap on his head taking all the time he could, to build up the suspense for the youngsters opposite who were now beginning to look somewhat uneasy. The face of Mark had gone rather ashen and Treavey could see he was beginning to regret his spur of the moment showing off by snorting insulting piggy noises towards Treavey.

Treavey slowly and assertively walked across the road towards the group and looked directly at Mark, and with a very stern tone said, "Gentlemen, have we got something to say?"

"Er, no, why, we haven't done anything," Mark replied in a voice where, if he could have visibly backtracked, he would have been pulling a J turn back in time to avoid the whole awkward incident ever happening in the first place. Treavey already knew he had this won.

"Mark, I'm surprised at you, I am," Treavey replied in slow and very concise words, "because when you were arrested by me for fighting some time ago, I couldn't stop you blubbering in the back of my car, so I was wondering why you suddenly felt so much braver in front of your 12-year-old friends here?"

There was silence, followed by a snigger from a couple of Mark's older friends. Mark looked mortified, standing there with his mouth open but with nothing to say.

Treavey was going for the coup-de-grace. "And I'm surprised with you Mark, as you couldn't tell me more about where to buy cannabis and other little pieces of information on your friends. You couldn't have been more helpful."

Okay, this was, in fact, a lie, but in some other country no doubt, the police would have jumped out of their car and pummelled the offending youths with large sticks leaving them for dead, or in some, they may have even disappeared, so a little tall story about blubbering in the car and being an informant was more than acceptable in his mind, certainly in a town like Perranporth where there would be few repercussions for Mark, anyway.

He left Mark protesting his innocence to his friends that all this wasn't true, but his friends had gone noticeably quiet. How did the officer know they smoked cannabis, what else had Mark told him? All of Mark's refuting didn't seem to convince his friends. They didn't trust him anymore.

"How very unfortunate," Treavey giggled to himself as he made his way back to the car. Mark wasn't going to be doing that again in a hurry. He was certain that lessons had been well and truly learned.

He made his way back to the station to fax the coroner's form off, that he had just filled in for the sudden death. A form 95. How ordinary a name for something which marked the end of a long, or even a short and tragic, life. A form which contained the personal details and events of the death, so the coroner had something to go on. As the poor chap hadn't been seen by his GP in the last couple of weeks, and it was never a good idea to assume the cause of death, he would have to have a post-mortem. Just in case Mrs Mitchell had been poisoning him, her husband's death would be treated in the same way as any other, just to establish and confirm that cause of death.

As he pondered the day, he pictured the sight of Felicity in her little yellow bikini and perfectly toned body and smiled to himself. Did she like him? He really wasn't sure, but he hoped so, oh my goodness he hoped so.

"Right," he pondered, "time I stepped it up a bit." He was looking forward to doing that, especially as she was working with him the night shift tomorrow. He couldn't wait.

Chapter 9

Snogs and burglars

"Is it me or does she just look incredible tonight?" Treavey thought as he watched the vision of Felicity seemingly glide through the office to start the night shift with him. For once, he was truly excited to come to work. How had it been, he hadn't noticed her like this before?

Okay, he had always fancied her as such, but she seemed to be unattainable. What was the point if he was just going to be rejected and anyway, he had always hoped he wouldn't partner up with someone from the police because home life would become rather monotonous having nothing else to talk about apart from work? Or was it the yellow bikini and her confident smile and greeting a couple of days earlier that had made her so attractive to him all of a sudden? Was he just an enthusiastic puppy wanting the reward he probably could never have?

He couldn't wait for Bomber and Micky on the previous shift to leave them to it. He now had her to himself for a whole nine hours. The door slammed shut and Felicity didn't waste any time.

She glanced up at Treavey finishing off his cup of tea and said, "Nice day on the beach the other day, Treavey? Meet anyone nice?"

Treavey was stunned for a moment, then questioned he was perhaps looking into this too much and perhaps she was simply having a friendly joke with him, as it may have been a little bit embarrassing for her when in normal times, she was to be seen in shapeless, rather unflattering, and baggy police uniform.

"Yes, I did, Felicity, I met someone I know really well, see her at work quite regularly, a lovely girl, quite attractive in fact. She was looking quite hot too, and we had a short but very nice chat." He paused for a moment and then continued, "Yes, Grace was there, the homeless woman?"

Felicity gawked at him, a little confused for a moment, having thought he was initially coming on rather stronger than she had expected but then burst out laughing as he delivered the punchline, almost choking on her tea.

"A good start," Treavey thought. "and boy, does she look amazing."

They began their patrol around the town with Felicity driving. She turned the heating up with her foot behind the dash and grinned at Treavey. "Can't believe you got me with that Treavey, you are such a little sod!"

It was past midnight now and the holiday pubs were closed. It was probably going to be a rather quiet night, although no one would dare say the 'Q' word as it was well known in the policing world that once that word was mentioned then all hell would break loose, and they would have the busiest night for months.

They continued past the pub and onto the cul de sac where Dawson lived. You never know, they could catch him lifting heavy packages from his car into his house or vice versa, and it was somewhere else to go anyway.

There was his Vitara car, parked where it usually was. It looked unlikely he was going anywhere tonight. A few moments later, they ended up parking on the beach car park, looking out to sea. The moon was behind them, and its clear light had lit up the whole sky, reflecting the surface of the sea right up to the horizon it seemed. The herring gulls were asleep with their beaks buried deep in their duvet feathers, boosting their energy levels for another day of scavenging and robbing holidaymakers of their ice-creams tomorrow. Treavey made himself more comfortable in his seat. Felicity was resting with her hands remaining on the steering wheel.

He decided to mention the white elephant in the room once more.

"Just think, I saw a half-naked Felicity walking past this car just a couple of days ago, looking like a top-class model, she was."

"Half-naked? Your cheeky git," she giggled. "What a lovely day off that was, just chilling out on the beach and enjoying the sites..." she paused for a moment. "...and the sites in this car park aren't too bad either. There was a guy I saw almost about here I've fancied for quite a while. Good body on him, wouldn't mind getting my lips around his if you know what I mean Treavey. He's hot, I mean, really hot."

Treavey moved his eyes right, without moving his head to subtly glance at Felicity. He wasn't believing quite what he was hearing. Was this the moment for the first kiss? He saw she was looking straight at him, beaming from ear to ear and she continued, "Yes, there was some hunky lifeguard here who had just got himself an ice cream. An amazing body, he had!"

Treavey realised he'd been completely hooked, chewed up and then spat out by Felicity, and it was her revenge for the way he had caught her out earlier with his Grace comment. They both laughed, enjoying the moment, Treavey silently wondering whether part of what she had said was true. Her eyes told him she found him attractive, but was that him reading too much into it?

"Golf 31, can you attend Perranporth campsite urgently, please? There is a report of a group of three intruders taking the portable TVs out of the vacant caravans. We believe they have just fled the area. The helicopter is making its way from a missing person enquiry in Penzance so they will come by on their way back up to Exeter."

"En route!" replied Treavey, whilst Felicity guided the car out of the car park and turned left towards the campsite. Both officers were looking at the moving traffic with two or three occupants inside coming their way but to be fair, the offenders would probably be heading up the hill out of Perranporth as they themselves were coming up from the bottom.

Newquay and Truro units were making their way towards to see if they could intercept them, but it was a long shot.

"Whiskey Victor from Golf 31," Treavey shouted up, "Do you have any descriptions apart from three intruders; any vehicles, and can we have a dog en-route please?"

"Standby," the comms operator snapped back, "I'm just passing a large log."

Treavey couldn't resist it. "You are passing a large log? I hope it isn't too painful."

Felicity shouted, "Treavey! That's disgusting man! You'll get yourself into trouble!" They snorted with laughter, maybe enjoying each other's company a little too much.

Treavey added, "Well, she deserved it, this job is the priority at the moment. Wait, there's Dawson!"

"Leave him," replied Felicity, "We have to go to this burglary."

Treavey looked frustrated that Felicity hadn't spun the car around after him, after all, why else would he be out and about at this time of night? "But the intruders will have gone, Felicity."

Felicity returned a serious expression, "We don't know that, and Dawson will most probably be yet another wasted stop-check."

They drove into the campsite where a security guard was waiting for them.

"Felicity, do you fancy waiting here in case they come out and I will have a look around to see where they have been trying to get in," Treavey suggested. He was gradually getting over his disappointment of not going after Dawson.

"Fair enough mate, I'll have a look at the CCTV. Did you hear the dog is way off?"

Treavey walked to the location he'd been directed to whilst the other security guard checked out a possible escape route through the hedge. It was late, and there were no holidaymakers out and about anymore. The majority were all tucked up in bed ready for another day on the beach or in the pool the following day although he could hear the distance boom of music in the clubhouse which had some late hangers-on in.

He continued down a steep narrow walkway towards a large group of static caravans shining his torch on the caravans around him. He thought he'd heard a noise, so he stopped and listened, then moved on again, keeping his torch off to not alert any intruders in the exceedingly small chance they were still in the vicinity. He was turning things over in his mind. He didn't want to mess this up.

He was thinking hard. "I should wait for the dog unit, but they are going to be ages yet, and we could lose them if they've come back for more, plus, there have been loads of people walking around here, including the security guard so I'm not sure we are going to get much success here anyway."

He was contemplating all options as he walked around the end of another large static caravan.

"Shit!" he exclaimed out loud as he realised, he was now looking into the faces of two teenage burglars with portable TVs in their hands standing next to a pile of TV's they'd been busy collecting from the vicinity.

"Stay where you are!" Treavey shouted and shone the torch in their faces.

They looked stunned for a moment so Treavey took the opportunity to update the Comms operator and waited, but he quickly realised he was some way off from the office where Felicity would be making her way down from and other backup was some distance away too. He looked around him but couldn't see the numbers on the caravans and the two burglars were slowly realising they had a very good chance of taking charge of events.

"Hang on Copper, what are you going to do about it?" the larger one smirked, suddenly looking very confident. "I mean, there's no way you could identify us, we can do what the fuck we like to you."

The other wearing a baseball cap decided this was the time to play the upper hand.

"Yeah copper, where are your mates then, all the way out here, hey? What the fuck are you going to do about it, want a slap do you copper, want a slap? Well, you're fucking going to get one."

"Firstly, just try it pal and I'll stick both of you on your arses, but I suggest you just stay there, you are both nicked, suspicion of burglary, the place is surrounded, anyway, I'm just one of the ones who have come in to flush you out."

Treavey was talking in the most convincing way he could put across, almost believing it himself until,
"Bollock's man, we could give you a fucking good beating and still get away from here and take all this stuff."

Treavey acknowledged he was losing this game and was quickly trying to decide his next move.

The teenager continued, "So little piggy, where's your back up?"

The situation was decided for them because right at that time, a monstrous noise came from the heavens above as an alien beam of light with the strength of a spaceship behind, illuminating both offenders and Treavey where they stood. Treavey's torchlight paled into insignificance, so he switched it off. He was just as stunned with what was going on, and then he heard a booming voice from the heavens.

"You are both on camera, we have your faces very clearly recorded, you will do exactly what the officer tells you to do."

The two young men watched in awe towards the skies but were blinded by the massive light which was raining down on them. They were rooted to the spot and in contrast to some moments earlier, now looked like two, ten-year-old school children. Treavey felt all-powerful. He wasn't used to getting the assistance of the police helicopter because it was stationed so far away, but boy, was he glad to have it there tonight. By the time Felicity turned up, both were lying face down on the ground, one handcuffed to the other, with their spoils beside them. Felicity reminded Treavey,

"What about the third? There are meant to be three."

"Good shout Felicity," Treavey replied, and he got on the radio. "Can I ask any unit attending not to go on foot, and when the dog unit turns up, can we ask him to attend our location, please. I suspect the third offender may have been to this area to drop a TV or two off and made off for the next. We'll have more chance of catching him with the dog and I don't want to spoil the track."

It was about 10 minutes later, Dave, the dog unit, attended with his dog, Finchy.

He quickly got out of the van and already Finchy was excited, bouncing around the cage in the back. He knew it was time to work and get a result and Treavey knew if anyone it would be Dave and Finchy together. It was completely up to them now. The harness was on in a flash and the long leash was clipped on, and now Finchy was pacing the area.

"Which way did you get here Treavey?"

"Straight down the narrow bit and round the left-hand side of this caravan Dave. I haven't been anywhere else," Treavey replied, now glad he hadn't trampled around the whole area and having to confess his sins of destroying any fresh track there may have been. Before he knew it, Dave

147

was gone with the dog, the long leash fed out, and Dave abruptly tugged away into the darkness grasping the end of the leash. The helicopter occupants above knew their job was to keep the suspect pinned down and to prevent the burglars from making a break for it. They had enough of a head start on Finchy already. Felicity joined Treavey and they both waited for any developments.

"I've got a broken caravan window here, number 58E, for your info."

A little later, a similar message came and then another. Just as everyone was wondering whether the third had made their escape, or indeed whether there ever had been a third, barking could be heard above the noise of the helicopter.

"Fantastic Felicity, now that's a good sign. Come on Finchy, what have you got?" Both officers waited in anticipation, hand on their radios, willing the update to come in, and indeed it did.

"One detained hiding under a caravan, number.... number 78B for the log." Dave updated with some glee. "If someone can take this one off me, I can have a search for any other caravans they've broken into."

Treavey thanked the helicopter crew over the radio for coming to his assistance, and jokingly asked, "If you could patrol Perranporth the same time tomorrow night, that would be useful!"

"Yes, apologies we weren't a little earlier for you..." the helicopter observer replied, "...but we had a little problem with aircraft traffic in the area, and had to wait for it to clear but happy to be of assistance Golf 31."

The helicopter carried out a dramatic bank to the left, gaining some speed whilst it lost height before swooping off, up and away into the gloom of the night, the clattering of the rotor blades being the last sign of the metal alien ship which had just come to his rescue.

Having sorted out the logistics with securely taking three prisoners to Newquay Custody, Treavey and Felicity

148

began the process of completing the paperwork needed for the interviewing officers the next day. A hand-over was going to be submitted to CID for the following morning, which hopefully wouldn't be passed down for the Response units to deal with, as Perran only had two officers working and it would be them dealing with it. Another unit had been busy obtaining a statement from the caravan site security, and then of course, their own statements had to be completed too.

They checked the pile of paperwork they'd managed to produce and left it with the night turn sergeant in Newquay to pass on for the early turn. It was always a relief to complete everything, but they knew there would probably be complaints about the quality, usually by those who had not worked a night shift in years and had forgotten it was the equivalent of being drunk, but with fatigue instead. Tiredness on night shift was often made worse if, after a night shift, and attempting to get some sleep at home, the neighbours were using screaming hedge trimmers outside the window on a summer's day. The effect could be understated until pointed out it was the equivalent of a hedge trimmer being used outside a window for several hours at three in the morning for office workers.

Treavey manoeuvred the car out of the car park and turned onto the quiet streets of Newquay which hadn't woken up yet. Seagulls were dragging out the contents of dustbins which had been put out for collection. The contents were being pulled out by the great birds who were unceremoniously scattering nappies, mouldy bread, and chip cartons across the whole street. They threw their heads back to screech with glee, which brought more of these grey and white sleek birds swooping down to join the affray. Not a feather out of place, the smoothest of textures around their faces, necks, and chest, and with the aerobatic skills of a high-performance military helicopter to aid them with their attack plans, they rarely failed in their intentions.

Treavey turned along the road which bypassed the villages of Crantock, and Rejerrah, and continued on to Perranporth, and as he coasted down the steep hill, he saw Felicity was sleeping beside him. He took glances at her face whilst she slept. He was able to study her in a way not possible if she had been awake, so he made use of every second. He studied her incredibly soft silk-like skin and her rosy lips, so perfectly shaped, just slightly apart. She looked at peace. He drove as gently as he could for some time taking glances at her, wondering what it would be like to kiss her, before deciding she had had enough relaxation and he was now going to carry out a little trick on her.

He drove into the rather large beach car park in Perranporth and lined up at one end of it. There were no people about, no onlookers and no cars in the car park so this was perfect. He slipped the clutch but used no revs, so the car rolled along at about 4 mph and Treavey opened the driver's door and simply stepped out. He knew that if this went wrong, he'd be in a whole lot of trouble, but he felt it would probably be okay if he was careful. As Treavey ran alongside the car as it progressed through the car park, he adjusted his pace to be level with the boot of the car and then banged on it hard with the flat of his hand. What happened then was to behold and Treavey wished he could have recorded it for prosperity, but there again, it was probably just as well it didn't.

Felicity woke up abruptly and first wondered why she was in the car park heading slowly towards the beach, then she wondered where the driver had gone, and in her slumber still, she then wondered whether she was fast asleep still or whether she was going to end up upside down on the beach itself.

She let out a high-pitched scream which was the signal for Treavey to open the door and jump straight back in and take control of the car, which indeed he did, whilst attempting to stifle the belly laugh that had erupted in him like a small earthquake.

"You complete bastard, Treavey," Felicity shouted at him, softly punching him on his arm. "You totally shit me up then. How could you? I was so confused!"

They eventually got back to the station at 6.00 am and Treavey was still laughing to himself, proud at his accomplishment which had taken some risk but had fully paid off. They both emptied the car of their items and sat down at the large report-room table. Wolfy had followed them in and had settled down in his usual place, enjoying the safe warm environment. He and Felicity held a cup of tea in their hands and stared at each other. Treavey no longer felt tired. They carried on with a longer stare than would have been comfortable in normal circumstances, looking straight into each other's eyes, almost daring the other to break first.

Treavey smiled and broke the silence, "Hell, that was a good job tonight, and it was good to get that paperwork done too. No doubt there'll be complaints why 50 statements weren't taken from the occupants of the caravan park, or we forgot to write the exhibits list, hell, did we forget to do the exhibits list?"

Felicity laughed; "No babe, I did that!" She beamed at him. "I've enjoyed tonight, Treavey, and I'm glad you ended up okay at that campsite with those burglars. I was worried about you. Could have been interesting if the heli hadn't turned up."

Treavey paused, thinking for a moment. He realised it had been a close-run thing. He sniggered, "Yes, I managed to bullshit them for long enough for the heli to arrive. I told them we had the whole place surrounded!"

They both laughed as they knew how ridiculous that sounded.

"That would probably have taken half of Cornwall's units on a night shift," he said, standing up and walking over to Felicity to daringly put his hand on her shoulder. She looked up at him.

"What are you thinking?" she asked, looking confidently into his eyes with a wonderfully relaxed smile. Treavey paused, wondering at what level he should go in. Straight for the kiss, or just a polite reply of some sort? The rather hot atmosphere was broken by a tapping at the door.

"Shit, it's Grace for her shower," Treavey shouted out loud. "Oh bollocks, Felicity, you aren't meant to know about this. She isn't meant to come tonight." Treavey opened the door to Grace and showed her towards the shower. She was looking so much better. She acknowledged him and thanked him, before disappearing into the bathroom.

He returned to the main parade room and saw Felicity with a face like thunder. "I know, I know. She's an ex-cop, you know, Felicity. I know I shouldn't, but it isn't harming anyone."

Felicity looked incredibly angry, "What the actual fuck Treavey, you've just let a tramp come into the police station for a shower. I use that shower you know."

"Shush, she may hear you, she's more of a friend, to be honest. She lost her children and husband in a road traffic accident and then lost her job in the West Mids Police cos she went off the rails. It all checks out too. She lives here because she remembers it from when she used to come on holiday and there's nothing, she doesn't know about what's going on in Perranporth."

Felicity stood up and walked over to Treavey moving closer towards his face. She was so close to Treavey's face, he could smell her fresh sweet breath and the scent of her perfume.

"Wow, that smells incredible," he thought to himself, but he had no idea what she was going to say to him. She looked angry, but then compassionate and sweet. He was very confused, and almost pinned up against the wall as she leant in further towards him and whispered,

"You know what I think? I think this," and she moved in touching her lips onto Treavey's. He tasted her tongue gently touching his, which sent a shooting, tingling sensation through his entire body down to his toes, and before he could react, she was moving towards the kitchen again talking as if nothing had just happened. "Another cup of tea, Treavey?"

Grace walked into the Parade room looking rather sheepish. Looking somewhat shocked, Treavey cleared his throat and said, "Grace, this is Felicity."

"Good morning Felicity," Grace said. She had her towel and some belongings under her arm. "I'm sorry if I startled you. You can completely trust me guys, but I'm on my way out now. Oh, one thing Treavey, I have more to tell you."

"Yes, Grace? What have you got, oh it's okay, Felicity is with me on this?"

Grace shuffled her belongings, so they were more comfortable under her arm and walked closer to Treavey as if she were a spy passing information between an informant and an MI5 agent. "I never see Dawson around and about at that time of night usually, but last night, he was driving his Vitara jeep thing through the town and fast, I mean, he didn't want to be stopped and he didn't seem to care if anyone saw him, not that there was anyone to see him but me of course. Whatever he was up to, you know the drugs and all that, he was definitely up to it last night."

Treavey looked devastated, "Oh shit, he must have been on his way back from when we saw him en route to that job Felicity. What time was this, Grace?"

"Time doesn't mean much to me, and I don't have a watch, but I would say it was about 2 hours ago. Well, I must be off now; got to start work soon."

Treavey and Felicity looked at her rather bemused, and Grace just chuckled. "You guys," she replied, enjoying the moment, "What do you think. Mayoress of Perranporth? Who'd employ me, although I do smell nice now, thanks to you."

The door clicked behind her as she disappeared. Treavey glanced at Felicity, studying her soft lips which had just been against his, and said, "A good night overall, but Dawson got away with that one, Felicity. We need to have a plan next time. I want him red-handed. Where the hell does he get the drugs from? How many overdoses last week?"

Felicity stroked the top of Treavey's hair and looked fondly into his brown eyes. "Oh, I think the guys went to three of them last week. They are dropping like flies, darling. Dropping like flies. Micky went to two of them and he was looking pretty down about it all."

Treavey was thinking hard. "I think we all need to work together on this now. CID are too far off from here to be able to get stuck in, and they don't work nights here, so we need to get this sorted amongst us. We need to have a bit of a meeting to establish what we all have. You never know, we could have enough for another warrant."

Felicity seemed dismissive. "Yeah, we could, but what do we know, Micky and you heard something from the Bradford brothers that night."

"You heard about that?" Treavey was surprised.

"Yes, nothing remains a secret around here, Treavey, and we know Dawson may or may not have anything to do with it, but he drives his car through town fast from time to time, oh, and your tramp friend says they are up to it but hasn't actually seen anything."

"Grace. Her name is Grace," Treavey said rather defensively.

He realised there wasn't very much to go on but pushed on. "And we have the fact he was hanging around the airfield that time and made off from me, and we have the

154

minor detail of a whole lot of people dying from drug overdoses around here, too."

"Yes true, Treavey, but that's hardly enough for a warrant is it? I reckon if we put our minds together and concentrate on this, we could achieve something. Personally, I suspect it's someone bigger than the Bradfords or Gary Dawson. They wouldn't have the know-it-all to do this on their own. I bet it's Londoners or someone like that. We should keep an eye out for them."

Treavey knew it made sense what Felicity was saying. She was no fool, and that made her even more attractive.

The door burst open, and Gordy and Micky walked in. "Quiet night?" Gordy enquired whilst they put their coats away and headed towards the kitchen.

"Hardly a job all night..." Felicity joked, "...apart from three in custody for burglary, mostly down to our hero Treavey here. I think the hand-on teams are going to take it on, but you may want to check in case you get dumped with it halfway through the morning."

Micky answered without a flinch, "We can do that if that's what happens. Nice one guys."

He plopped a couple of tea bags in some mugs. "Anyone die last night?"

The radio broke the relaxed atmosphere of clinking cups and boiling water. "Is there an early turn unit on duty yet Golf 31, there's what looks like a drug overdose which has just come in, can you let them know?"

Micky sat down quickly looking devastated. "Oh, my goodness guys, we have to sort this mess out. Those are normal people dying out there."

"You are absolutely right, Micky," replied Treavey. I think we need a quick chat before Felicity and I go home. We must get to the bottom of this.

155

Chapter 10

Car pursuits and lifeboats

A few days later and the call had gone up, as it was getting pretty busy in Newquay and they'd run out of units. A few too many stag dos had met up and were unable to contain their drunkenness on a hot sunny afternoon and a suspicious death at the location had soaked up the units available, so more units were required to assist from the surrounding areas. There were additional officers allocated to Newquay in the Summer months to cope with the huge swelling of tourist numbers, and even though the tourists were mostly harmless generally, it also meant there were more victims to prey on if you were a criminal looking for your next target.

Treavey was blue lighting it with Gordy from Perranporth, hoping that crime would stop in Perran today as there wasn't going to be much of a response available for the rest of the day. He'd just started a late shift with Gordy who he hadn't managed to crew up with much recently, so it was going to be good to re-establish connections with him. Gordy was a stickler for the rules, a robot of a man almost, who spat traffic tickets out like confetti with monotone robotic instructions. He liked the gym and was always immaculately dressed topped off with a very sharp, short ginger haircut. He could be quite formidable. When he laughed, it was like a middle-weight Frank Bruno laugh, relatively silent, but deep and with a controlled regular beat to it.

They drove at speed into Newquay up a very steep Trenance Hill and down onto Mount Wise which guided them down Marcus Hill with the old Methodist church on the left and into the town itself. It was extremely busy and Treavey could sense there were pockets of hostility about. Treavey and Gordy didn't want to be taken up with arrests too soon, so some discretion was required. The first skirmishes they saw happened very quickly. A bit of 'handbags at dawn' involving some men ripping their shirts off exposing their pale white and rather flabby bodies. It didn't quite give the intention the impressive ripping of cloth was designed to achieve, but this was lost on these men who had nothing left to aim for but to force the respect from others. They just weren't particularly good at it.

Gordy was revelling in jumping out of the car and getting between two groups of squabbling, drunken men, holding his arms out like a Traffic Officer stopping oncoming traffic from both directions. Treavey soon followed once he'd safely secured the car and there was a little bit of pushing and shoving but it soon subsided. No one, it seemed, was in the mood to fight with the police today.

It was very hot and both officers were sweating in their white shirts. The trousers were black and heavy so absorbed the heat like a solar panel, but the caps they wore not only instilled authority but also protected their heads from the glaring sun. Leather gloves looped over their belts showed they were ready to fight if required, so acted as a warning to those who thought these county cops would be a light touch, compared to their city ones.

The control room told all units to look out for a Black Range Rover. It was believed to be in the area delivering drugs to a group of Liverpudlians. They may be tempted to drive through the town first to take in the sites of the pubs and clubs for later on, being disarmed by the apparent lack of police. This information had come from a registered informant, so it was emphasised any stop had to give the impression of it being a standard stop-check.

157

"How come these drug dealers drive such distinctive vehicles?" Treavey asked Gordy, not really looking for an answer but Gordy humoured him with one anyway,

"Because they're arrogant twats?"

"Sounds fair," Treavey replied, before steering the car around a bend leading out of the town centre, and along Fore Street towards the front of the 'Sailors Arms' club.

"I've had some fun in that club," Treavey mentioned as he slowly manoeuvred himself through the throng of people clogging up the road. "It was great growing up after school and meeting girls who suddenly took an interest in you, being a late developer and all that!"

Treavey grinned at Gordy in the passenger seat who said nothing.

"Okay, most of the time I walked in there single and left at 1.30 am still single but on the odd occasion when I did get lucky, it would be down to Towan beach for a bit of extremely irresponsible skinny dipping, before the real fun started."

Gordy raised an eyebrow at Treavey and asked, "So did you have much to play with once you'd come back out of that very cold sea?"

"Well, you know," Treavey replied, "If you have a little spare, it helps!"

Gordy choked slightly before laughing, "Oh fuck off Treavey!"

Both officers were enjoying the moment and their company whilst they reminisced over some good times.
Suddenly, it all kicked off in front of them and both officers were on the radio calling for back-up and were out of the car. Treavey threw himself at a much larger thick-set man with the gate of a grizzly bear and who was looming over a substantially smaller and skinny teenager.

Treavey shouted at him, "Oy, oy, oy, just calm down, just back off, walk away, down there, go, just go."

He didn't give the man a chance to argue as he pushed him down the road away from the trouble. Gordy had the other two men in control, one in each fist by the scruffs of their necks. He reminded Treavey of a father separating two squabbling siblings and could hear Gordy clearly in his authoritative tones, "Gentlemen, this is where you don't want to cause trouble because the rest of your holiday will be being spent locked up and will turn out extremely expensive for you. Do I make myself clear?"

He sounded like a foreboding teacher everyone remembered at school. The one who never raised their voice and who never needed to. Both officers returned to their hastily abandoned car, the rather startled family holiday makers were carrying on about their business after having an enforced impromptu ringside seat to the disturbance. Before they got into the car, they took a moment to look around them.

The town was indeed a lovely seaside town, smelling of salt and sun-lotion, against the background of blue skies, white fluffy clouds and blazing hot sun with the incredible waft of fish and chips filtering through the air to add to their symphony of senses. Added to this, the gentle drone of the waves crashing on the shore not far below them, and the delightful and excited children's screams as they enjoyed frolicking in the waves. Some children and even adults had never seen the sea before, let alone played in it. This made both officers savour the moment, times like this should never be taken for granted.

They drove the full length of Fore Street past the surf shop 'Two Bare Feet,' and on towards the 'Red Lion' pub at the top of the harbour. Nothing was going on there apart from families enjoying steak and chips under colourful brewer advertising sunshades, outside in the sun. A live band's music was spilling out from inside the pub. It was a fun atmosphere, and Treavey commented somewhat enviously, "Blimey, wouldn't you just love to pop in there for a cold pint of cider?"

159

Gordy replied in a monotone, "Oh yes mate, that would be just perfect." He was staring straight ahead and let out an uncharacteristic shriek. "Range Rover!"

Treavey straightened himself and made himself more comfortable in his car seat and slammed his foot down on the accelerator without hesitation as the Range Rover they had been keeping an eye out for, screamed up Tower road, past the catholic church and back into the town. The car was taking the bends in the road as if on rails. Gordy flicked the switches for the two tones and the blue light whilst Treavey negotiated the same right-angled bends whilst losing as little speed as possible in the pursuit. This was going to be a tough one, but he had a small chance at least, against such a large vehicle.

Gordy declared the pursuit on the radio and updated Comms on their position and the speeds they were driving. The Black Range Rover twisted as it deviated from one road to another, attempting to shake the police car from its tail but without success. Within two minutes or so, Treavey realised he was not going to lose this pursuit unless he messed up in a big way. He'd managed to keep up with it as it flew along the back road that ran parallel to the main street. This was useful as it was avoiding the busy high street which could cause a real danger to the public and he may have had to call the pursuit off. The pursuit carried on towards quite a busy part of town including the main post office where there were shops either side and a lot of holiday revellers, but at least it had fewer pedestrians milling around than in the town centre.

It was now 'foot down' all the way out of town, along Henver Road making towards the outskirts of Newquay. Gordy was calling in Traffic units coming from Bodmin some 20 minutes away, and unfortunately, there were no other panda cars nearby to assist, so it looked like it was going to be completely down to them for the foreseeable future. The Range Rover looked as though it had two occupants, that would be a handful if they made off on foot.

Gordy shouted, "If they starburst Treavey, we'll go for the driver first, but we'll try for both of them if we get the chance."

"I'd go with that Gordy," Treavey replied as he swung the patrol car down the hill towards Porth, diesel engine straining on its highest revs.

Treavey shouted to Gordy again, "He's going along the coast road, I reckon. Get Traffic to try to cut them off up the line."

"Will do," snapped Gordy and he was immediately on the radio. There was no point in asking for the helicopter as it was in Exeter and the pursuit would be well and truly over before it got anywhere near to them.

The pursuit began to settle down. It was just as fast, but the officers were able to relax a little, knowing they had it in hand.

"I used to work in that pub there," Treavey calmly commented as the cars flashed past the 'Mermaid Inn' set on the edge of Porth Beach.

It continued towards the other side of the valley, up the very steep hill, which allowed the panda car to catch up with the Range Rover, which was itself, now struggling to maintain momentum up the steep incline.

"Jesus, this could go on forever, Gordy, what's our fuel like? Oh, I see we are good with that," Treavey thought aloud and settled in for the long drive which was feeling like rallycross along some of the most stunning coastline in Britain.

There was no time for Treavey to take in the view, but Gordy took a glimpse of the late afternoon sun shimmering on the vast blue water to his left side and many meters below. They were on the top of the soaring cliffs driving flat out around the meandering coastline, above miles of gently frothing waves which would eventually, having built themselves up, collapse onto the golden sands of the beach below for their finale.

161

Gordy updated the radio operator, "Golf 31, we are at 70 mph, distance 60 meters, subject vehicle's driving isn't too bad apart from its speed, heading down the hill towards Watergate. Any update on Traffic please?"

The Range Rover slowed to negotiate the very tight left-hand bend as it arrived at the bottom of the hill of Watergate. It lurched heavily over to the right-hand side as the bend caught the driver out slightly and slewed over to the opposite side of the road narrowly missing an oncoming VW camper van. The surfer occupants openly showed their shock and disgust with gestures. Treavey watched the oncoming driver's expression go from fury to comprehension as he saw the police car following close behind.

Treavey shouted, "We've got him!" as he watched the Range Rover dive left down the slipway which led directly towards the beach, famous for its surfing and huge expanse of soft sand.

Treavey pulled back slightly, ready for the decamp from the car in front. It slowed too, being careful to avoid a couple of rather hippy looking surfers making their way up from a surf.

"Fucking slow down man!" shouted the middle-aged surfer with long blond straggly hair and Bermuda style shorts.

He looked at Treavey with just as much disdain as the cars continue to the bottom of the hill at a slower pace. As they approached the end of the slipway, the Range Rover slowed to an almost stop, and Gordy unclipped his seatbelt in readiness. Then the Range Rover was off again, accelerating at speed before unexpectedly plunging onto the soft sand and with all four wheels spinning and gaining purchase, was making good progress through to the firmer sand beyond. For a very few seconds, Treavey felt he could follow but the realisation soon hit him it would be impossible to. He had to stop and watch the large black car he'd been pursuing so successfully become a tiny black dot in the distance, as it made its way back towards Newquay once more.

Gordy remained staring out of the screen at the dot and said more in statement form, "Where in the hell does he think he's going?"

"Absolutely no idea," Treavey replied resolutely. "There's no way out that way. The cliffs will eventually block them off from going any further. I guess we just wait here."

They knew any drugs in the car could be either buried somewhere or just thrown over the sand or into the incoming sea. They could then return and be arrested with few concerns, apart from owing a lot of drugs to someone, and having committed traffic offences and of course failing to stop for police, but these were relatively minor offences compared to possession with intent to supply a class A drug. Treavey was watching his one chance to solve the drug supply mystery disappear into the distance, and there was nothing he could do about it.

Gordy sounded resigned to the fact they'd lost the job, "By the time this gets to court, it'll be something like, 'Oh sorry Mr Police officer, we just panicked and didn't know what to do' and the Magistrates will probably go for it too."

The radio shouted out at them, "Golf 31, we have search and rescue coming as we are concerned, they're driving along the coastline with a fast-incoming tide. The vehicle occupants will be mistaken if they think they can get out the other side."

"Holy shit Gordy," Treavey replied excitedly, "you don't think they believe they can drive back to Newquay, do you? Not unless that car can climb vertical cliffs it won't."

The comms operator shouted up again. "Golf 31, we need you to meet the Sea King helicopter on the beach so you can assist in detaining them if they get stuck. They don't want to have drug dealers fighting them in their helicopter."

Treavey looked at Gordy with an excitable grin.

163

Gordy slowly put the Bakelite telephone receiver mic to his face. "Yes, I think we can sort that out."

They waited patiently, watching the naked midriffs from bikini-clad sun-kissed girls walking past their open car windows. "Oh, my goodness," Treavey commented under his breath.

Gordy quietly replied, "This is heaven. What a place we work in."

"Yep," replied Treavey.

There was nothing more he needed to say. They had one of the best views in Britain stretching out before them and half-naked beautiful people walking not one foot away from their eye line. Life felt good right now.

A few moments later they could hear the very distant sound of what they thought must be the helicopter arriving from over the horizon.

"I think that's it," Treavey said, pointing through his windscreen at a tiny spec in the distance against the blue sky beyond.

They got out of the car, locked it up, and started walking down to the beach. It was difficult walking through the soft fluffy sand just off from the bottom of the slipway in such heavy boots and they felt the holidaymakers staring at them. Sunbathers nudged each other, all trying to guess what the officers' next move would be.

The tracks of the Range Rover stretched away into the distance along the base of the cathedral like cliffs, and now the tide was far enough in, it was soon devouring those same tracks in the sand. There would be no return for the Range Rover. It was inevitable the sea would soon claim it's expensive reward, and maybe a couple of lives too.

The two officers were slightly more relieved to feel the firm sand under their feet as they walked nearer to the tide line where the sand was firmer. The two officers scrape a large letter H into the sand to give the pilot somewhere to aim for where it was clear of holidaymakers.

"Maybe we should call everyone off Gordy," Treavey shouted, "I mean, they'd be no loss to anyone, and it would save the taxpayer an awful lot of money."

Gordy ignored Treavey. "It's going to get a bit noisy in a minute, here it comes."

The huge red and grey beast from RNAS Culdrose came to a hover above them and slowly manoeuvred down onto the sand just in front of them, its engines maintaining its revs to a crescendo of noise as a crewman jumped out from the large open side door and beckoned the officers towards him. They jogged towards the helicopter bending their heads by a few centimetres, clearly unnecessarily and achieving little but it seemed the right thing to do to keep the deadly blades from taking their heads from their shoulders.

They attempted to skip onto the airframe but ended up climbing rather awkwardly into the doorway, hooking their backsides onto the floor in the doorway and rolling into the cavity beyond. They found themselves a canvas seat on the side of the aircraft and fell back into them. A medic dressed in khaki green overalls and helmet was showing them how to secure their helmets and harnesses.

Both police officers were in a strange environment, like two schoolboys on a school day out; their eyes flicking this way and that, and not saying a word apart from; "okay" and "yes", as they were secured in by the medic. Treavey looked towards the bulkhead into the cockpit where the two pilots were at work, with the myriad of very rustic looking dials, like the control centre for an old Russian nuclear power station.

The winchman jumped onto the aircraft with much more finesse than they had themselves. He was dressed in the same helmet and overalls just like the medic and he crawled over to the two officers tugging their straps. He then beckoned to the pilot who raised the lever on his left side to lift the helicopter off the ground before the whole air frame tipped forward gently and quickly gained height.

165

Treavey took stock for a moment. He didn't expect to be in an aircraft when he joined his shift earlier today. He realised what an incredible job policing could be, certainly, a variety it would be difficult to find in any other job.

The aircraft banked sharply to the left to follow the coast towards Newquay, its nose pointing slightly downwards for maximum speed. A pump of adrenaline pushed into Treavey's bloodstream as he forgot he was not James Bond for a moment. He looked through the window gazed out to sea towards Newquay town. There was a streak of white foam in the water which led from a distant faint blue line. At the front, he saw a black and orange shape of an inshore rubber lifeboat bouncing across the uneven surface towards them.

Gordy gestured to Treavey telling him he could see the Range Rover below. The helicopter banked around to the right heading out to sea before circling again to face the cliffs and enough for Treavey to see the dark shape of the Range Rover abandoned at the base of the cliffs at the cul-de-sac of jagged rocks meeting the sand and incoming waves. There was nowhere else for them to go and there was no retreating through the surf which had crept in behind them. The two occupants were unsuccessfully attempting to climb the cliffs but even they must have known it would be futile when they had reached just a few meters up and felt enough fear to persuade them to return and wait for their inevitable capture.

"Problem," the winchman shouted in the ear of Treavey. "We can't land as the tide is too high where they are. The lifeboat is going in to recover them, but it means we need to put one of you on it first with the medic escorting you down. Fancy it?"

Treavey desperately wanted to take the offer but looked towards Gordy, "I'll give him first shout."

Gordy enthusiastically took up the offer, much to Treavey's regret, and it wasn't long before he'd been strapped into the harness. Treavey handed over his

166

handcuffs to Gordy so he had two pairs. Gordy shuffled over to the edge strapped to the medic and a few seconds later they had both gone, being controlled by the winchman lowering Gordy and the medic towards the inshore lifeboat below. Treavey watched out of the tiny window as the lifeboat travelled at a steady speed below them and Gordy was transferred to it on the wire.

The medic was soon back in, joining Treavey and the winchman again. The helicopter backed off away from the scene slightly so all the occupants could watch the goings-on from a distance. The lifeboat rode at speed taking a gap between the waves and beached onto the sand next to the Range Rover. The two men were walking down from the cliffs towards them. It looked as though they were resigned to the fact they were caught and had no fight in them. This was no city life.

Treavey asked the winchman. "Just in case they kick off until they are in the boat, can we just monitor? It would be good if one of the lifeboat crew could have a quick look in the car to see if there are any drugs in there. Anything obvious at least. Gordy the police officer will have to stay with the prisoners you see."

It seemed an age for the two to be detained and the car to be searched. Nothing obvious was found in the car but they'd had time to dispose of it around the vehicle or hide it between the boulders. The Range Rover was now looking very isolated, almost ready to be taken by the waves. He felt uneasy the two were not handcuffed but he could understand why the lifeboat crew were unhappy about cuffing them on the water. There were enough of them to throw them overboard if they kicked off. It seemed they had already hidden the drugs. The offenders were unlikely to be able to recover them later but, in the meantime, the coast guard could have a good try with a drugs dog later when the tide had gone out again. That would be in approximately 6 hours but it would be dark then so it may have to wait until the following morning.

167

The Range Rover could have been taken out to sea by then but otherwise, would have to be recovered by a recovery truck if they could find a suitable one. They wouldn't want to lose that as well.

The helicopter gained some height and Treavey saw the inflatable bounce over the surf and then level off at speed heading towards Newquay harbour several miles away from where there would be more officers waiting to receive them. The helicopter banked right and Treavey got a wonderful view of the tops of the cliffs and the coast road as he was returned to the 'H' they had made in the sand. It was ignored this time as the pilot was able to go quite a bit closer to the slipway than before and gave a show to the onlooking locals and holidaymakers. Treavey felt slightly embarrassed as it may now have looked like he was the one being rescued, after all, where were the prisoners or his partner? This thought took the shine off his somewhat 007 arrival, but he gave as cavalier a wave as he could to the crew before jogging back towards the slipway. He was very quickly out of breath running up the slight incline in the very soft sand, once more, but his ego prevented him from stopping for breath. The helicopter powered up within seconds and was soon gone but not before it could be seen following the line made in the water by the lifeboat.

"Nice one, they are checking up on them," he noticed. Only the slight hum of its engines could be heard as he unlocked his car.

"Officer," he heard from behind him and he spun around to see a nervous young couple in their mid-20's with a small child with them holding a plastic bucket and spade in his hands. "Can my son have a look at your police car please, would that be okay?"

"Yes, of course, he can. Here, he can sit in the driver's seat," Treavey replied, before lifting the shy but rather awe-struck little boy into the seat before pointing out the lights, sirens and the radio to him.

This reminded Treavey of the Newquay Police Station open day when he was ten years old, which had hooked him into wanting to join the police. He'd had a look around a police car, just a Ford Escort but he'd thought it was magical. Here he was, showing this little boy and parents his own police car and they were getting as much joy as he had got, not only from when he himself was ten, but just now from a similar experience he had just got from a helicopter ride. Everything was relative.

Treavey reversed up the narrow lane back up to the main road and slowly made his way back to Newquay to meet Gordy back at the harbour. The prisoners were already on their way back to the station in a police van. They couldn't complain about the adventure they'd just had. They wouldn't have had that in London.

He pulled up outside the Lifeboat station. He could smell the unforgettable scent of seawater and fish, with the addition of some diesel perhaps from the fishing boats coming in and out between the tourist sight-seeing boats. Sailing dinghies such as Topper's, Laser's and Mirrors were flitting about in the afternoon sun, either being launched into the water or dragged up the beach on their spindly trailers.

He made his way into the lifeboat house and was led up some stairs to the lounge area where Gordy was wrapped in a space blanket and drinking a cup of tea.
"You okay Gordy?" Treavey asked, rather confused at what he was seeing. He was looking at someone who resembled more of a casualty than a police officer.

"Treavey mate, you made the right decision. It was bloody wet and bloody cold. I couldn't wait for it to be over."

Treavey laughed. "Oh my god Gordy, you look drenched! Are your pants wet? There's nothing worse than having wet pants!"

Treavey was enjoying every bit of this and Gordy knew it.

"Most definitely," he replied, "most definitely just a little bit damp!"

The two made their way back to Newquay station running the same route out through the centre of the town to refresh their memory on how it all started. Treavey was recovering from the adrenaline rush they'd just had.

"You know, Gordy," he said, looking rather thoughtful, "We need to make sure they try to search that car before the tide takes it."

Gordy replied almost instantly, "The car's going to be a goner where it is, and so will anything in it, but I've asked the coastguard to have a go and see what can be done but they've not committed. I was trying to get a police dog and handler down there but it's proving difficult at the moment. If you needed to hide drugs, you'd use the ground around you to do that, right? You aren't going to get rid of them for the hell of it, are you? You'd mark the spot somehow, and bury it under some rocks out of the reach of the tide, wouldn't you? We need a dog."

"You'd give it a go," Treavey agreed. "Yes, there's half a chance we could find it with a drugs dog, but if they hid it intending to recover it, then our lot needs to get there first before they get bail and recover it themselves."

The two got back to the station and started the paperwork. Gordy was still rather uncomfortable in his damp underwear, but also keen to get the work done as he knew custody would be chasing them up wanting to get rid of the suspects as soon as they could. It was only a minor offence after all. They had no evidence that it was drug-related, although they knew it was, so without that evidence, they had merely committed some traffic offences and failed to stop for the police, so they weren't going to get much in court, either.

Treavey was on the phone to the control room trying to arrange the coastguard to assist with the search for the drugs. He was disappointed but understood their reply. "So, as it was not life-threatening or body recovery, they couldn't get involved in police work, what, not even to treat it as a training exercise?" He looked pensive and was listening to every word over the phone. "Fair enough Sarge, I can see why, no problems. I'll speak to the patrol Inspector here to see if they can arrange a search tonight or tomorrow morning with a drugs dog when the tide is out."

Treavey looked frustrated. Without definite intelligence, it was going to be tough to convince a dog handler to take a long walk along the beach to search for these drugs.

"Hang on a moment, that's it!" shouted Gordy. "Which dog handler do you know who wouldn't want a nice walk along the beach as part of their working day? Let's forget the search team, if the drugs are there, then the dog will find them, we don't need a search team."

Gordy was on the phone straight away calling the dog unit. The call was short, and Gordy's had a grin on his face. "Job done, they are checking the tide times and doing it first thing. Bloody top guys, they said they'll do it later tonight on the first low tide before the prisoners get bail."

There was nothing they could do now apart from the paperwork. They attempted to hand it over to CID, but they weren't interested at that point. After all, it was only some road traffic offences so if anything, they needed to speak to the Traffic Department. Traffic was spoken to and the officers got a little bit of advice for the interview but nothing they didn't know already. Treavey knew from the start it was going to be down to them, so he decided with Gordy to just get on with it. They started with a basic interview and asked the custody sergeant, who was keen to empty his cells, to keep the suspects in custody until they managed to check the area for drugs with the dog.

Six hours after the arrest, they were back at the location in the darkness where they parked the car and met up with dog handler Dave. Dave opened the rear doors to his Ford Escort van and out bounced an extremely excitable liver and white spaniel.

"Come on Lucy, let's go for a walk, come on girl," Lucy bounded onto the beach into the darkness and the officers began their long walk towards the scene into the eerie gloom using their torches like searchlights scanning the skies for demons hidden within the oppressive cliffs above. They could hear the white noise of the waves crashing in the distance, and as they moved away from the main beach and moved further along the coast, the white noise became louder with pauses between the build-up of waves rising to a peak before gently toppling over into a shadowy white froth, which then dissipated into a soup of white foam rolling towards their feet.

The officers could walk in comfort as they were not going to get cut off for some time now. It gave comfort when there was a considerable area of wet sand laid in front of the tide line, showing the tide was in the process of retreating from the beach, rather than approaching the dry sand to soon engulf it.

Lucy seemed to enjoy lolloping along the sand, before diverting into the water for a splash, and then back to circle her handler, repeatedly checking he was still there and hadn't strayed too far from her. She simply felt this was the most wonderful walk after dark.

It was not long before they saw a rather unnatural shape ahead of them in the gloom. The torches struck out into the distance and illuminated what was left of the Range Rover. It had been completely engulfed by the incoming tide before being pushed onto its side. Several tonnes of metal played with like a cat teasing a mouse. There was no competition. The car looked destroyed, with huge dents in every panel, and an appearance it had been in the sea for years. It had moved a good 100 meters in the water before being spat out further along the coast.

Treavey coaxed the others to move a little further along the cliff line. The air was cool and crisp in his lungs, but he'd worked up a sweat by now.

"Just a bit further I reckon. I recognise that outcrop over there."

Gordy joined in, "Yes, it's further on, I marked the position with a long length of seaweed just above the tide line. Here we go, there it is."

Gordy and Treavey held back, not wishing to destroy any scent for the dog. Dave called Lucy back and chatted to her. Lucy's childish and playful manner instantly changed to work mode and her whole demeanour changed. Her nose was on the sand and she was rapidly pacing over the rocks at the base of the cliff, pausing occasionally to have a sniff in the air before losing interest and searching for a more promising scent elsewhere. It looked as though there was no pattern to her searching and her handler called her to go over the same area once or twice, so he was satisfied she hadn't missed anywhere.

She bounced like a mountain goat around the base of the cliffs before catching a scent slightly higher up which interested her. Her body was rigid as she scrambled up a steep incline to a small ridge about 6 feet above the baseline. Dave called her back and scrambled up to the ridge himself. The other two watched him with some expectation, but there was no change of expression on Dave's face. It looked like the result was going to be disappointing.

Dave scraped around where Lucy had been and pulled a rock away which tumbled down off the ridge and rolled to a stop at the base.

Dave shouted in excitement, "Good girl, who's a good girl Lucy, there's daddy's girl."

He pulled a large package the size of a small briefcase, wrapped in cellophane from the ledge and slipped down the slope a little. Lucy sprinted off with the toy she'd just been thrown by Dave which was what she'd been after all the time.

Dave carefully placed the package on the ground at the feet of Treavey. "I think their stay at her majesty's pleasure has just got a bit longer, don't you?" he said with a look of glee on his face.

The three of them shared the chore of carrying the package back with them to the car. It was not long before they were back at Newquay Station writing statements, and with a huge lump of what looked like heroin deposited on the desk of the Detective Sergeant, and after a short phone call to custody, they now had a considerably lighter workload for themselves. CID were suddenly very keen to take the job on.

Before he left Newquay Police Station, Treavey ran up the stairs to have a quick chat with the DS, a seasoned cop who had pretty much seen everything in his time. His weathered face gave away the years of poor attention to his health and his rather rosy and mottled nose showed he was struggling with coping with his alcohol intake.

"Good job here Treavey, well done for going back there again," he commented as Treavey waited at the door politely to be asked in.

"Thanks, Sarge. I wondered what you thought about whether the gang have anything to do with our supplies in Perranporth?" Treavey asked, feeling like a schoolboy at the door of the headmaster's office.

"Unlikely I'm afraid. The delivery to your neck of the woods is a strange one. It's obviously coming from somewhere, but all our informants haven't a clue where from. They knew about this delivery, but they don't think it was heading to Perranporth."

Treavey felt despondent which the DS saw. "Don't worry about it Treavey, it's clearing up a lot of crime in your area as they all pop off with drug overdoses. They aren't breaking into cars or houses to feed their habits anymore and with someone like you and Gordy over there,

174

it won't be long before you find out who it is anyway. Just don't be too quick about it."

Treavey quietly laughed under his breath but felt uneasy. He wandered away from the office feeling a bit down. He questioned himself. "That DS has been around for a bit. Maybe he's lost a bit of humanity. Hope I don't get like that. Maybe it was just dark humour. They are someone's kids at the end of the day."

It suddenly dawned on him. "Court day tomorrow. Best get prepared for that, now. This job is all over the place. Chases one day, then looking all smart in court, giving evidence the next."

Chapter 11

Death and defendants

Treavey was standing in the witness box. He was dressed in his tunic and had put his custodian helmet down beside him on the desk. He surveyed the rather drab looking room with several empty seats for an observing public who rarely came. There was a huge elaborate colourful wooden crest on the wall behind the magistrates, presumably there to remind people of the severity of the occasion. Without that austere reminder thrust in front of you, you could have been in a local town council meeting. He took the oath on the bible that had been handed over to him.

"I swear by almighty God, that the evidence I shall give will be the truth, the whole truth and nothing but the truth." He was desperately trying to hold back the next line which all the urges in his body wanted him to say. "So, help me God!" in a strong American accent but he resisted the temptation. He didn't think the American addition would go down too well.

The bench of three magistrates were to his left and they were looking directly at him as he gave the oath. He felt the middle-aged one in the centre looked very confident, just by the way he was shuffling the papers in front of him. He looked to be the more approachable of the three. The one to his left was an elderly woman who wore small square rimmed spectacles at the end of her nose and a scruffy grey-haired bun tied to the back of her head. The autumnal coloured woollen cardigan matched her stereotype perfectly, giving the impression of being a strict librarian. The other was an even more grey person, practically bereft of any interest or distinction at all.

"Your Worships, I am PC 3908 Michael Treave in the Devon and Cornwall Constabulary currently stationed at Perranporth Police Station."

He knew his lines and Treavey shut up to await the first question from the prosecution. It would be an easy ride at this point, but the cross-examination by the defence was the fun bit. Treavey was thinking hard, pensive, but very much enjoying the anticipation of the battle ahead. If it was too easy, it could be a trap, but what if it was something that exposed him, or even just looked like he was being exposed as a fraud.

Treavey generally enjoyed appearing in court because he had had a great tutor who taught him several rules; "Firstly, just think all the magistrates and the defence solicitor had their skirts or trousers around their ankles this morning and were taking a dump. That takes the mystique out of them immediately. Secondly, only answer what you know. If you don't know, say you don't know. If you made a mistake, say you made a mistake and that way you will never have anything to hide, and standing up there speaking freely is a nice place to be.

The prosecution stood up, running his finger down his notes, and holding his lapel with the other hand. He'd dressed in a very smart pin-striped suit, no doubt with the intention of looking like a Rumpole of the Bailey.

"Officer," he said in loud and confident tones, "So you were driving along the main A3075 driving towards the direction of Truro but near to Perranporth and you noticed in front of you a red BMW 318i motor car registration B581WOD, is that correct?"

Treavey looked at the magistrates as was custom and replied, "Yes Your Worships, that's correct."

The prosecutor continued to outline the case, "...and you tried to cause this vehicle to stop as you recognised it was being driven by the defendant who you knew to be disqualified from driving, is that correct?"

"Yes, Your Worships, that is correct."

The prosecutor straightened up and then summarised the events from his pad. "So, tell me if any part of this is incorrect. I see no point in dragging this out as Their Worships are terribly busy people. You switched on your blue light and the car drove off at speed. You attempted to keep up with the car, but you lost it in the back lanes around Perranporth airfield. On returning to Perranporth you located the car parked and abandoned, and you checked the vehicle to see if it was secure or open, yes?"

Treavey was happy to fill in the details. "Yes, Your Worships, I approached the car and tried the doors and boot, but they were all locked. The glass was intact and there was no sign of forced entry. I assessed the ignition area from outside and could clearly see it was undamaged."

"Right," the prosecutor looked directly at Treavey, "So in your opinion, there was no sign at all the vehicles had been broken into and as far as you could see, the person who had been driving the car, had been in possession of the keys?"

The defence stood up sharply, "Objection Your Worships, he cannot know what the officer was thinking at the time."

The prosecutor immediately replied, "I'll then perhaps put it in another way, officer, did you see any signs to show the car may have been stolen?"

Treavey clearly and loudly replied, "No, none at all. It looked as though it had been parked by the driver and secured."

The prosecutor continued, enjoying his flow a little too much perhaps. "So, then you think, 'well, I'm not leaving it there,' and so you attended the address of the registered keeper which was less than two miles away and waited out of sight watching to see if the defendant arrived back, is that correct?"

"Yes, that's correct, I wanted to see if the driver returned home and whether he had the keys to the car in his pocket which would confirm my suspicions he'd been the driver at the time."

"Go on," encouraged the prosecutor.

"I waited for about half an hour and then noticed the defendant returning home, so I approached him, and he looked startled, and he was sweating. I searched him under the Police and Criminal Evidence Act and found some keys which I later found to be the ones which opened his car and started the ignition. The defendant just replied, 'No Comment,' for the whole time I was with him and again in the interview. As I suspected him to have been drinking, I carried out a station procedure and he provided a result of 92 micrograms of alcohol in 100 millilitres of breath, the legal limit being just 35 micrograms."

The prosecutor rounded up the incident putting forward a conclusion damning the defendant with being so reckless as to drive nearly 3 times over the drink-drive limit and whilst he was disqualified from driving, which showed utter contempt for the law and the courts.

He finalised with, "No further questions."

Treavey felt good for a second but it soon dawned on him he'd just experienced the easy bit as it had been his side which had been asking the questions. He knew it was unconventional to bring a case like this to court. There was a lot of circumstantial evidence with very little physical evidence. It would have been extremely easy to say he had recognised the driver but that wasn't his style. He remembered what his tutor had said, and what if, just what if it hadn't been him driving after all. There could be nothing worse in his mind than to prosecute someone and get an innocent person convicted.

The defence stood up. An older man who had a certain swagger about him. He looked very confident which unsettled Treavey a little. "Just stick to your advice," he thought to himself. "Don't let him faze you."

"Officer, I appreciate you are an exceedingly observant police officer,"

Treavey knew immediately he was being flattered, and to be incredibly careful he didn't fall into the trap of getting too comfortable. The defence was not here to make friends with him.

"You lost sight of the car which my defendant claims he wasn't driving, yes?"

Treavey knew he couldn't sugar coat it. "That's right," he replied.

Treavey was remembering his tutor's words, "Keep the answers short if you can."

The defence continued, throwing his folder onto the desk, and turning to face Treavey, almost to show this case was already won. "So, you can say that anyone could have been driving that car, yes?"

Treavey didn't want him to highlight the negatives but ignore the rest of the evidence. "At that time, I had a very big suspicion it must be him as I knew he was disqualified, and the car was completely locked, and the defendant had the keys on him, having found him very sweaty." Treavey was pleased he just about got it all in before being challenged.

"Just answer the question, please, PC Treave. But at the time you saw him, you didn't see the defendant driving and you didn't see him get out of the car once it had stopped."

Treavey had no choice but to say; "Correct."

"Okay," the defence continued, "so you say the car was locked. The doors and the boot?"

Treavey replied, "Yes, the doors and the boot."

"And the sunroof, was the sunroof shut?"

Bam! That came out of nowhere. Treavey knew he hadn't mentioned the sunroof in his statement, and so it would look a bit strange if he just confirmed it now. "Stick to what your tutor said, Treavey," he thought.

"The sunroof? I must admit, I don't remember seeing a sunroof or checking one. All I can say is I checked the car for a break-in, and any form of damage and I couldn't find any. I was satisfied the car was completely secure."

"Thank you, no further questions." He replied curtly.

Treavey was surprised he ended so quickly. The court officially released Treavey, but instead of leaving the court, he remained at the back of the court to listen to the summing up. The prosecution did a good job with that too, mainly emphasising the defendant had not said who the driver was if it hadn't been him, and there was definitely a motive for the defendant to run from the police, with the fact he was drunk and disqualified. There was no explanation as to why the defendant was in the right place at the right time with the keys to a fully secured car and dripping in sweat which would have matched the time it would have taken to run from the car back to his home.

The defence was clear that nobody could prove it was his client in the car, at the time PC Treave saw the car mobile, and that was the end of the matter as far as he was concerned. Treavey had felt annoyed with himself for not noticing the sunroof. It niggled him as he felt a bit of a fool by having to admit that in court. The defence could have taken full advantage of that, but they didn't.

"Why was that?" he wondered.

Treavey drove slowly back to Perranporth from the court in Newquay satisfied with the surprise guilty verdict. Of course, he was guilty, but magistrates need to hang on to any reason to suspect a reasonable doubt, and that could be watered down to really no doubt at all, but a benefit of the doubt being given. It was human nature, especially when you see a puppy-eyed defendant saying he didn't mean to, or it wasn't him and the nice police officer must be mistaken.

"But that sunroof," Treavey thought to himself. "I mean that sunroof, you are slipping, Treavey." The panda car meandered back up the main coast road towards Perran. He carried out a check on car registration. B581WOD and the answer came back immediately.

"Golf 31, Bravo 5,8,1 whiskey, Oscar, Delta comes back as a red BMW 318i, new owner since one week ago, now registered to a Mr Richard Dutton, of 15 Southgate Lawn, Perranporth. A quick check shows he's not known on our systems, Golf 31?"

Treavey thanked the operator and headed to the address. The original offence had occurred 4 weeks ago, so it would have to be a new owner. Maybe the defendant had realised he was going to be convicted and have an extended disqualification period and decided to get rid of the rather distinctive car. It was just fifteen minutes later when he appeared outside a smart semi-detached house. There on the road outside was the BMW. It was as faultless as he remembered it. He parked up adjacent to the house and walked over to the car parked a few feet in front.

He casually looked at the roof of the car and his jaw dropped. "There's no sunroof. There's no fucking sunroof!"

Thoughts whirled around his head as he walked back to his car. He was angry but thank god he had kept to his tutor's advice. "Can you imagine if I'd said, 'Yes I checked the sunroof.'" He knew what the defence would have said, "Officer, this sunroof you checked doesn't actually exist, so that's not true is it, and if that's not true, what else isn't true?"

It would have gone badly downhill from there. He felt immensely proud of himself. He'd beaten the defence solicitor. He had avoided an almighty landmine which would have blown him off his feet. He had survived and not only had he survived, but he had also won. Christ, he loved court.

"Officer, is there a problem?" a voice came from behind.

A man was walking out of his house towards Treavey. He looked, shall we say, law-abiding. One shouldn't stereotype perhaps, but of course one did if you wanted to be a good police officer, and it was usually pretty clear to him if someone was on the right side of the law or not.

"Nothing to worry about sir. Is it Mr Dutton?" Treavey enquired, thinking fast to decide how much to tell him.

"Yes, that's right."

Treavey decided honesty was the key and told him of the court case he'd just had. "Nothing to worry about, but I just had to check, and fortunately, it seems I am not going mad after all."

Mr Dutton smiled warmly. "They tried to have one over you because they damned well knew you had nothing else. Try to get you to say something they could prove wasn't the case, however well-intentioned you were, then it weakens the whole case. Take it from a solicitor, it's all about who wins on the day, not necessarily to do with what was right or wrong."

Treavey pricked up his ears, "A solicitor?"

Mr Dutton nodded and smiled, "Yes, I've bought this car for my son. I realised the chap I bought it from wasn't the most reliable of people." The friendly chat was broken by the radio.

"Any Perranporth unit able to attend a sudden death, believed an overdose?"

Treavey wished he'd gone straight back to the station as he'd have had the car empty by now and would be on his way home. He couldn't ignore this though.

"Yeah, 3908, not sure I have a call sign, just returned from court, is there no other unit?" Treavey asked wistfully, hoping another local unit keeping their head down might perk up.

"Sorry 3908, we have no one else available at the moment. Golf 31 is attending a road traffic accident on the A38 so will be some time. Would you be able to assist?" Treavey knew he wasn't getting out of this one. This job could take some time as well. There's usually a lot of waiting around, so Treavey already knew he was going to be late off. It could give him a clue as to where the drugs were coming from though.

Within 10 minutes, Treavey was walking up the narrow staircase to a rather grotty looking flat. He'd already said goodbye to the paramedic who'd left the scene. The flat was made up of an old ex-local authority semi-detached house with one ground floor flat and one first floor. He followed a rather pert backside of a young woman, about 23 years old up the dirty wooden stairs into the bedsit above. The smell hit his nostrils, a dirty smell of unwashed bodies and dust and grime from many years accumulation. A vacuum had not travelled this threadbare filthy carpet in many a year. There was a door which used to be white but was now cream with nicotine stains and the grime from thousands of hand marks down the leading edge to reflect the lack of basic care this flat had received. The girl led him into a bedroom and stepped aside to present the scene.

There was a mound of a stained and filthy duvet and an extremely pale leg protruding out of it at the bottom. It was rigid with rigor mortis and so Treavey knew the death was between 6 to 12 hours ago. He exposed the male's body to look for obvious wounds. He gauged the man to be in his late 20's but the face was now resembling just a carcase. No sign of life or even that it used to be alive at one time. It was like a lizard skin shed for a newer one, but this one had had no replacement. Treavey often marvelled about how dead someone looked. You could never tell someone's character when they were dead, as in if someone walked towards you, you could get an idea of what their demeanour was like, how kind they were, or whether they had attitude. But when they were dead, the soul was gone, and all clues with it.

184

The man's arm was hanging down the side of the bed and it was deep purple, along with his buttocks, caused from where the blood pools from gravity to the lower parts of the body.   Treavey examined the body from top to bottom.   It would be embarrassing if the undertakers found a knife sticking out of his back.   Treavey looked at the bedside cabinet and observed drug paraphernalia on it.   A cannabis grinder and a discarded spliff cigarette, a dirty needle but no other signs of drugs.   There was a prescription receipt for methadone, meant to be instead of heroin, but so often became an 'as well as'.

No attempt at CPR had been made by the paramedic. What was the point when the body was as stiff as a board? Treavey looked at the girl.   She would have been quite pretty with her fine blond hair around her rosy complexioned face if she hadn't had such an abusive life perhaps.   But her face showed a history of drug abuse, with lack of nutrition and a lack of will to make herself look presentable any longer.   What her parents must have originally hoped for.   Treavey had the impression she had come from a middle-class family; had probably got into the wrong crowd as there were some clues which showed she had relatively high standards at one time and still maintained some.   A pretty silver picture frame with a photo of a financially comfortable looking family in it.   A vase of fresh flowers stood on the table bursting with colour amongst the gloom of the room, and she wore fitted Levi Jeans which flattered any shape she still had.

Having requested CID to attend, routine for a death such as this, he prepared his first question to her. "What's your name, my love?"

"Mary," she replied, as she continued to stare at the bed with the body of her boyfriend on it.   She looked as though she was in shock, but she also seemed to be resigned to the fact her boyfriend was dead; almost expectant.   Her reaction surprised Treavey.

"That's a lovely name," Treavey replied, and she sniggered in response. It seemed others had been surprised at such a delicate name, too. Almost as though she had let it down.

"Can you tell me what's happened, I will need to fill in a form with some details from you?"

Mary told him how they had taken heroin together the night before. He had not had any for the day, so he had taken quite a large amount in the evening but not enough to kill him, or so they had thought. When she woke up in the morning, he was lying dead beside her.

Treavey goes for it, "Mary, where do you buy your drugs from? We think there's a particularly neat strength about or I suspect it is particularly cheap in this area for now. Look, your boyfriend is dead now. Don't you think it's time to end all this, to get yourself off these drugs?"

She paused and looked as though she was going to blurt everything out to him, but she hesitated and then paused some more.

"Some guy in town. Look, I'll never write this down, but I'll tell you now it's cheap as chips. The deal is we don't tell anyone anything. That's why so many people are on it now. Coke and smack, you know, heroin by the truckload. We suspect it gets here in many ways such as car, plane, and boat, but we don't really know how."

Treavey threw caution to the wind, "Who do you get it from, off the record?"

Surely, she'd clam up now but he did have a good rapport going with her so there was always a chance.

"I didn't say this, but that Dawson guy, and he has two runners for him who are brothers; they live near the station I think."

She turned away and walked into the lounge, picked up a tin of tobacco and started to roll a cigarette from the tobacco.

"Don't think he'll mind me taking his tobacco, do you?" She attempted a grin.

Treavey looked around the lounge area but decided not to sit down. It didn't look any cleaner than the bedroom, worse in fact.

"You know Mary, people do give the habit up love, it'll take an effort, but you can do it. I suspect you don't want to be living in a similar state in 20 years if you make it that long."

She took a drag of her freshly lit roll-up and looked at Treavey directly in his eyes. Her dazzling blue eyes surprised him. "Christ this girl is beautiful, well, would have been beautiful at least."

She replied to him, "Look, I know, this is shit. I need to get help but there pretty much is none. I've tried to get it. Stuart tried to get help too, you know, that dead body in there and look how it ended up for him."

"Tell me you didn't inject him yourself," Treavey asked her.

Fortunately, she was educated enough to know what to say.

"Of course not. That would be an offence of supplying drugs, wouldn't it? That would be a serious offence."

Treavey wasn't out for offenders here. Yes, he should be carefully interviewing her, but he felt sorry for her too. She seemed like a nice girl. At the end of the day, it was Stuart's choice to take drugs, and he alone fucked his life up, whatever other reasons he had to help him along the way, but ultimately, he killed himself. Treavey didn't want this girl to end up in prison because of it. He wouldn't lie, but he wouldn't lure her into an admission either.

The CID officers walked up the stairs and surveyed the scene. Treavey told them what Mary had told him, and the officers asked Treavey to make sure he put an intelligence record in on it so it would be in the system officially. "Yes of course, but it only confirms what we already suspected. Are you guys able to put surveillance on Dawson and the Bradfords at all?"

187

The reply was a chuckle. "No chance Treavey. The manpower for that would be incredible, we could hit their places with more warrants, but we think they are stashing it elsewhere. We need to find out where they stash the stuff."

"But surveillance would lead us to their stash, no?" Treavey insisted again.

The CID officer cut him off. "Two hopes, Treavey, one is Bob, and you know the other one."

Treavey left the CID officers to it, passing the doctor who arrived to certify death on the way down the stairs.

"He's up there doctor, the one who hasn't breathed for about 6 hours, is beetroot purple and is stiff as a wardrobe door. When are they going to let the paramedics do this for you?!"

The doctor grunted and continued up the stairs. A quick fifty quid for him no doubt but they'd have to change the system one day. Treavey heard of some doctor having to come out to certify dead, a head separated from its body on a railway track the other day. I mean, how much deader than dead could you get before they say, "Okay, we'll assume they are dead now, and save the busy doctor some surgery time."

Treavey got into his car once more feeling surprisingly quite refreshed from his long day. The court case felt a long time ago, but he was now into overtime and thought he may as well nip down the town and see Grace on the way back to the station. He drove to the seafront and then to her favourite spot, but she was not there. He checked another couple of places, but again she wasn't there. He began to feel a little concerned. "Surely, nothing's happened to her, right?" he hoped. No, he was sure one of the others would have said something. He drove south up the hill along from the beach to a lovely observation point which looked over the whole of the beach and up the coast, scanning miles and miles of sandy coastline. It looked stunning against the backdrop of the crisp blue sky and occasional fluffy white clouds.

There she was sitting on a bench, no doubt dedicated to some person who had looked across at the view just as she was now, but many years prior. He pulled the car up and sauntered over towards her. She was looking content and well in herself, apart from being semi-permanently tipsy perhaps, but she had a lot of history to try to block out. Treavey couldn't blame her.

"Hey, gorgeous!" Treavey risked an over-familiar greeting, as he felt he knew her quite well now.

She spun her head around to watch him approaching, slightly surprised and inquisitive to see who it was speaking so warmly towards her.

"Hey, how's my favourite Perran plod? How are you Treavey?"

He sat next to her and they both took in the view spread out before them.

"This has got to be one of the best views in the world Grace, no?" Treavey remarked with some enthusiasm.

"Oh well, I've not checked most of them out to compare, but I suspect this one is a good start for now."

Treavey got down to business. "Now Grace, I have a surprise for you."

"No," she replied, deadpan.

"No what?" Treavey enquired surprised at the rather immediate answer.

"No, I won't marry you Treavey. You smell far too fresh for me, and people will talk. They'll think I will mislead you as a mature woman."

Treavey burst out laughing but Grace stared at him with a very straight face, and said, "What, what are you laughing at?"

Treavey checked his laugh and looked at her rather confused for a few seconds before Grace laughed herself.

"No dear! Don't worry, it was a joke!"

She paused as Treavey chuckled in relief, feeling rather naïve that he'd fallen for her joke. Grace straightened her expression again and said sternly, "Yes, of course, I'll marry you."

Treavey's smile disappeared again before she burst into laughter again.

"Oh, Grace, stop playing with me. I've had a long day! Anyway, what I'm trying to say is I've got some good news for you. You may be insulted but I thought it may help. You know everything which goes on in this town right? The information you gave me about Tommy and Billy Bradford and Gary Dawson seems to be confirmed. I can't get you anything for that as I need a result, but I have registered you as an informant. This just means if you come up with some information on that lot which gets a good result, then you could get some money."

Grace stared at Treavey who wasn't clear by her expression whether she was pleased or insulted.

"Darling Treavey, you know I'd tell you anything, anyway right?"

"Yes, I know that Grace," Treavey replied. "But I think it'll help you and I think you deserve a bit of a break, but you mustn't put yourself in danger, right? I'd never forgive myself."

"Oh, don't worry about me. No one sees me." She gazed into the distance up the coast and her mind seemed to wander slightly. "No one looks at me or knows I'm here apart from you, Treavey. You know I'm extremely grateful to you for that. You are a special kind of person."

They both sat there for a few moments, happy in their silence. Watching the excited families on the beach below making precious lifelong memories, scanning the coast into the distance of flat soft sands and the dunes behind which fed up into the long grasses protecting the campsite from the vicious storms which blew in from the Atlantic. The sea looked inviting with its pale blue, turquoise and deep green shades, with surfers frolicking in the waves on their newly bought white polystyrene boards, the older tourists on their slim plywood boards and the women wearing swimming caps to keep their perms dry. Seagulls with wings outstretched were gliding in the warm breeze above the lush, green bunches of thrift grass, taking in what they could view below, and with a gentle tip of a wing, swooped across hundreds of yards of beach to take up another thermal, before rising on the air-current once more and returning towards the two of them.

"I could stay here forever," Treavey said.

"It's not so bad in the summer," Grace replied, reminding Treavey it could be a very tough life being on the streets for most of the year.

He stood up and took one more look at the view and as he was just about to leave, Grace said, "One more thing Treavey, you see that large rock, almost an island when the tide is in around it?"

Treavey could see there was a funnel of the sea which flowed between them and the rock when the tide was in but was free to climb on when the tide was out.

Grace continued. "Last night, I saw a red canoe paddle out at high tide, and it paddled out past that rock until I saw it meet up with a small boat. It hung around there for a bit, but I couldn't see what it was up to. All I know is it purposefully met up with it and then it returned to the beach. Strange I thought, especially as it was 11.00 pm."

She had left the bombshell until last.

"11 o'clock! Jesus, Grace, that's quite late. Did you say it was a red canoe?"

"That's what I could tell from the torchlight from the boat anyway," Grace replied. "It was definitely up to no good, especially as it was quite choppy and not a pleasant evening for a relaxing paddle. Bloody dangerous in my view."

Treavey thanked Grace and headed back to the car. He slowly drove back to the station where he was

191

disappointed to find there was no one there to share the information with. He had to look out for this red canoe now. Was it every Thursday evening the boat was having a meet at 11.00 pm? He'd have to make sure he was there next week to see if the canoe turned up on the beach. Treavey felt it had been a good day today, a very good day overall. Before he went home, he submitted the information from Grace using the correct procedure to protect her identity. He liked to conclude the day by completing his paperwork if he could, rather than to leave it until the next day. Far less chance of forgetting to do something important and getting into trouble.

He gently stroked Wolfy who was stretching out on the warm windowsill and headed off home, now excited for the week ahead. At least he had a lead now.

"I might just catch those drug suppliers, it may just happen, and it could even be next week," he said to himself quietly, as he started his car up, and glanced across to the Bradford brothers' house before heading home. "That's enough police thinking now," he thought to himself. "I'm on late shift tomorrow. Right, off duty now. Nice thoughts, nice thoughts, no police thoughts."

Chapter 12

It's just too much

"Ah hell, this is going to take some time," PC Greg Baddock, known as Bomber, shouted as he slammed his pen down on his paperwork. "Treavey, I'm trying to get this fucking file done and some idiot decides they want to threaten to skydive off the edge of a cliff."

A moment of silence followed as Treavey gathered his things to start his late shift. Bomber was still on his early shift.

"I'll jump into the car with you Bomber, we'll just have to negotiate them down more quickly than usual, mate."

Bomber scooped a couple of items together including his coat and helmet which he always wore in preference to his cap, he preferred the tradition of it and headed towards the door.

"Okay Treavey, if it's any consolation, I do feel bad for having just said that, but that file of mine is late, and I need to get it done soonest."

It was a grey day. The occasional glimpse of sun, but otherwise pretty dull weather. Treavey knew the struggle the tourists were going to experience if there were too many days like this in a row. A sunny day on the beach cost parents a homemade sandwich, maybe a pasty, and an ice cream, but a day like today or even worse when it's raining, well, that cost a lot more. The bonus is they could end up in places, experiencing sites they never thought they would, such as driving to Dairyland near Newquay on a rainy day to see the multiple milking systems where the cows all march in and attach themselves to the machines and get milked automatically. It's what the tourists come on holiday to see! When else would something like that attract someone's interest, but it all costs money for the whole family to go, of course, and can add up by the end of the week.

Maybe the doom and gloom of the day had coaxed another to want to end it all. All the locals tended to love Cornwall, but if suffering from depression, it could be extremely difficult to get some help here. The isolation could be intolerable for many and often people would find themselves in a position where the police were being called as a last resort.

The officers turned up in the area where the person had last been seen. They parked the car in the cliffside car park, where Treavey had thought he had heard the ghostly Merlin engines of a Spitfire that night, when in fact it was a light aircraft possibly attempting to land in the storm in the nearby airfield. The details of that night came rushing back and there were still some unanswered questions, such as why that light aircraft was out and about on that ridiculously dangerous night. The best of pilots wouldn't have considered flying in that weather, so it was little surprise when he was asked to attend a plane crash in the trees nearby just a short time later. Dave, the dog handler, had indicated there was something within the plane which could be drugs, but nothing turned up according to Felicity who had taken over on the early shift. So frustrating and still very strange.

"Treavey!" Bomber shouted. "You're away with the fairies man. Come on."

Both officers made their way over the mounds of pink thrift towards the greyness and mizzle of the cliff edge. They walked on the same paths worn by rabbits, foxes and badgers cut deep through the thick fern and gorse which protected them from the deadly drop just hidden from their view. As they trampled through the thicket and got a little closer, they saw the shadowy dark shape of a girl sitting close to the edge of a rocky outcrop. One step further, or a shuffle of her backside and she had a sheer drop below her, not into the sea, but onto the black jagged rocks some 40 metres below which would have been unsurvivable.

She was motionless, dressed in jeans and a little white cotton top. She had a slight figure, was in her early 20's, probably, and she had long fine blonde straight hair which swished about her face like the sea playing with the seaweed on the rocks. She brushed it aside once or twice, but then sat motionless once more.

"What do you want to do, Bomber?" asked Treavey?

"I feel a bit bad for what I said earlier..." Bomber said reflectively, "...so I'll take this one mate. I'll talk, and you do some digging on her once I get her details, yes?"

"Sounds like a plan mate. Well, good luck."

The officers moved slowly forward together so as not to startle her and push her into a sudden reaction. The last thing they wanted to do was to panic her. Their progress slowed as they approached within 20 metres of her. They'd got a lot closer than they had originally hoped which they were relieved for as it was incredibly tiring negotiating with someone if they were too far away to hear properly. The concentration could be exhausting, and no real rapport was usually achieved.

Bomber started the negotiation. "Hello. It's the police here, we are here to help you. My name is Bomber. What's your name?"

It came to Treavey like a bolt of lightning that he recognised the girl. He gripped Bomber on the shoulder and quietly said, "I'll take it from here Bomber. I know her. Her name is Mary."

Treavey shuffled around Bomber on the narrow path cut into the gorse. Its spikes managed to find their goal through the thick police trousers jabbing him in the calf with sharp shooting stabs.

Treavey continued, "Hey Mary."

The girl made no reaction, said nothing, and didn't move. Only her hair swished in the sea breeze, which rushed up the cliff pushed on by the Atlantic. "Mary, I came to your flat when your boyfriend died. I am here to help you and to talk about things. We can make things better, I promise you."

She began to move her hands into her pocket and Treavey soon saw the familiar movement of a cigarette being rolled. She remained silent which unsettled him. It could be a good sign with her rolling a cigarette to have a conversation, settling herself in for a chat, or it could be the last roll up before she jumped.

"Mary, I can only imagine how sad you must feel at the moment. How unbelievably depressed you must feel having lost your boyfriend. Nothing I will say now will make this all go away immediately, but what I can say..." Treavey checked himself to see if he was making things worse, "...what I can say, Mary, is you will feel better in time to come. This grief will fade, and you will remember the happy times with him instead."

Mary turned her head towards Treavey, "What happy times? My life's fucked. I want to start again."

"There's no reset button, Mary, but there are ways to make this one better, and for you to be enriched by your experiences, yes, even horrible ones, so that maybe, you could help others in similar positions as you are maybe. You will feel better eventually and be glad you didn't end your life."

Treavey turned to Bomber and gave him some details to check with the control room before attempting to move forward a little, but without even moving her head, Mary demanded, "Don't come closer, or I'll jump. I'm going to do it anyway. I've had enough of this life."

"You know, Mary, there are many people who have felt exactly like you, but they have turned their lives around, they are highly successful people now, and they are happy, you have to believe that. You will have a family one day, your very own family. You don't want to give all that up."

Treavey felt more desperate and was lunging for any positives he could. She just was not interacting so he couldn't expand the conversation, gain a rapport, or gain her trust.

The greyness of the sky just added to the depression. If only it were a jet blue sky with a warm sun and a gentle summer breeze on their skin, pure white fluffy clouds coasting across the blue canvas, then perhaps it would help her believe there was too much to live for. They stood there in the greyness with no progress being made and extraordinarily little coming from Mary. She was just sitting there, and no one could know what she was thinking or feeling.

"Come on Mary, love. We can make some plans. I can get you some help."

"There's no help. I don't have the strength anyway," she replied quietly. "I don't want to be here anymore."
Treavey paused a moment. He was running out of things to say. He looked at Bomber behind him and said, "New tac mate, do you want a go?"

Bomber nodded his head and manoeuvred himself halfway around Treavey but stopped dead. Treavey wondered why Bomber had paused in such an awkward position.

"Come on mate, these thorns are doing their best to bleed me dry."

Treavey's attention was on Bombers face now, just a few inches from his own. Bomber's harsh, rugged face had turned pale, and he looked as though he was going to burst into tears.

"Oh no, Treavey, oh no."

His voice was gentle and soft but so solemn it was almost unrecognisable to Treavey. Bomber was transfixed, gazing into the distance towards the rock and he confirmed the worst.

"Mary's gone."

They both shuffled their way towards the cliff edge through the relentless gorse, still trying to make out the tracks from the nightly wild animals to lessen the impact on their skin under their trousers which offered little protection. They both stood where Mary had been sitting and they leaned over to where she had jumped. What it must take to jump from somewhere such as that. To think there was no other solution was so sad, devastating in fact. Their eyes scanned below for where the body could have landed but there was nothing obvious.

Treavey spoke up, "Once the body clears that ledge jutting out, Bomber, you see that grassy outcrop, then there's no hope for her, but..." Treavey paused for a few seconds of contemplation. "...you don't think...?"

Bomber took on the rest of the sentence, "... that she could have slid down to that ledge and rolled towards the face of the cliff instead of going straight over?" he added, before continuing with, "Well I can't see her body at the bottom."

He got on his personal radio and requested immediate attendance of the coast guard, lifeboat, and helicopter. There was an exceedingly small chance but perhaps they were not being realistic to even contemplate it. At least they could recover her body for her relatives.

Treavey stood tall, looking straight out to sea, reminiscing on the short relationship he had had with Mary.

"She seemed such a kind girl. Two deaths in such a short time, her, and her boyfriend, and all down to drugs. What a complete and utter waste of life.

Some 15 minutes later they could hear the now familiar thumping of the Sea King helicopter blades cutting through the damp air from Culdrose Naval Base.

"771 Naval Air Squadron to the rescue again," Treavey declared. "Come on boys, do your stuff."

Some coast guard personnel had turned up in their blue boiler suits and were holding their radios to their ears listening to the helicopter and lifeboat transmissions. The grey and red beast of a helicopter was hovering like a clumsy bumblebee before turning 90 degrees and flying across the scene slowly before facing the cliff again and drifting across once more to scan for signs of life. It looked like the pilot and co-pilot could be reached out to and touched whilst they pointed at different areas on the cliff face, whilst the deafening engines repositioned them with such delicacy. The lifeboat had arrived too and was searching the shoreline below.

"Whilst they can't find a body, then there has to be hope I guess," Treavey mumbled to Bomber. "You did see her jump didn't you Bomber, I mean, you don't think she's slipped away without us seeing, do you?"

Bomber stared straight at Treavey and replied with some indignation, "Mate, unless she can fly, she was on her way to a long way down. I saw her just topple over as if it were effortless for her." He paused, contemplating what he had just seen some moments before. "It was quite eerie, Treavey. I don't want to see that again."

Again, that rough, tough exterior of Bomber was slipping. The real human underneath was revealing himself.

"They think they've seen something, about halfway down." One of the coastguards said, who was looking rather more animated now. "They are going to send someone down to have a better look and if they can't get there, we'll set up a line and go down ourselves."

They waited whilst the helicopter dragged its tonnes of metal around just above their heads. They felt the warm rush of air from under the rotor blades blasting into their faces and knocking them back slightly. The men on the cliff settled themselves against the force as the helicopter remained motionless above them. The medic was expertly lowered with a stretcher from above by the winchman leaning out of the helicopter. The medic came level with them at first, and then continued further down the cliff.

Treavey couldn't help thinking of the sight the medic had to prepare himself for. How he prepared himself for the ugly mutilated sight of death he may see before him, before returning home to his family with those same thoughts swimming around his head.

The line went slack, and the helicopter banked away from the cliff heading out to sea, disappearing into the haze of the greyness for some moments. Its chattering engines changed tone as the sound was redirected by the rotors which caused the helicopter to pitch and level off once more. It was almost silent on occasions before coming back to a crescendo of battering noise and loud shouting again. It seemed such a brutal tool, with little finesse, yet contained a beautiful soul as it scanned the cliff to save human life. The medic was busy at the point of that ledge and everyone held their breath in anticipation. All had discussed at the top of the cliff, whether the fall had been survivable. Much talking about whether she could have slid down to that point, or whether she could survive it if she hit the ledge directly. It was all surmising.

The helicopter returned to the same spot it had been in earlier, and the winch was lowered once more towards the ledge. It was a few moments before the helicopter pulled gently away from them towards the sea and the heavyweight at the base of the wire eased away like a trapeze from the danger of the jagged edges of rock, the wire shortening as it did so until the medic with the full stretcher was entering the inside relative calm of the helicopter being assisted by the winchman. It wasted no time in banking hard to the side and gaining speed towards south Cornwall again. It was heading for Truro hospital, gaining height and speed as it slowly disappeared into the clouds. There was no time for goodbyes. That same medic would be clearing the casualty's airway, getting oxygen into her, and plugging

200

any wounds she had to stop further blood loss. She would be in an operating theatre within minutes.

The coastguard chatted amongst themselves for a bit and slowly began to drift away. They collected their heavy gear as they went and before long it was just Treavey and Bomber left alone on the cliff. The only sign of the lifeboat was the narrow white wake left in the water from where it had once been.

"She could actually make it, Bomber," Treavey exclaimed hopefully.

"There's always a chance." Bomber replied. "Not sure she'll be in any condition to be happy about it, mind. Has she made her troubles twice as bad now?"

They both returned to the station for what was formerly known as a debrief perhaps, but otherwise known as a simple chat over a cup of tea. Bomber looked a little shaken from what he had witnessed, but his shock was eased knowing perhaps he hadn't witnessed the imminent death of someone, especially a kind, warm‐natured and pretty girl. Should it make a difference? They discussed this very point. Bomber dived in with both feet.

"If she was ugly, a pain in the arse and rude with it, I think I would get over it more quickly, to be honest with you. Don't ask me why, it's just a feeling."

Treavey sipped his tea and continued with the topic, "Do you think we miss people on how much of a loss to society they are then?"

Bomber paused in contemplation. Then he seemed confident in the answer he was just about to give. "No mate. She probably is not officially a loss to society at this stage of her life to put it bluntly. I think it is human nature to gravitate towards nice people. It may be physical, as in an attraction physically which reflects warmth and safety, or to the nature of their character of course. You will miss them more than those you have little interest in."

201

"So, people are pretty two dimensional then, Bomber." Treavey threw in.

"Quite the opposite. So much is taken in and analysed by the human brain. Our natural instincts are honest, truthful, and ruthless if you like. It isn't swayed in the slightest by social pressure to be attracted to something or someone because we are told to."

Treavey thought for a moment. "So basically, you are saying we want people, who we want to mate with, to survive more than those we don't feel are compatible with us, and we want those who have similar thoughts to us and enjoy our company to live more than those who drive us bonkers and wind us up."

"Well..." Bomber realised it possibly wasn't quite as simple as he thought, "...sort of like that, but we don't wish the others dead, well, most of the time, it's all down to preference, isn't it? We are animals at the end of the day. We want to have sex to produce children who will stand the best chance in life to progress our genes, and we'll put up with the rest."

"Put up with the rest," Treavey repeated whilst chuckling to himself.

Bomber laughed too and added, "Yes, put up with the rest. The ones we don't want to bonk, we put up with!"

They both laughed together realising the callous nature of what they had just said, but also sharing a realisation that that was pretty much what it came down to, and there were not too many environments where colleagues were willing to share such thoughts. Perhaps those who saw violence and death on more or less a daily basis tended to be a bit more blunt. They saw anything else as being a waste of time. Life was too short. They couldn't be bothered with it all.

Bomber looked at the pile of paper and picked up the biro he had dropped on the desk a couple of hours before. He stared at it for a moment and said, "Sod it. I'm going home." He shuffled up his papers, putting them in a yellow cardboard folder and slipped the mass of papers into his already bulging skippet before making towards the locker room. He had got his civvie jacket on and was out of the station in less than three minutes.

Felicity walked through the door.

Treavey's heart missed a couple of beats and he suddenly felt much happier to be at work. She looked beautiful in her civilian clothes as she made for the cloakroom.

"Hi Treavey!" she shouted as she disappeared into the cloak room.

Treavey shouted, "Cup of tea Felicity?"

A faint reply was heard, "Yes please, I'm having a shower. Want to join me?"

Treavey took it as a joke and assumed the door would be locked. If he wanted to make his pension, then he knew it was not the appropriate thing to do, but who would know? He opted for making the cup of tea instead.

He waited at the report room table with the two mugs of tea. It was his second in just 20 minutes, but he felt he would look awkward if he had nothing to drink with her.

She came out of the locker room and nonchalantly said, "Damned Treavey, I was waiting for you to scrub my back, where were you?"

Treavey couldn't hide his embarrassment.

"Only joking Treavey, I love playing with you." Treavey's whole world of reality came crashing down around him again. She was going to be a tricky one to suss out.

Felicity expertly tucked her long blond hair into a bun and sat down near to him. "Hey, Treavey, I have some news, just a word of warning really."

Treavey was concerned as it was never good news when someone spoke like this. "I was hearing from someone, I can't say who at this stage, but they told me that some vagrant was passing information to the drug dealers from this station."

"Shit!" shouted Treavey, "You are fucking kidding me. Tell me that isn't true, no fucking way."

Treavey felt devastated he had been made to look such a fool. He put his head in his hands and lent forward resting his head directly on the desk. "That just shows me to trust people, to see the best in people. That bloody woman double-crossed me, and she used to be a copper too."

Felicity put her hand on Treavey's shoulder and as he straightened back up, she touched his face affectionately. "Don't worry sweetheart, she fooled me too. I let it happen. I mean I was uncomfortable with it, but I let it happen by not stopping her coming in here for a sneaky shower. She must have seen some stuff on the walls, the mugshots and maybe she's has eaves-dropped some of our conversations."

"But I was always so careful," he replied. "I always made sure there was nothing said or to be seen whilst she was in the building."

Felicity got up and walked over to the window. "Don't worry Treavey. I suggest you don't mention it to her. Just say there have been some clampdowns recently and it is too risky to have her in here now."

He felt so annoyed with himself. "I just don't understand it. I could have fucked the whole investigation up. More people could die if I was the cause of delaying catching the suppliers. Shit, I have been so double-crossed. She must think I am such a pushover."

"Just leave it now Treavey. Forewarned is forearmed. Don't mention anything more about it if I was you, but I think that is why we have been so unlucky with catching them. I suspect that when she sees us going out of town on a job, she signals them to move the drugs. That's what I think."

"We should nick her," Treavey replied angrily.

"For what? Anonymous information about something we have absolutely no evidence for, and it would only get you, and possibly me, in the shit anyway."

Treavey threw himself back in his seat. "Bollocks, I fucked up there. After all I did for her too. What a mug I've been." He sat in silence for a bit and said, "What do I do about Thursday?"

Felicity pricked her ears up, "Thursday?"

Treavey informed her what Grace had told him about the red canoe going out to sea at 11.00 p.m. to what looked like a drug drop.

"I suggest that's to throw you off the scent mate." She replied rather too formally for Treavey's liking.

Where had the 'sweetheart' gone? Maybe it was because he had looked a fool in her eyes. Quite a turn-off, really, and he could not blame her for it.

He stood up declaring, "I need to go out for a drive, fancy coming? I've had a shit day so far."

"Sure sweety," Felicity replied, slamming the empty mug on the desk. "We need some air."

Treavey felt a lot better already. She had used the word 'sweety' again, and she'd soon be sitting right back next to him in the car. Perhaps this shift would improve after all.

It was a dull atmosphere outside. Little likelihood of any sun in the next few hours. He drove the panda car out of the rear car park turning onto the road towards the seafront. It was always a good place to start. They chatted for a while about how unfortunate it was for the families having to dig deep in their pockets on a day like today to entertain the kids.

Felicity said, "Most of the kids and teenagers will probably be in the campsite pool and the adults will probably be getting drunk at the bar."

Treavey concurred and added, "That's where I'd be. A lot of these people will be leaving here on Saturday, going back to the factories and their offices, so they are going to make the most of it in the meantime."

They both headed into the beach car park and had a quick look at the uninviting dullness of the beach. The seagulls were going to have to do without the ice creams and pasties today. Treavey saw the large rock or what may be called a small island where the canoe had paddled past according to Grace.

"So, what about Thursday? I am going to give it a run and expect nothing but hope for the best. Fancy coming along to waste a couple of hours?"

"No, not me, Treavey, nothing's going to happen, if the source is Grace. You should be more careful who you trust, mate."

The word 'mate' was back again. Treavey decided to push for some answers, as he still felt very confused.

"Who told you about Grace, Felicity?" Treavey enquired determinedly. Felicity kept looking ahead at the rather drab scene ahead of her, the grey sea blending perfectly in with the grey sky, with only a thin line of white foam on the crest of the waves far out to separate the two.

"I said I wouldn't say anything..." Felicity paused, as if wanting to say more, but feeling she shouldn't, and then continued, "...but if I said it was the older brother, then, strictly speaking, I have kept my word."

"Billy Bradford?" Treavey exclaimed, "You are kidding me, he's the one we think is doing it, along with some others."

Felicity calmly replied; "Or are they? Put enough confusion into the mix and it detracts from the main offender. Maybe it is Grace. It could all be her cover?"

"Oh, that's ridiculous," Treavey snapped, but thought for a second, feeling very confused, "No, that's all ridiculous, I'm not having that."

Felicity smiled at Treavey, "Yes, I know it's ridiculous, but we have to take things people say at face value, and then check it out. You know, check and challenge. Otherwise, we could just be on another wild goose chase."

"Agreed there," replied Treavey.

He was so annoyed with himself. He thought he was making progress, especially with what Mary and the cliff attempted suicide had told him. Mary had tied in Dawson and the two Bradford brothers too, without naming the brothers perhaps, but it was clear it was them she meant.

"Right, forget Thursday then, I'm not wasting my time," snapped Treavey.

"You know, if you want me to come along Treavey, I'll give you a hand, even though it's my day off, I'd be willing to change it for you.".

"No, you're alright. I'm early turn that day, so I think I'll stick to that."

They drove off from the car park to where he had last seen Grace at the top of the cliffs looking over the beach from the park bench. She was not there. She was probably getting some shelter somewhere else. What was the point of sitting there, if there was nothing to look at but greyness?

Felicity looked across at Treavey. She could see he had had a terrible day. "Don't worry Treavey, I'm sure we'll catch them. It can't go on as it is, can it? You look so handsome when you are thinking."

Treavey did not feel in the mood for flirting. He'd had a bad day, and it had got worse, but hopefully he would learn that Mary would survive at least.

"I need to check up on Mary before I finish today," he declared, "I'll call the hospital later, to see if she's stable. It is amazing what they can do nowadays. Hopefully, she hasn't damaged herself even more now. I mean, if she's in a wheelchair, can you imagine?"

"Golf 31," the radio burst through the solemn mood.

"Can you attend number 3 Hollins Close for a domestic? We've had a call from the neighbour who's reporting loud screaming and shouting from the address."

207

Treavey slammed the gear stick into first and accelerated hard, flicking on the blue light and two tones. Felicity calmly reported back, "Golf 31, en-route. Any previous on the address?"

Comms came straight back with a reply. Tapping could be heard in the background as the operator extracted more information from the screen.

"We've had 12 previous visits since 1985, and it was the same surname then. Standby... yes, the gentleman at the address is a Mr George Butler. He has... 21 convictions, mainly for theft, assaults, domestic assaults and one GBH pending."

Treavey shuffled his bottom in the seat. "This could be a tough one, Felicity. Better be on guard."

Felicity pressed her transmit button and spoke assertively, "Can we have a van en route just in case please, as a contingency?"

"Already called for and will be about 25 minutes, Golf 31."

Nothing more was said as they screeched around the bends and junctions, overtaking a slower car on the main street causing the driver to jerk their steering across in alarm.

"Needs to look in his mirrors," Treavey commented before swinging into Hollins Close and cutting the two tones.

They pulled up on the left. "Has to be the second house, right?" he shouted, as he jumped out of the car, and having waited for Felicity to exit first, locked the doors.

They fast paced it to the front door, but all seemed quiet for now. No noise or shouting could be heard. Treavey felt obliged to go in first as the door was open. "Hello, hello, it's the police."

A woman of slight build, about 30 years old was standing before them having just slipped out of a nearby room. She looked terrified, and her eyes glanced to and fro, across to where she had just come from and back at the officer. Something was up, so Treavey gently took hold of her arm and pulled her towards him passing her on to Felicity who was directly behind him. He poked his head around the corner, so he was now gazing into the lounge itself. He saw an exceptionally large, strong man sitting in the armchair, motionless. There was broken crockery on the floor and an upturned coffee table. The size difference between the two occupants was extensive. It seemed the woman was his partner, and first impressions were this man preferred to be dominant in the relationship.

The guy was in his mid-30's, overly broad stature and had thinning wisps of ginger hair and a scraggly beard looking as though it had been stuck on in patches. He was a huge slob of a man who didn't take care over his appearance. He had got comfortable with his lazy lifestyle and needed a partner to feed his addiction of selfishness.

Treavey went in at a low level. "Hi, I'm PC Treave, what's your name?"

The reply was short and curt. "George."

Treavey explained to him why he was there and tried to establish what had happened but made little progress. He was aware the man was playing the victim.

"She attacked me," and "She's mad, they all are," and "It always comes back on me, doesn't it?"

Treavey saw Felicity in the corridor and walked out to meet her. She was rather ashen and spoke softly to him.

"She's scared to death Treavey. He's grabbed her around the neck, and she has got the marks to prove it. She seriously thought she was going to die this time."

Treavey glanced across to the pitiful figure of the woman who was stooped over at the end of the hallway next to the front door.

"Okay, tell me when that van's arrived will you, he could be a handful when I have to nick him."

He walked back into the room and the man was already standing there staring wide-eyed at him, his chest pushed right out, his fists clenched and his face red with rage. "Oh shit, he heard me."

"You fucking what, you little shit?" The gorilla of a man shouted, with spittle flicking from his mouth like a sprinkler.

He looked solid and ready to fight. There was no negotiating this one down.

You think I'm being nicked again, copper? You'll have to fight me, pal, and you'd better be better at it than you look."

Treavey knew he had to act fast and play it cool at the same time as he knew he was on the back foot. It was going to be all or nothing. He pulled out his wooden truncheon from the sleeve sewn into his trouser pocket. The truncheon wasn't very effective to hit anyone with, or even threaten anyone with to be honest, but he saw it being used very effectively by his tutor as a poking stick to great effect once, but it had to be done with conviction.

He called his colleague in, "Felicity, I'm sure you could have a chat with this gentleman, could you?"

Felicity appeared in the doorway looking rather confused as to why she had been called into the room, and the thug turned towards her whilst Treavey continued, "Yes, he wishes to say something to..." at which point Treavey took the element of surprise and thrust the point of his truncheon with his full strength straight into the man's solar plexus immediately doubling him over and causing a huge gasp of air to be exhaled.

Having had him distracted with Felicity, and catching him in mid-sentence, it was enough to win the element of surprise, but now he had to continue being just as effective. Treavey was on to him with the cuffs trying to snap one clasp on him and Felicity was taking up the clues she had just seen in front of her with no warning and flew through the air on top of the bundle of chaos which was now happening in the centre of the lounge.

There was a lot of swearing and shouting and the officers found themselves grabbing an arm each, which was quite effective until the raging, wounded animal tried with some success to roll over on to his front and draw his knees up and attempt to raise his mass into a fighting position. The beast was gaining some control of the situation when Treavey had to step back having lost the limb he was claiming but saw an ideal opportunity of Felicity on all fours just like he remembered from the playground at school. And with a forceful push from Treavey, over the thug went, right over her back with his head slamming into the plasterboard wall behind, punching a hole in through the plaster with his ginger speckled balding head.

Both officers were on to him shouting and screaming, Treavey being more alarmed by Felicity's language towards the man than the other way around. All three laid there for a moment gasping for air.

"Hello," they heard someone say from the front door and in walked the police van driver. "Oh," the police van driver said whilst taking in the scene of devastation before him. The officers with shirts untucked with missing buttons and clip-on ties ripped off, and a large man whose head was still partly inside a cavity wall. "I see you've all been having rather a lot of fun in here."

All three looked up at him and Treavey calmly replied, "Yes mate, something like that, we just got a little bit bored waiting for you to finish your cup of tea before you came along to see if you could assist."

Treavey looked around at the male he was now straddling. "Oh, didn't I tell you? You're nicked!"

The thug was led out to the van. He had no fight left in him.

Felicity got into the passenger side of the car as Treavey put the keys in the ignition and said, "Glad you picked up on the best move in the book! It should be in the home office book of moves if it isn't already."

As usual, the woman who was living a continual state of a bullied victim could not find her way out of the cycle of abuse. Felicity had tried to get her to make a statement, but she wasn't having any of it. Felicity looked straight ahead as they drove towards the station to start the paperwork, although there would not be much, now there wasn't going to be a case.

"The trouble is Treavey, mate, I see why they don't press charges. She pushes the panic button when she thinks she is going to die, and she realises he's completely lost it. Then the police turn up wearing superhero cloaks and take away the immediate threat and that's it, the panic goes, and she loves him again. He promises her he won't do it again, or she knows she is in enough trouble later when he gets out of the cells, but he will be a lot easier on her if she doesn't press charges. It's all a bit shit mate. You can see why they don't write statements. There has to be a way around it."

Treavey drove on in silence. He knew he had just about got away with that one. He nearly got his head knocked off his shoulders, so he was in no mood for sympathy.

"All I know, is I don't have as much paperwork as I would have had and after a bloody long shift like today, I'm grateful to her for that."

Chapter 13

The Cornish shipwreck

"To hell with it, I'll only regret not doing it if I don't."
It was 10.00 pm a week after Grace had supposedly witnessed the red canoe acting suspiciously in the bay. He was already halfway through the shift. Treavey was packing a few things into his own private car. He had swapped his early shift for a late one on this Thursday night to try to catch the late canoe paddler smuggling drugs into Perran. He hoped so anyway, but he knew it was a hell of a long shot. Sgt Sash agreed for the change, which was helpful, especially as he was always away at meetings and at Headquarters on certain projects, but he was particularly good at supporting his officers, all the same. It made all the difference. He agreed the canoe intelligence needed covering, even though Grace could be in on it and it could be a complete waste of time, but it was probably more useful having him on a late shift to help Micky later anyway.

Micky opened the rear door of the station to join Treavey in the car park. "Taking your car are we Treavey?"

Treavey explained the panda was going to stick out like a lighthouse on a foggy night so he was going to take his own car instead.

Micky smiled at him and suggested, "or... maybe we could walk the whole half a mile down to the front?!"
Treavey broke a smile, "I guess we'll just have to call a taxi when we discover a massive hall of drugs in that canoe!"

Both officers began walking down to the seafront with their civilian jackets over their white shirts. They may have passed as waiters if spotted by a holidaymaker, but it certainly wouldn't fool hardened drug smugglers. It was good to be with Micky again though. He was good company and was a steady hand on the tiller.

Treavey knew Micky had taken a keen interest in the drugs issue in Perran since they had been sitting under the window of the Bradford's house eavesdropping on their conversation. Very little progress had been made, however, and several more drug-related deaths had taken place in the small town since.

It was getting dark as they made their way along the empty pavements into the town. In order not to be too obvious, they skirted around the edges of the centre to get to the beach. Micky had some binoculars with him, which Treavey acknowledged were going to be crucial. Finding a good spot was going to be tricky; somewhere they would be able to see what is going on, and to see who is in the car park ready to pick the consignment up at the same time.

"You know it could have been perfectly innocent last week," Treavey commented nervously. "I mean, they could have been out for a paddle…"

Micky glanced across and said "…and coincidentally bumped into a boat in the darkness near the jagged rocks. It is more likely to be untrue than true, I agree though. If they turn up this week, then we will be lucky because we don't know it's every Thursday for starters, but if it does turn up, I reckon we are on."

"It suddenly sounds very unlikely indeed," Treavey responded rather despondently.

The darkness had fully crept in without them noticing. It was a beautiful mild late August evening, and it was coming up to 11.00 pm already. The tide was three quarters the way in, giving off a beautiful atmosphere of tranquillity, the business of the day on the beach now a distant memory.

Treavey felt uneasy. "We are just too far away here," as they made their way along the dunes slightly, which gave them some cover but also allowed them to see what was happening in the car park.

"Yes, it is going to be difficult, Treavey, but we've got to make the most of it. The sarge has informed the helicopter, Oscar 99, just in case the boat turns up, but we know it will probably be empty by the time they turn up but at least we will be able to identify it. That is, if we can identify it ourselves to give them a description, of course, and looking out there that is going to be almost impossible. We should have given Grace a police radio!"

They found themselves nestled near the lifeguard hut looking out to sea and having half an eye on the car park, but they realised they wouldn't notice anything happening until someone turned up with a canoe on the beach, if, indeed, they did at all.

It was not long before they heard the low decibel thumping of an engine ticking over and it was coming from out to sea.

The officers look at each other. "You don't think... do you?" Treavey asked expectantly.

"It's a boat, Treavey, just a boat, let's not get too excited." Micky settled down making himself more comfortable in the sand.

Treavey was getting more excited. "We need to get closer; this is no good being here. If it is the drugs, we have no description of the boat to give to the heli."

Micky shrugged his shoulders, "If it is the boat, and they are re-stocking Perran with its weekly supply of class A drugs, then at least we'll have the delivery, and we'll have to leave it up to Oscar 99 and the coastguard to figure out which boat is the one involved."

Treavey was silent for a few seconds. Micky also sat in silence listening to the throbbing of the boat coming nearer to the shoreline but still out of sight within the darkness, and then he slowly turned around to Treavey to see him half-naked standing next to him.

"What the...?" Micky exclaimed aghast at what he was seeing.

He watched Treavey strip off his trousers leaving just his boxer shorts on, tiptoe towards the back of the lifeguard hut, returning a few seconds later with a considerably large surfboard under his arm.

"Got to take a closer look. Don't nick my clothes, Micky!" Treavey said as he struggled with the board down to the shoreline.

He glanced back at where Micky was in the darkness and temporarily regretted his decision as his feet touched the icy water. He dropped the board into the water as soon as it was able to float free and put enough weight on the back of it, so the front protected his naked torso away from the waves gently rolling in. Once he was waist-deep he committed to jumping on the board as he pushed it forward, lying on his front whilst paddling either side with his arms. There was sufficient board surface area to keep his feet well out of the water, which gave him some protection from the chill. Fortunately, it was a mild evening, and the wind was being kind to him.

He felt his way through the darkness on the water, feeling quite creeped out by the icy darkness listening to the water slapping against the underside of the board, and being aware of the deep water below him, never quite knowing what was hidden below. There was something rather ghostly about the sea at night. The depth beneath became more sinister at night. Treavey made sure his feet were out of the water away from those imaginary sharks. He paddled gently, stopping occasionally to listen to the engine of the boat, but he could tell it had stopped, but he could now see a white spot of light beaming out like a needle prick in the backdrop of pitch blackness. He paddled towards it for a time which seemed to go on forever, the cliffs raised high on his left like a huge shadow of foreboding, a depression bearing down on him. He did not like it at all. Why was it that the atmosphere of night-time in the sea created this hell on earth feeling?

Treavey realised he was getting awfully close to the boat. He could see it was a white yacht, probably about 30ft in length and it had seen better days. His eyes had become accustomed to the lack of light and all was becoming clearer. He drifted around to the hull of the boat to see the nameplate on the bow. He felt like a Royal Marine in the second world war spying on the Germans. His adrenaline was up. He knew he had got to keep an eye out for another boat or canoe which may interrupt his observations, so with the yacht pointing out to sea, Treavey ensured he was ahead of the bow, so it would be unlikely he'd be seen whilst it remained anchored.

"Seaguard," Treavey repeated to himself reading the name on the bow. "Seaguard is the name. Got it."

He couldn't report the information back to Micky as he did not have his radio with him for obvious reasons, but his ventures had so far paid off. Now, if the canoe did turn up, then he'd got them. If it didn't turn up, then the boat could be full of drugs, but there was no way he had enough to warrant a search on the boat. He could only tip off HM Customs, but would there be sufficient on duty to do anything at this time of night? Was it better not to blow his cover and to catch them later instead?

Half an hour had gone by, which had felt like just a few minutes for Treavey, who was looking out for any action whilst trying to think what options he had. He glanced up the cliffs to see if he could see Grace sitting on the bench as she had been the previous week. This was a time of clarity so he could think things through.

Thoughts rushed through his mind. "It didn't make sense if she was passing information to the drug dealers as Billy Bradford had told Felicity. Why would he tell us she was doing that? And if she was, then why did she tell me the boat had come for a meet with the canoe last week, unless she was having fun and she knew this yacht had nothing to do with it, but then he would have been a terrible judge of character. No, something was wrong, and it felt a total mess at the moment, yet this yacht was here today so something was right, too. I just wish I could get this yacht searched. Hopefully, a canoe will turn up soon and I can watch it being loaded with drugs."

Treavey began to shiver. It wouldn't be long before his limbs seized up, but he couldn't paddle around too much to keep warm either.

He was waiting and staring at the name of the boat. "Seaguard, Seaguard, that's a strange name but they tend to be, often named for personal reasons. Maybe it was a security thing, to help the sailors feel secure and guarded against the danger of the sea."

He stared some more at it, waiting and listening. The penny dropped. He couldn't believe it, "That name, Seaguard. It spells drugs backwards; yes, it has other letters too, but it definitely says d r u g s. They are all there. Are they taking the piss?" His thoughts were broken by the starting of the boat engine again, and it was heading straight for him.

Treavey paddled furiously to the side and watched the rather tatty looking yacht pass at a steady speed and slowly disappear into the night.

"Right, back to the beach, find out whether Micky has seen the canoe, and inform the Coast Guard or Customs to keep an eye out for that boat, whoever is interested. It's got to be registered somewhere."

On dry land again, Treavey made his way up to the lifeguard hut where Micky was still waiting.

"Well?" he asked Treavey, with his customary raised dark, bushy eyebrow on his balding head.

The way Micky asked that meant he had not seen any canoe either.

Treavey was feeling despondent. "It was a shit looking boat named, pretty much, 'drugs' mate. We need to update

Customs cos if it's a no show because the canoe was tipped off, then the boat should have some drugs on board.

Micky got up and stretched his arms. "Sure Treavey, but we have to bear in mind it could just be some boat which came in for a bit of rest whilst they sorted out where they were going to go next to rest up for the night."

"Yes, or that," Treavey replied feeling rather damp, cold, and despondent. Both officers, and with Treavey fully dressed, headed back up to the police station.

"It had to be done Micky, we had to cover it. We couldn't just let it happen and us not know about it."
Micky carried on walking without dropping his pace.

"Mate, I'm impressed with you surfing off like that, I think you're a total nutter of course, but impressed all the same."

Once they got back, Treavey was on the phone to the control room Inspector. He wasn't going to let this lie. A considerable conversation took place but as he tried to explain the evidence, he could feel the interest dropping off from the Inspector on the other end.

"Yes, I could speak to Customs and no doubt trace it for you and find out which port it's from, but we don't have resources to do raids on boats willy nilly. To be honest there is no evidence of drugs on this boat, just that you saw it moor up for an hour in a bay, before moving on."

When he said it like that, Treavey could only agree the evidence was simply circumstantial. There was nothing concrete at all.

"I like the boat name theory though," the Inspector said, laughing as he said it.

This job was going nowhere fast. It was a dead end. Treavey put the phone down and looked at Micky who was enjoying gently stroking Wolfy.

"Wolfy is a good stress reliever," Micky said softly, "He always makes things okay again, Treavey, you should try it sometime!"

Wolfy's indignant expression made Treavey feel his efforts and theories were rather wayward and that perhaps sleeping was a much better way of sorting the world's problems out. Perhaps the cat had a point.

Treavey poked his head up. "Do you fancy a cup of tea?"

"Yes, I'll have tea, thank you," Micky snapped back with a smile.

"Ah yes, of course. Tea coming up," and Treavey disappeared into the kitchen.

Micky scanned the police computers for the latest crimes. It was a system he was getting used to, a huge advancement to the paper system where police officers had to go to an intelligence officer to find out any information. The green print on the dark background on the screen was a view into any of the crimes and intelligence available in the force. Treavey could see the benefits. Other forces were still lagging behind Devon and Cornwall and he had heard the system they were using was superior to many others.

Treavey returned with the cups of tea handing a cup to Micky. "Mate, I'm having this and am off home after. I'm on earlies in the morning with Felicity."

"Fair enough," Micky replied, "I don't blame you, get home and get your head down."

It felt like it had only been a couple of hours when Treavey was wiping the sleep from his eyes and dragging himself into the station at 6.00 am the following morning. He glanced across to the lovely looking Felicity who was trotting in behind him. They both said goodbye to the leaving night shift, Bomber and Rambo. Both pussy cats at heart when you got to know them, so their nicknames sounded a bit ridiculous really. Treavey discarded his jacket and headed for the kitchen. He felt someone was close behind him, froze and slowly turned around to see Felicity leaning into him as he prepared the tea.

"Morning Treavey," she said softly as she stood well within his personal space. She seemed to be lapping up the awkwardness she was creating with Treavey. He made as if he wasn't that bothered about her being so close to him as if it was completely normal behaviour, but he was sure she wouldn't have done it to anyone other than him.

He smiled at her and returned to making the tea. The phone rang.

"Unusual for this time of the morning," pointed out Felicity. "Must be the control room. It could be a bit of a complicated job if they're ringing us."

She answered the phone. There were a few seconds of pleasantries followed by a period of listening intently. Treavey was sipping his tea and watching her face to see if she gave any clues away. There was nothing for a few moments, no change of expression but then the blood seemed to drain from her face. Treavey knew it was going to be a decent job, something pretty big. After a few, "yep... yep... uh-huh," she put the phone down, leant across to Wolfy and gave him a loving stroke as he snoozed on the table.

She glanced up at Treavey, who in anticipation, was now beside her. "Mate," she paused momentarily.

"Sweety, there's a shipwreck down at St Agnes Head. A small yacht has hit the rocks and broken up. I am told it's like confetti out there. A dog walker reported it this morning. The lifeboat is around there now and has located two bodies. They want us to go up there and stop on-lookers from getting too near the edge of the cliff. They don't want to add to the deaths."

"The Seaguard?" Treavey inquired.

"They don't know which boat it is, Treavey. I'm sure the coast guard will be working on all of that. Let's get to the cliffs. Hopefully, it's some of those scrotes delivering drugs to this place. That would be good, wouldn't it? It would get rid of some, although they are probably just the couriers. Christ, I hope it isn't a child involved, you know, a family."

They both rushed out of the station slamming the door behind them and drove to the stunningly beautiful location at St Agnes Head.

It was a beautiful day. The footpath was well-trodden as it was late in the season, and as both officers walked towards the sparse group of people looking over the edge of the cliff, they were struck by some of the best views in the world. The herring gulls were gliding effortlessly on the warm breeze, their soft grey and white contrasting with the turquoise green of the crystal-clear sea below. As the gulls glided towards land, they were lighting up against the jet-black cliffs which jutted out from the calm waters below, and both officers could so easily forget the reason they were there.

The contrast between what should have been an idyllic scene of beauty, with them inhaling the warm scent of sweet sea air deep into their lungs, and what these holidaymakers were having to prepare themselves for in the unfolding action below, couldn't have been greater. They didn't get this action in their home cities and towns, watching heroes in lifeboats dodging the jagged teeth of the rocks ready to rip a deadly slash into the rubber hull of their delicate boat.

The Sea Kings of the sky had been back to oversee the operation and to pluck those from the sea who would otherwise have perished, but the graceful beasts of the sky had already attended and had bowed away, ready to attend again if required, but there was no life to be saved here today.

A thin white foam was all that was left to show where the sea had impacted the cliffs, but then there was something else bobbing in the water too. There was debris from the hull of a sailing yacht, what looked like pieces of polystyrene floating on the surface, and then a jagged piece of fibreglass swirling and twisting in the currents. Treavey and Felicity made their way through the small crowd who voluntarily opened up in front of them to let

222

them through, and then the scene before them became quite clear.

The boat was ripped in half across its middle. It had had quite a battering through the night from the waves. This hadn't just happened. This had been a violent attack by the waves which must have built up since the evening had started and it was not clear at all on what side the boat would have originally been. Too much was missing. Only a piece of the bow was left, caught on the rocks but the rest was gone. The view into the hull was clear and apart from the debris swimming around inside, there was nothing left of any structure and certainly no contents.

Treavey spoke to the crowd, "Hello guys, as long as you don't go further than this line, we are happy for you to remain here. They are removing bodies from the base of the cliffs so all those who don't wish to see anything like that, I suggest you step away now." There were nods of appreciation as the officers decided to walk towards another small group of holidaymakers who had decided to take a view from further along the cliff, but could see the work by the lifeboat in recovering the bodies at the base of the cliffs.

Felicity spoke first. "It's pretty clear the boat hasn't made it around that headland. They must have hit it in the darkness. What the hell are they doing sailing around here at night if they don't have the navigation equipment or skills? They have to be drug dealers."

She gets on the radio, "Victor, this is Oscar 31 here, can we ask the lifeboat to have a scan around for packages of drugs near the base of the cliffs too, just in case they've floated in. It's a small chance, but as you know, we've had quite a drug problem in Perran recently."

The controller fully understood the reasonable request and informed her they would pass it on. Treavey commented that it was probably a good idea to get the police helicopter to have a look as well, later on.

223

Once they had got to the spot along the cliff where the other tourists had congregated, they could understand why they had gathered there. They had a clear view of the inshore lifeboat manipulating something large into the inflatable boat whilst choosing the best time between the waves to approach. It was distinctly an adult they were hauling in, and after some time manoeuvring the boat against the current pushing them towards every rock around them, they managed to get it aboard.

One of the crowd spoke up. "Oh, so that's a second one then, the poor souls."

Treavey swung around to acknowledge a holidaymaker, a portly middle aged man, dressed in a summery checked shirt, walking boots and beige chino shorts.

"So, they have two bodies in the boat now do they, two adults?"

The tourists nod in confirmation. They all watch the inflatable carry out a fast 180-degree spin in the waves and power up to full throttle ripping a groove in the calm water as if it were a jet boat, heading straight for St Agnes to their Lifeboat station where the bodies would be taken on from there. There was no need for first aid today.

Treavey and Felicity paused for a moment, as did everyone. They watched the boat disappear and they all slowly turned away, the holidaymakers to carry on their holiday and the officers to make their way back to the car. Nothing much was said. There was a melancholy mood between them. It was always the same where death was involved. This was the desperately sad side of the job, but as was often the case, the incident had left more questions than answers. "I wonder who they were?" Treavey said, but that question was partly answered almost immediately.

"Oscar 31, the boat was called the 'Seaguard' for your information. We are making some enquiries on it with the

Coast Guard." The composed soft female voice from the control room cut the atmosphere.

Treavey's gloom disappeared immediately. "I knew it, what did I say, Felicity?"

She genuinely looked impressed with him. "How the hell did you know that, Treavey? You thought it was that boat this morning. Did you throw a rock at it from the clifftop last night or something!?" She said with some amusement. "So, go on, tell me what you know."

Treavey realised he'd got himself into a bit of a corner by not involving Felicity with the developments from the night before.

"You know that time when I told you about Grace telling me about the canoe collecting a package after dark, from a yacht that came in last Thursday, and we discussed whether we'd change shifts to see what was about this week?"

"Yes, and I offered to change my early turn shift to a late shift to help you, but we decided not to bother?"

"Well, yes, about that…" Treavey broke out in a grin and continued, "…well, I knew the chances were next to no chance that it would be around again this week, or that if it was, it was probably something quite innocent. Well, I went down there with Micky who was working anyway to have a look, and the next thing, I'm on the lifeguard's rescue board paddling around the yacht which came in again, assuming it was the same one anyway. Micky stayed on the beach to see if the canoe turned up and, well it didn't, but I got close enough to see the small scruffy yacht which turned up was called 'Seaguard' which, just so happens to be an anagram of the word 'drugs."

"Does it?" Felicity looked a little annoyed. Probably because so much had gone on and she had been left out.

Treavey realised the anagram side of things was a little stretching it. "If you take a few letters away and read it back but then it does."

"Blimey, well, it's done now, and it seems they've met their end at the foot of our cliffs. That'll teach them. Hopefully, as I asked comms to do, they'll send the helicopter up to have a look for any drug packages." Felicity said, having lost all enthusiasm.

The door chimes sounded, and Treavey went to the front to see who had just come in. "Hello Grace, how are you?"

"Hello darling, how are you,Treavey, I'm pretty good myself, thank you."

Treavey was pleased to see her, so he could recap what had happened. "I'm glad you've come in, Grace, I wanted to talk to you about that canoe which turned up last Thursday. Remember the one?"

"Yes, I remember the one. The one who was taking drugs off that boat, the boat which sunk around the corner last night. Two bodies on it right?"

Treavey was no longer surprised with how she knew so much already, or at least how quickly information had got around Perran. "Did you see me paddling around last night when the yacht came back?"

"Yes, I was watching. I saw your mate on the beach too." Grace was quiet, a matter of fact, about it. "I bet that water was cold, Treavey, it's just a shame that canoe never turned up."

"Yes, Grace, that would have been beneficial for you if it had. I could have got you some money. Unfortunately, the information has to come up with a positive result."

Grace shook her head, "Oh, I'm not worried about that, it's obviously up to no good, but I know from my time in the job, the snouts have to come up with the goods, not just be right. So, Treavey, did you stick a delay mine to the bottom of the hull or something?" Grace looked deadly serious. Treavey looked astonished but just as quickly, Grace broke a smile.

"You silly billy…" Grace replied, "…you thought I was serious, didn't you? No love, their greed, stupidity, and

226

lack of nautical skills killed them. Just as much as the two in that plane flying around in that weather a few weeks ago. Did you find out who they were?"

Felicity popped her head around the corner, unfortunately, Grace, we can't divulge that information. Is there anything else we can help you with?"

Grace was backing off towards the door. "No dear, no, nothing else. Just chatting to my favourite officer Treavey."

She gave more of a grimace than a smile and left the station in the direction of the seafront.

"You have to be careful, Treavey. She's a honey trap you know."

"What do you mean?" Treavey asked, looking rather bemused.

Felicity frowned and placed her index finger gently on his chin, "Oh sweetheart, she's using her good looks and body to flirt with you to get the information she needs."

She giggled and walked into the kitchen to make a couple of mugs of tea. Treavey followed her in.

"I know you are joking, Felicity; I think you are, I hope you are, but it's made me feel a little queasy, thank you very much."

Felicity was setting out the two mugs with a teabag in each. She kept her head down but turned it slowly to the side to look at Treavey rather seductively.

"Maybe I'm jealous of the attention you give her, Treavey. I want you to be all for me, you see."

"Oh Felicity, you are such a piss-take. I just don't know how to read you."

He walked in beside her and waited for her to fill the mugs with hot water.

"Women are complicated beings you know, Treavey."

She poured the milk slowly, "Maybe just one day you'll have to risk making a move and see what happens."

She stirred the mugs with a teaspoon and pushed one mug towards Treavey for him to take.

227

"One day I might, and we could both be embarrassed," Treavey replied, feeling like an awkward schoolboy in a playground having just caught a girl in a game of kiss chase.

He took his mug into the report room thinking intently. He tells himself off, "Come on Treavey, how many signals do you want for god's sake? One day you'll have to find the bollocks, or she'll get bored waiting for you to make a move."

Chapter 14

Crossed wires

August was coming to the end and Treavey was on his way to the address of a Pakistani couple. They were in their late 50's and he had the unenviable task of passing them a death message. To tell them their son was dead, killed in a car accident in Birmingham. It was a stupid collision really, it only involved him and a friend. He drove the car into some roadworks on a motorway, getting confused with the cones lining the lanes and the car went from 80mph to zero instantly as the motorway maintenance had dug a deep trench in the lane, which the car had driven into. The occupants had suffered from nasty brain injuries, where the brain separates. He was dead, but his friend whose details were unknown, was in the hospital with serious injuries.

"These are the worst ones," Treavey warned himself.

He was trying to compose himself as he negotiated the bends and junctions as he got nearer to the address. He had a drink of water with him just before he went into the house as he knew his throat would go dry.

"Right, I've got to try to pronounce his name correctly too, damn it. 'Farroqi', no that's his surname. And his first name again, right, Basil, okay, that's easy."

He checked with the control room on the detail. "How have we confirmed this chap's details who is deceased, Victor?"

"Golf 31, the deceased has a full driving license on him with that name, and the address you are going to. There is also a passport with his name on it and a photo with that, Golf 31?

"Received, thank you, that's enough for me, thank you, Victor, I will be there in a few minutes."

He parked the panda car outside the address. It was smart semi-detached in quite a proud street, as some effort had been put into the gardens. Having taken a large gulp of water, he slowly walked up the garden path to the front door and took hold of the large doorknocker. He gazed around him and straightened his cap on his head. "I wonder if it will be the deceased's mother or father," he thought to himself, his mind going two to the dozen. He was feeling uncomfortable with the heat from the sun and felt sweat dripping down the centre of his back.

"Christ, these people are going to remember this for the rest of their lives. In the next few seconds, I am going to rip their poor souls apart. I'm going to change their family forever. God, why am I doing this job?"

The door opened. There was a small woman in brightly coloured and patterned traditional clothing standing in the doorway. She invites him into the house where her husband was sitting in the lounge area. He stood up and welcomed him into the house, gesticulating for him to sit down. He looked much older than he was. He looked frail, and he seemed to have aged another 10 years since Treavey had entered the house. He had thinning hair, was slightly crouched over, and was wearing clean but rather worn-looking clothes. He was not a man for wasting money.

Treavey took a deep breath as he placed his cap on the settee next to him. He began to speak.

"Mr. and Mrs. Farooqi, have I got that right?"

Both nodded at him, their expressions were of concern. Treavey knew they realised they were going to hear some bad news. It was just going to be how bad it was, so best put them out of their misery quickly.

"Right, well, Mr. and Mrs. Farooqi, I have some terrible news for you, I am afraid, there was a collision near Birmingham on the M5 involving a car which we believe your son was driving, and I'm afraid he died at the scene. I'm so sorry."

Both of them stared at him for a moment, the gentleman put his hand on his wife's arm, and asked, "Which one?"

Treavey panicked, "Oh shit, how could I have done this to them," he thought to himself. He spat out the next sentence, "I'm so sorry, I'm afraid we strongly believe it to be Basil. We have sufficient information to say it is him."

Treavey waited for a reaction. He could see the gentleman trying to hold it together, sitting as proudly as he could, but he was beginning to crumble. His wife looked even smaller than she had looked before. A petite woman, who was now sobbing quietly to herself, burying her face in her scarf. Treavey knew at this point, he could have said that unicorns would come through the windows and serve them tea and they probably wouldn't have taken it in, or they may have just replied, "Yes, quite."

He gave them a little time to take the information in, and then began to tell them what would happen from then on with regards to the Coroner and identifying the body formally, but that was enough information for now.

He had already written down the contact details of the officer in the case in Birmingham for them. He passed it over to the husband, who looked slightly more composed than his wife who was shaking uncontrollably in grief.

As he took the piece of paper from Treavey, the father said, "Thank you, officer, this cannot have been easy for... Basil!"

Treavey was a little confused, "Easy for Basil?"

The man looked as though he had seen a ghost, but his face quickly broke into a smile, as if a weight had been lifted off his shoulders, "Basil, Basil, Basil, welcome home, my boy!"

Treavey spun around to see a tall, slender young man, who was looking just as confused by the whole thing.

"What's a matter Dad?" he asked his father. He looked genuinely concerned about what was going on in that little lounge. "Officer, what is going on here?!"

Treavey felt a flush come over him. He wanted to run out of the house, but he knew that just was not possible. It flashed through his mind to see how he could have messed up so much. Where did he get it so wrong? No, there was nothing obvious, he had got the correct first and last name and the address was on the identification, with a photo ID. Treavey looked on motionless as he saw the parents hugging their son, weeping uncontrollably. He felt devastated at what he had just caused.

They eventually all sat down, and it was only a few moments before relief turned to anger.

"Officer, you see my wife and me, we were grief-stricken at the loss of our son, and yet here he is, sitting before us, like a miracle. Like a miracle, but how can you have got this so wrong?"

Treavey knew excuses were not going to work here.

"Mr. Farooqi, I am so sorry, I cannot explain how this terrible thing has come to happen. I am so relieved your son is alive and well, on behalf of the Devon and Cornwall Police, I most humbly apologise. I just don't understand, the man who died had a passport with the name and photo of Basil and a driving license with the details of Basil and the address of this house."

Basil immediately left the room and Treavey continued chatting to the parents. He wanted to be sure of things, before he dropped this on to the control room to update the West Midlands Police. They had royally messed up, but Treavey was feeling relatively relieved that, even though he was taking the flack, it hadn't been his mess up.

The wife suddenly spoke up, "We must celebrate, we have been given another chance, I am so happy now. I felt the genuine feeling of grief, and yet now I am happy, so happy!"

She clapped her hands together, sitting there with such relief on her face. Suddenly everyone was feeling so much better. Basil was back, but his face was deadpan. He definitely was not looking as he should.

Treavey sat back, staring at Basil, and quietly exclaimed, "Oh no!"

He had realised what may have happened. Things were just about to get worse. Basil was silent for a moment longer, trying to find the words; his parents looked confused, both sitting down now and waiting for their son who had come back to life, to speak.

Basil began to speak, "Officer, my passport and driving license is missing, and I think I know who's taken them."

Treavey sat up and listened intently waiting for his dreaded thoughts to be confirmed.

Basil continued, "Mum, Dad, I think Ameer has taken them. I think it is him who's got my things. I mean, he can't drive, and he asked if he could borrow them so he could hire a car to meet his friends in Birmingham. I told him no. Mum, oh no, I think it's him."

"But the photo ID?" Treavey asked.

"He looks like me, he's only a year younger than me, always been in a bit of trouble. Oh Dad, Mum, oh no, I think it is Ameer.

This was more than his mother could bear. She ran out of the room sobbing like a baby. All thoughts of how she should compose herself gone. His father was sitting with his head buried in his hands completely grief-stricken. How the hell were these people going to get over this.

Treavey felt he had done enough damage. Having updated the son Basil on what would happen and explained the importance of a formal identification which had to follow, he left the house, opened his car door, slumped back into his seat, and sat there in silence for a moment staring into space. The only thought he had was, "Well, what a total fuck up."

He put his finger on his transmit button, but hesitated. "No, I need to get my head straight and get back to the station. That couldn't have gone worse if I'd tried." He drove the panda along the residential roads slowly, peeling onto the main road which took him back towards the police station. He knew there was no one there. The weather which had been hot was now overcast, fitting his mood. The whole town looked drab and dirty right now. The sun had disappeared behind a huge bank of dark grey clouds, but Treavey didn't care. He felt utterly depressed.

He made himself a mug of tea and slumped into the seat in the parade room staring at Wolfy lying in his usual spot by the radiator.

"Look at you Wolfy, not a care in the world have you mate? You just need to decide which place is warmer than the next, it's not a bad life is it, mate?"

He put his hand on the transmit button on his radio and began. "Victor from Golf 31."

"Golf 31, go ahead."

"Yes, Golf 31, regarding that death message, I passed it."

"Received Golf 31, obliged."

"Just one thing Victor, once I'd told both parents Basil had been killed in a car crash whilst in possession of identifying documents, he walked into the room."

"Who did Golf 31... I don't understand."

"The deceased walked into the room."

There was a slight pause. Treavey could imagine the expression at the other end of the radio.

"From Victor, so that's... good... no?"

"From Golf 31, yes and no. Yes, because his parents thought they had lost a son and were jumping around for joy, happy there had been a mistake, and no, because we then worked it out from the missing documents belonging to Basil, his brother Ameer, who was only one year younger and looked similar, is probably the deceased instead. One son had come back to life, but then they found out the other one had died instead. I cannot describe the emotions that poor family has just been through."

Treavey knew that now and then, there were certain radio transmissions the rest of the airwaves would stop what they were doing and would listen to intently, and this would have been one of them. He knew that each officer, either listening in their cars, on foot patrol, or in their stations, would have stopped what they were doing and were now thanking their lucky stars they had not been put in the position of Treavey. It was toe-curlingly awful.

The comms operator replied one more time; "I just don't know what to say. That must have been awful for you to go through that. We'll pass it up to West Mids Police."

He finished his mug of tea and sat at the table in silence for a bit, watching the belly of Wolfy gently rising with every breath. It was so peaceful to watch, and the sight seemed to put things into perspective. How he wanted to curl up himself, in the warmth, with no inhibitions and just sleep forever. What that little black fluffy body and such perfectly formed face must be feeling right now, feeling completely trusting of his surroundings, enough to shut his eyes to the world, then to go out for some sport, hunting small birds and mice for fun, not for necessity, and to return for a proper meal, either here at the station or his real home, or indeed both. He was looking well-fed.

He remembered following his cat around the cliffs of Cornwall when he was a child. He spent three or four hours following it, just seeing what he got up to. There was a lot of walking and stopping and sniffing around the fields and cliffs, and lots of remaining completely still intently staring at what seemed to be nothing, before moving on again, and then climbing a certain way down a cliff towards the beach which alarmed him at the time.

Treavey was enjoying the greys, greens and yellows of the cliffs diving into the blues, greens and whites of the sea below. The cat was more interested in the sounds hidden beneath the spongy mounds of thrift and long grasses. With his cat knowing no boundaries, Treavey had to leave him to continue when he went further along the cliff line into the grounds of a grand hotel called the Glendorgal, a beast of a hotel that stretched over the cliffs with huge granite chimneys set above Porth beach.

Treavey snapped out of his daydream. He needed to change his mood, or just have someone to chat to. He had had quite a summer season so far and it had not all been good. Drug overdoses, suicides, children killed in road accidents, and now a complete disaster of a death message. The whole season had been a disaster in fact, or was this just normal in a seaside resort on the coast of Cornwall?

He drove his panda into town again and found himself drawn to driving towards the southern side of the beach, up the steep hill to where Grace had preferred to sit recently, to view the vista of the beach which stretched up the north coast. As he turned the corner, he was relieved to see her sitting there. It was a comforting sight for him. He just did not believe the information he'd heard from Felicity about her being an informant for the drug dealers. There was always a niggling concern; was he being groomed by a very clever lady perhaps? But when he looked at the information she could have heard or seen from being in the station or what he had told her, there was nothing at all. Nothing of use to anyone. No, he was convinced as much as he could be, she was an ex-cop who had lost her family and fallen on hard times. Anyway, he liked her, and he was sure he wasn't that bad a judge of character.

"Hi Grace, got two minutes?"

She shuffled herself along the bench by a couple of inches, wearing a wonderful smile, "Yes, my darling, it's always good to see you."

Treavey sat down next to her. The clouds were still casting a gloom over the sea and the coastline, but there was still hope for some hardy holidaymakers, their day wasn't ruined yet, and they were sticking around to take advantage of any improvement in the weather. They were on their holidays and by hell, they were going to spend a day on the beach.

The wind had blown up a little more and people were using their striped colourful windbreaks as barriers against the cold wind. Several together in a circle formation would protect them from marauding raiders, or rather keep the young children in, and guarantee a territory they could defend. Another emergency windbreak with these large families, consisting of the main family along with grandma and grandpa, would soon make up a roof to the whole set up if the rain started to come down. You could see the fathers were enjoying it even more than the children, as they suddenly had an excuse to build a den once more.

Treavey and Grace sat there in silence for a while. It was clear why Grace had chosen this spot. It gave almost a bird's-eye view. Watching the grey shadows with the sun behind the clouds rushing across the dunes at 100mph, then a glimpse of sun bursting through, teasing the public into thinking there was some hope again, before snatching it away once more, as if it were a colourful stick of rock being taken from a child's hand having just been gifted to them.

"What's on your mind, Treavey?"

"Nothing much, Grace..." Grace could sense he was going to say more. "Well, you know. Bad day and all that. One of those days where, through no fault of your own, you destroy a person's life and their future forever, then they are the happiest they've ever been in their life, before

237

moments later, they are thrown into the depths of grief again."

Grace said nothing for a moment. Treavey knew he had made no sense to her at all. She took a breath and in a dismissive tone, replied, "Sounds like an average day for a copper, that. There are rarely any winners in the job you do."

More silence. There was something quite therapeutic watching the Cornish sea building up slowly into each white ridge of a wave before it could grow no more and tilt over breaking up into a white foam which chatted amongst itself before running out of water to progress any further; the white foam having nowhere to go but to bury itself into the sand to disappear forever. Treavey could feel his blood pressure calming. Things generally felt better now. He needed this.

Grace broke the silence. "You have to be in the right place at the right time, Treavey. Those drugs were coming in by plane, and then by boat when the plane crashed in that weather. Both have faltered now, but they will get it in, and they want to avoid the roads, so either they will use another boat, or they'll have found another plane by now. It seems to be well organised, even if they have some buffoons bringing it in. I've had word the drugs either went down with that boat, or it was recovered by others before the dog walkers reported it shipwrecked. You won't find it though; I know that much."

"The only problem with that, Grace, is the plane wasn't carrying any drugs when it crashed."

"How do you know they hadn't already dropped it, Treavey? If it was not picked up by whoever was waiting for it to arrive on the airfield, it probably ended up in the sea. It was a shocking night wasn't it, but I hear it definitely arrived with the drugs on board? Can't you put a lump on Bradford's car, or Dawson's? Get a pattern of where they are going at night?"

"Fine chance of that, Grace, we have no set evidence or intelligence to say they are the ones up to their necks in this. We could never get authority for a tracker on their cars."

"Yes, fair point. Circumstantial evidence alone, however clear and obvious, just isn't enough, is it?" Grace replied forlornly. "I'm glad I'm out of it now, Treavey."

Treavey felt the time may be right to dig a little deeper. "I'm so sorry you lost your family like that Grace. I just can't even begin to imagine."

"Yes, well, it's all done now. I had them for a while and life was almost as good as it could be. I was working hard in the police and then that happened. It was simple and quick. No one deserved it, but it just happened. A little like that little boy who died a few weeks ago, just down the road."

"But you lost everyone Grace. I mean…" Treavey realised he was perhaps going too far.

"I didn't lose everything, Treavey. I introduced myself to alcohol, and we became great friends, and it has been my comfort ever since."

"Really?" Treavey asked half under his breath.

"No, Treavey, but it numbed the pain, and then replaced it with some more problems, like losing my job and being thrown on the scrap heap. I am just happy I am not a drug addict, to be honest with you. It could have so easily gone down that road, but I knew it was the end of me if I did."

Treavey felt rather honoured to be let in to such a private side of her life. She seemed to be quite composed about it. "So, how is your life now, Grace?"

"There are some tough bits, but I like the anonymity of it all now. Nobody sees me, if they do, they avoid me, so it's not too bad. I mean, how many lounge windows have a view like that, Treavey?"

She pointed out into the distance. Treavey thought that any lounge may be more beneficial for her than no lounge with a lovely view, but she did not see it that way.

"Right, thank you, Grace, I'll catch you later. It was nice to talk to you."

Treavey sauntered back to his car and set off for the police station again. He felt calmed by the chat he'd had with Grace, but it was slow progress. He was just going to have to get lucky, but he also knew he had to make his own luck too. He wasn't going to catch the hand-over whilst drinking tea in the station. On his late turn and night turn, he was going to spend every spare minute at the airfield or along the coast and on the bench to see if another yacht came in. He would also have to find some quality intelligence on Gary Dawson and the Bradford brothers.

He was just about to pull out onto the main road in the town centre when a blue Astra sped past him, the driver was not wearing a seatbelt, so he pulled out behind him and had to put his foot down to catch up with the car. He flicked the blue light on, half hoping he failed to stop. It would be nice to have a pursuit right now to get some of the frustration out of him. The car pulled over almost immediately and came to a stop on the side of the road.

Treavey's blood was pumping but he knew he had to calm down a bit. He sat in the driver's seat of his car for a couple of seconds, cleared his front seat of items, and then got out of the car. He walked slowly up to the driver's side of the car and the driver wound down the window. He was about 45 years old with greying hair, wearing blue jeans and a grey Adidas T-Shirt stretching over his gut. His expression was one of annoyance.

He was the first to speak, "Yeah?"

"I've stopped you because you were driving too fast for the centre of town and you weren't wearing a seatbelt sir, so I wonder if you could pop out so I can have a chat with you in my car."

He reluctantly got out of his car and followed Treavey to the panda car; Treavey invited him into the front passenger seat.

Once back in the police car, Treavey began explaining the circumstances, "I was coming out of the side road when I saw you driving above the speed limit across the front of me without wearing your seatbelt. Can I ask you…"

"Prove it, can you prove it, mate?" said the man, breaking Treavey's flow.

"Right, okay, I cannot prove you broke the speed limit, so I am just going to give you advice for that and deal with you for your seat belt."

"So, do not give me any advice, I don't want any of your advice, I mean, how old are you for Pete's sake, young enough to be my son and I wouldn't listen to him for advice either, so if I'm getting a ticket, get on with it, so you can waste my time for as little time as possible. Some of us have work to do, you know."

Treavey's heckles were raising but he knew he had to keep cool. It wouldn't be good for this to turn into a shouting match. He remembered his tutor saying, "If you meet Mr. Aggressive who wants to fluster you, just take your time, take extra time, there's no rush, so you don't miss anything."

He settled himself in his car, stared out of the window for a second, and began again. "Right, in that case, could I see your driving license please?"

"Nope."

"Okay, so is this car registered to you by name?"

"Yes, hurry, I'm busy."

Treavey slowly picked up the radio receiver and squeezed the handle to transmit. He ran the registration number through and waited for a second. Treavey pressed the receiver tight to his ear, with the volume down so the man could not hear the reply.

"Golf 31, your check comes back as a Blue Vauxhall Astra, registered to a Mr. Sean Black from number 6, Queen Elizabeth Drive in Newquay."

Treavey glanced across at the man in the passenger seat. "Okay, what's your name and address please Sir."

"You've got it there, so just get on with it."

Treavey took on his tutor's advice and put a patronising tone to his voice so Mr. Black wouldn't think he was succeeding in intimidating him.

"I'm sorry, Sir, it seems you don't understand why I am asking you. You see, I need to ensure you are the owner of the car, or indeed have permission to drive it you see, so, now, what was that name and address again?"

"Sorry, are you stupid or something, check the number and then you'll get your answer, haven't you got anything better to do?"

"I'm sorry sir," Treavey replied in soft dulcet tones, showing he was not flustered by this in the slightest. "You see, I don't know that you haven't just stolen it from up the road and are now trying to fool this very polite and patient young police officer into thinking it was your car, now you see, unfortunately, if you insist on not telling this nice police officer your full details, you're going to leave him no choice whatsoever but to arrest you, and to take you back to the station in Newquay, or Truro, whichever is the busiest, in order to establish your correct credentials. Now does that make any more sense to you?"

Treavey realised he was sounding incredibly patronising now, but after the day he had just had, he didn't care.

"You said you'd take me to the busiest station; you mean you'd take me to the quietest station!" The man was laughing, making a joke of Treavey's presumed mistake.

"Oh no sir, you misunderstand me once more. You see, if you insist on wasting my time by failing me the simple task of confirming your name, date of birth, and address, then I will ensure I waste as much of your time as I

242

possibly can, and don't think you'll be getting a lift back to your car either. Now, shall we start again?"

The man spat his name and address out at a million miles an hour. It was so fast, that Treavey had no chance of even hearing it, let alone writing it down. A year ago, perhaps Treavey would have tried to end this confrontational situation as soon as he could, and get the whole experience over as soon as possible, by just accepting this was probably the same man as the registered keeper, but he knew there was just as high a chance he was trying to deflect Treavey from him having no insurance or that it was a stolen car.

The man spelled his details slowly, very slowly, so Treavey was writing the letters down and having to wait for him to continue. B... l... a....c.... k.

"We are getting there now aren't we Mr. Black, but I still feel you think we are in a playground back at your old school, but I'll play your game until I run out of patience which, believe me...." Treavey turned his head very slowly until he was facing directly at Mr. Black, "... is very soon."

Mr. Black stared at him for a moment, then changed his tone. "Well, well, how come you are picking on me for a fucking seatbelt, that's my choice, isn't it? I mean, my mate heard about someone who was thrown free of his burning car and survived, and he'd have died if it hadn't been for him not wearing his seat belt."

Treavey had heard this a million times, so didn't even turn his head from his paperwork, but continued writing.

"You see Mr. Black, I have heard that so many times, that either this country has thousands of burning cars on their roofs with drivers having been thrown out of them, which incidentally, I haven't been to one or even heard of one, or someone is using the same made-up story as everyone else and incidentally, seat belts have saved thousands of lives more."

Treavey finished filling in the line for the HORT/1 document for Mr. Black to produce his insurance within

243

seven days, then continued, "...the other aspect is that the public doesn't want to pay for your comatose backside to be laid up in intensive care for 6 weeks at great expense to them, when you could have simply just have been an outpatient. Does that make sense?"

Mr. Black was silent. His mind was working fast to attempt to come back with something, but he calmed down considerably.

"Okay, you police are always moaning about how busy you all are, how come you aren't arresting all the murders and rapists instead?"

Treavey raised an eyebrow. "You are ticking them all off today, aren't you Mr. Black. I will tell you why, as long as you promise not to come up with the same well-worn cliches for the next poor officer who stops you, which I feel they inevitably will be required to."

He tapped his pen to emphasise a full stop on his pad and looked straight out of his windscreen.

"Why aren't we arresting them all? That's not very fair now is it, because I think you'll find we catch almost every single one, also, if you would like to point out where they all are, then I'd be pleased to go straight there and arrest them, and lastly, there are nearly 4000 road deaths in this country every single year and yet just a handful of murders and rapes as terrible as they are, so where do you think my time is best spent, Mr. Black?"

The battle was won. Mr. Black had realised he had picked on the wrong police officer. He grabbed the ticket for the seatbelt with the HORT/1 document producer and stomped off back to his car. He wasn't known for any crime, so Treavey thought he had quit whilst he was ahead and let him go without searching his car. There were no grounds to anyway.

"That's it," Treavey thought to himself. "And now for that cup of tea."

Chapter 15

You're nicked

The following morning, Rambo is bringing in a large tray of mugs of tea for the start of the shift.

"Right, you bastards," he declared with pride, "don't say I never give you anything."

"Like we don't give you anything, Rambo," replied Felicity, smiling.

Rambo was straight back at her, "Yeah, trouble is, it's always with a bit of chaos too, that's what you give me, Felicity, okay, as well as the odd mug of tea I'll grant you."

Rambo slightly misjudged the height of the table and slammed the tray down slopping the contents of a few mugs onto the tray."

Micky looked at the spilled tea pooling on the tray, "Nice production Rambo, but the delivery could be slightly improved upon."

Gordy did not even look up from his paperwork, emanating as much emotion this morning as a slab or Cornish granite. Felicity was hooting with laughter and leaned forward over Treavey placing her hand on his shoulder to reach for a mug. Treavey stood up and checked his skippet for paperwork. There was a handwritten note in there. It was from Rambo, "Can you contact Grace, she's got some information for you."

Treavey read it out and asked Rambo, "Did she say what it was about, mate?"

Rambo was leaning back on his chair sipping his tea.

"No mate, she just asked you to contact her. She said there wasn't any immediate rush."

Felicity casually spoke up. "Careful Treavey, I don't trust that woman. She is an alcoholic ex-police officer, probably the worst type to trust. They usually have an axe to grind."

"Na, she's alright, Felicity. I trust her, but I don't share anything confidential with her anyway, not that there's much to say to her."

"Didn't she tell you there was an exchange of drugs with a canoe and a yacht? No one else saw that canoe, and then randomly a yacht turned up the next week, but it had no drugs on board."

Treavey felt himself getting defensive. "I don't think she'd say it for nothing, and there was a good chance there were drugs on that yacht, but it was lost when it sunk. The sea was rough enough to get rid of it by the morning."

Felicity could see Treavey was not going to have his mind changed. "Just be careful, remember what the Bradford boys said about her."

Micky piped up; "Like they are trustworthy, those guys are up to their armpits in it with the drugs in this town. I was sent to yet another overdose yesterday. Just 18 years old she was. Poor girl. Her family was devastated as you can imagine."

Treavey could see no one was getting intelligence on the drugs imports very fast, and the only chance he had was to have as much information coming in as possible. He could see everyone seemed to be getting frustrated with it and felt they had begun to give up.

After his cup of tea, Treavey nipped out of the station on his own. He decided to walk, mainly as there were only two cars in the yard and they were being used by the others, and it was another lovely day in Cornwall, anyway. He enjoyed meandering down to the beach and chatting with the tourists. The smells took him right back to his childhood when he lived above a beach in Newquay called Lusty Glaze and spent every day of the summer on the beach surfing and sunbathing. He had run down to it after school as the tourists were beginning to return home, but there was still some fun to be had before his supper at 6.30 pm. The fun to be had was watching the wind brakes become swamped by the fast-incoming tide, taking towels and shoes along with it. The occupants of their windbreak islands would have an expression of total shock as the bitterly cold sea overwhelmed them and they would panic, running around not knowing what to save of their personal belongings first. And all to the sound of an appreciative audience watching from the safety of surrounding viewpoints.

As the tide got higher, and the occupants of the windbreak islands had retreated to the safety of the slipways, beach shop, and cafe, he would enjoy running from the slipway to the steps along the sand, which led up to some beach huts before the incoming waves caught him. Then he would try to get back again, and he would make it most of the time. It was all in the timing you see. Others would join in and get their timing completely wrong. The entertainment being the summer crowd could see they had got it so wrong in the unusually soft boggy sand. The oncoming doom was inevitable, almost in slow motion as the wave forced its way past their sunken ankles, taken over by another wave rising up their legs and overwhelming their waist and then torso with some force, soaking them from their shorts to the top of their shirts. The worst part being the cheering of the crowd in pure delight at the individual's downfall. It was almost gladiatorial, with the crowd pointing their thumbs down, and the victim was left to succumb to the icy water; before walking back rather bedraggled, up the slipway to safety.

Treavey was standing in the beach car park, breathing in the holiday atmosphere. God, he was lucky to be alive, he felt. He continued up the steep road to where he hoped to see Grace and was relieved to see her there, sitting on guard with every vessel safe in the unknown knowledge Grace was there to report anyone in trouble. He assumed

247

the position next to her on the bench, breathing quite heavily after the walk up the steep hill.

"Hey."

"Hey," she replied.

"Grace, I have travelled far, climbed mountains to be with you here today, and I'm hoping it wasn't for nothing."

Grace slowly looked around to face Treavey sitting next to her. She smiled, "Mountains?"

"Well, it felt like one anyway, certainly in this heat."

Treavey chuckled, having removed his police helmet with one hand and mopped his brow with the other. He enjoyed the cool breeze flowing up the cliff in front of him.

"Maybe I should have asked you how you are first, Grace."

"Not necessary, sweety. I am always pretty good. I wanted to tell you; you need to investigate a girl called Mary. She's got something to do with the drugs supply around here."

Treavey thought for a moment. "Mary?" He took in the name, "The only Mary I know tried to kill herself, but I understand she's out of danger and should be home soon."

"Sounds like her." Grace replied without changing her calm tone, and continued, "She tried to kill herself after losing her boyfriend, but I understand she owes a lot of drug money and I wouldn't be surprised if that's why she did it."

"No, she did it because her boyfriend died, I'm sure of it, I mean I spoke to her at the time, she was devastated, I'm not sure you are right there, Grace."

Treavey remembered Mary telling him about the involvement of some dealers who could only have been Dawson and the Bradford brothers. Why would she have done that unless she'd already decided to kill herself? She'd have been cutting her own supply off by telling Treavey who it was. She may have been clearing things up before she left this earth, perhaps.

Grace continued to take in the view. The sea was looking at its best today. The dazzling turquoise colours, a gently rippling surface, gulls gliding effortlessly across hundreds of metres before tilting a wing and coming to an instant but controlled hover, before arching their wings, lowering their feet and rear end to glide down to a steep but controlled landing on the cliff edge with pinpoint accuracy. She watched a herring gull land next to its mate amongst the Sea Pinks, throwing its head back with its beak wide open and screaming in delight at its prowess.

Grace said, slightly annoyed with the suggestion of Treavey doubting her information, "Treavey, it's up to you, but the word I hear is there was more to it than just her boyfriend dying."

Treavey had to add another suspect to the list for the drugs coming into Perran killing a lot of its inhabitants. Could it possibly be Mary? Had he been incredibly naive? He got up from the bench. Another useful chat, but was he getting any closer to solving this? Even the locals were getting worried about the number of deaths in the town. The local paper had printed it as the main story. Questions were being asked what the police were doing about it and he knew the bosses from Newquay would be putting more pressure on them to be more proactive.

With this in mind, he walked back down the hill past the beach again and into town, before making his way to Mary's flat where he had attended the sudden death of her boyfriend, Stuart, to see if she was back from the hospital. He would sound her out, see how she was coping, that is if she was back, that is. He needed to dig further. He was quite warm by the time he reached the flat, even though he was in shirt sleeve order, he could feel the sweat on his legs, and it was not very pleasant.

He rang the doorbell and waited not expecting a reply. There was a considerable delay considering the size of the flat. Was she in the toilet perhaps? But now he could hear steps coming down the stairs. There was another delay and then a soft female's voice emitted from the other side of the door.

"Hello, who is it?"

"It's me, Mary, PC Treave. Can I come in? I just want to see how you are?"

After another pause, the door cracked open and eventually fully opened. Mary turned around and led the way up the stairs to her flat without a word and Treavey followed her. She was looking worse than before, and she was limping badly. She looked battered and bruised.

"How has the recovery been, Mary?"

She huffed with an abrupt, sarcastic laugh. "Look at me. How do I look like I am recovering? I feel like I've jumped off a cliff."

"I guess you are pretty fortunate to be alive though, Mary."

She slumped back onto the sofa in the lounge.

"Fortunate is one word for it, I suppose. Not sure I am feeling quite that fortunate yet."

Treavey sat in the armchair opposite and hesitated for a moment, then, "I have to ask you when you jumped... any regrets as you fell?"

Treavey knew this could be considered extremely callous, but he felt there were many white elephants in the room that needed to be dealt with. It was not often you had the chance to speak to someone who'd gone through it.

"Do you know," she began, "... I did immediately regret it. It is very final, you see. And as I fell, I wondered if I should have just persevered for a bit longer. It is so final you see. No more chances after that, or so I thought."

Treavey was impressed with her honesty and wanted to find out more.

"And when I met you before, you told me who was involved in the drugs in Perran, do you remember?"

"Yes, I remember, but I'm not so sure now. I get mine from various places, but sorry if I don't want to end my supply by telling you where it's from."

Treavey felt she regretted telling him who it was from. It was obvious to him that the Bradfords with Dawson were top of the list. He decided to finish on an open question. "How are you, Mary?"

"You know, fucked up, boyfriend's dead, tried to kill myself and fucked that up, and I owe shit loads of money to the wrong type of people, apart from that, everything's dandy thank you, how are you?"

There were times like this that Treavey could see why people like Mary felt there was no way out.

"You know, Mary, you will look back in years to come when your life is so much better than it is now, and you will be so glad you persevered, you know. If anyone is threatening you, you need to tell us. We can be subtle, you know, we can offer you some help."

She leaned forward and studied Treavey's face.

"You know, PC Treave, why can't I meet someone like you, but your occupation may be a little tricky for me right now. I have a load of shit I have to deal with. I have half a chance coming up, so you can see how I'm doing after that."

"Just be careful Mary. At least you are not in prison right now. That would make your life a whole lot worse. Don't do anything stupid now."

He watched Mary's expression change to melancholy and pain ridden. She was silent for a moment and Treavey fought for the right words, but concluded it was best to say nothing. He waited a little bit longer, watching her. She looked so vulnerable. Her life had taken many turns recently, and each turn had been horrendous.

She took a deep breath and sighed, "I miss him." She slowly glanced up at him and smiled so beautifully. "But he's gone now."

251

She dipped her head back down again, clasping her delicate hands together gently. She shook herself out of her half trance, got up off the sofa, and stared at Treavey. It was time for Treavey to go. She placed a hand on his arm and looked directly into his eyes once more. Treavey was stunned by her deep blue eyes. "Don't worry about me PC Treave. Give me a few days and I should be in a lot better position. Then I can get on with my life again, hey?"

He left Mary in the flat wondering what she was going to do, but he was quite certain it was to clear a drug debt one way or another. Grace was right. Mary was expecting some money to come in soon to pay off some big debts. But how big, and to who?

He was soon back at the station, putting his custodian helmet aside and relaxing back into a seat at the report room table. Micky was there. "Good day, Micky?"

"Hello Treavey, I think I've made some progress." He replied in his usual slow, and controlled comforting tones. Treavey needed some good news. He sat up in his chair and asked with some anticipation, "Go on?"

"Well..." Micky was revelling in what he was going to say next. "...you know our little sit down outside the Bradfords house a while back, well, I may have been doing that a few times since, and having spoken to CID in Newquay, they are working on a warrant."

Treavey raised an eyebrow. "They were happy with you listening to Bradford's private conversations then?"

"I may have said I was casually walking back to the station and overheard them boasting about stuff, such as their involvement in their drugs killing half of Perran and laughing about how they'd have to be careful they didn't lose all their clientele."

Treavey replied excitedly, "Oh wow, but that's not a lie, is it? That's almost how it was. Were they really that stupid to say that?"

"Yeah, they think they are safe in their own home so why not openly enjoy their criminality? That, with the rest of the intel they have, is sufficient for a warrant and DC Lemon is busy getting that from a Magistrate right now. Are you about later, as he'll need some help?"

Treavey was a lot happier now than he had been. It looked like things were starting to move. He had heard of DC Lemon, a larger-than-life character, who enthused energy in everyone around him. He was the one who would take on this as a challenge, and he talked for England too!

"You never know mate..." Treavey continued, "...if there's enough of the stuff found to send them away for years, they may even start chipping away like little canaries. This could be it."

It was another couple of hours before they heard anything else. Much tea was drunk, and Treavey had finished his granary bread, cheddar cheese, and Branston pickle sandwiches he'd always had for his meal break since he had joined the police. It tended to hit the spot. The rough bakery granary bread, the sharpness of the mature cheddar along the sweet Branston pickle was always just the trick, on a hot summer's day or a winter's night. He had tried ham and mustard sandwiches which were lovely now and then, but he soon came back to cheese and pickle. There was always time for a treat some days, when he just couldn't be bothered to make them at 5.30 am. Nipping down to the bakery in Perran and buying a pasty with carrot cake was always a winner, but would have been too expensive every day on his budget. He was a creature of habit or maybe just loved cheddar cheese and Branston pickle.

DC Lemon entered the station with quite a commotion, his hands full of paperwork and exhibit bags. "Jesus, it doesn't help them being directly opposite, does it?" he exclaimed slightly out of breath.

"It has its drawbacks, but it means we can keep an eye on them too," replied Micky, sitting up and showing he was keen for what was about to happen.

DC Lemon dropped his paperwork on the desk and slumped back into the chair. He had been very busy and had just travelled from Newquay with the warrant which was now on the desk in front of him.

"Right chaps, Micky and Trea...vey, right?" he hesitantly asked.

"Yes, that's right," Treavey replied, "How can we help? Is it all still on?"

DC Lemon licked his lips and winked at Treavey, and Treavey quickly took the hint, jumping up and headed off into the kitchen to make some tea.

"Thanks, Treavey, sorry to be cheeky, you can call me Dick, by the way."

Treavey could see the humour it was meant in and had not taken offense. "Milk and sugar, Dick?"

10 minutes later, all three officers were going over the briefing. Dick sounded as if he had everything in hand.

"Right, sorry to come to you last guys, but as Felicity and Rambo are busy with an arrest, I have a couple of others on their way from Newquay. I have an exhibits officer, a man with the Bosher in case they decide to be shy about letting us in and I have another officer to help with the searches. Are you happy to come with us and do some searching too?"

Micky and Treavey both eagerly agreed, happy they had not been lumbered as the exhibit's officers. A complicated methodical job of endless lists, and if anything went wrong with the case, it was often because there was an issue with the exhibits. At least they could have the bit with the least responsibility and free of most of the paperwork. Perhaps Dick wanted that part done properly.

"So," Dick exclaimed on hearing on the radio the others have arrived from Newquay, and were waiting in the car around the corner, "It is 3.50 pm now, happy to go at 4.00 pm, everyone?"

Treavey felt a pang of adrenalin rush through his body. "This could be it," he thought to himself. He looked at Micky and said, "Well done for getting that information Micky, especially as you were fortunate enough to hear it just walking by!"

Micky winked at him. Both officers thought there was nothing underhand as such. They had just happened to hear it whilst sitting outside their house listening through the window and then Micky had heard more on his own, that's all. Nothing illegal, but the defence would have made a big thing of it and tried to muddy the waters somewhat.

Wolfy got up from his cushion and arched his back whilst stretching with an enormous yawn.

DC Lemon commented, "You have a station cat? That's so cool."

"Well, not exactly," Treavey replied, watching Wolfy step through the cat flap and disappear, "he's probably off to his real home to tell them of our plan. Maybe he's a double agent."

Treavey took the front door with Dick and another officer who had just joined them. Mick and the other officers disappeared around the side and rear of the house. Dick knocked on the door hard but there was a huge anti-climax for Treavey when Bradford's mother answered the door and invited them in.

"No smashing doors in today then," he thought. They congregated in the lounge area and Dick showed her the warrant. Her two sons sheepishly walked down the stairs. They resembled naughty schoolboys as they sat on their sofa next to each other looking very young indeed. An officer told them they were detained whilst the search was made of the house and garden. The boys sat in silence.

Dick divided the house up for searching and the officers got to work. Even if a house was relatively clean, searches involved dirty laundry and searching behind wardrobes and settees so there was soon a lot of dust floating about. They tried to keep it light-hearted for their mother who was generally helpful but extremely embarrassed about having her bedroom searched. One of the officers later admitted he had located her toy box, however spared her the blushes of mentioning it at the time.

Treavey had agreed with Micky to search the main bedroom of Billy, starting from opposite corners so they knew they would not miss anything as they moved around and finished at the other's corner. Treavey came up to the wardrobe and opened it. He pushed across the hanging clothes to see what was at the bottom and saw a series of large packages.

He laughed and commented to Micky sarcastically, "Well, I've found the drugs."

He was chuckling as no one would ever have put them in such an obvious place and, unfortunately, there was far too much of it for it to be drugs. He dragged one of the packages out from the bottom of the wardrobe and ripped a bit of the paper open expecting it to be books or similar. He stared, failing to take it all in for a moment. He, understandably, was not expecting this. He looked back at Micky whose backside was sticking out from behind the bed, before pulling himself out with a smile, holding a small piece of cannabis up in a clear bag grinning at Treavey declaring, "Oh look, drugs," before placing it on the bedside table.

Treavey looked at Micky, and feeling rather stunned, said, "Mate, you call that drugs?... I call these drugs!"

Micky stopped what he was doing and stared back at Treavey. "Shit mate, those are drugs. That is a lot of drugs. Shit, that is some drugs!"

Treavey placed the large package on the floor outside the wardrobe he had opened and said, "...and wait there,

Micky," as he dived into the bottom of the wardrobe.

"One, two, three, four, five and six, and seven…" he went on "Fifteen, and that one, that's sixteen, and in his bloody wardrobe mate, did they think they were hiding it in plain sight or something, not 20 metres from the police station?"

Treavey located the detective constable downstairs; Dick was in the lounge area holding up some cannabis to the two boys asking them whose it was. Treavey waited patiently, noting their silence at first, but then seeing the concern on the boys' faces as they both glanced over to him. Dick also glanced across to Treavey.

"Er, Dick, we've found something which looks like an awful lot of drugs in the wardrobe of Billy. And I mean, a lot."

Dick rushed up the stairs and was jumping around on the spot in excitement. Micky was beside himself with excitement too as it was his warrant this had come from. The search was completed but they all knew they had got what they wanted. Dick returned to the lounge and spoke to the boys with their mother putting on a calm exterior again.

"Right, we have found what looks like a rather substantial amount of drugs upstairs, therefore, we are arresting all three of you for possession with intent to supply a class A drug."

He cautioned them but Billy was already protesting, "What do you mean, you found it in my room, that means it's mine, it's nothing to do with the others. Why are you nicking my Mum?"

Dick was direct with him, "All of you have access to that room, so we have to arrest all those who live in this house, and that includes your Mum."

All three were placed in handcuffs and led out of the house to an awaiting police van, Bradford's mother looked completely out of place in her handcuffs, stepping into the rear of the van.

Micky commented to Treavey as they watched them leave, "Bloody hell, Treavey, we know she doesn't have anything to do with it; she looks like a fish out of water."

"Do we know that Micky?" Treavey replied.

Treavey did not take his glare off the van as it drove off and disappeared around the bend.

"How can she miss all of that going on under her nose, Micky. I mean you were outside the window and heard it. Does she hear nothing living in the house? A blind eye is just as bad."

They crossed the road back to the police station and sat in the parade room having washed their hands. They could not believe their luck, basking in the glow of success as Felicity and Rambo walked in, who noticed the atmosphere was rather odd.

Felicity was first to break the silence. "Why are your boys so chuffed whilst we've been working our backsides off with some crummy shoplifter who's probably going to get off with it again?"

Treavey took a deep breath and sighed. "We may have got a warrant with the information Micky was able to get, along with some previous intel, and we may have had DC Lemon up here, our new favourite DC in the world and we may have just..."

Treavey was milking this moment with everything he could muster, "...we may have just found a shit load of what looks like heroin in his bloody wardrobe, of all places!"

"Whose wardrobe?" Felicity demanded.

"Billy's. Billy bloody Bradford, that's who, so they've all been nicked, and I doubt with that lot the boys will be out for a very long time. Dick is pushing for a remand on the boys and I'm sure he'll get it."

Felicity looked excited, but Treavey noticed she was also slightly off with him.

258

"Sorry Felicity, we couldn't wait for you two, otherwise we would have loved to have had you along. DC Lemon, Dick, got the warrant and then it was all go."

"Oh yes, I understand Treavey," she replied, "Just a bit gutted I wasn't on the job when the case was broken wide open, I guess, eh Rambo?"

She looked across at him, but he was stirring his mug of tea, showing very little interest in the conversation.

"Eh? Oh, I think as long as they've been caught, that's all I care about," replied Rambo. "Looks like we won't be seeing their red Fiesta driving around for a bit."

Micky joined in, "That's been searched and is parked down the lane out of the way. Reckon it will be staying there for a couple of years I bet. I have got the key to it here, just in case it needs another proper search or needs moving. I'll stick it in our property store for now."

He came back from the cupboard and pulled out a bit of statement paper and said, "Let's hope DC Lemon can get them talking. We need to know who's the one in charge of the drug imports, and ultimately the deaths which have been happening here. This thing goes far bigger than those two little jerks in their house opposite us."

There were highs like this now and then in policing, when everything came together and the local police got involved in a job they would usually only hear about in the news. Treavey was driving home in his car thinking things over. It will be top news in Perranporth, and Newquay, and Truro, and, well, Cornwall and Devon, probably. He felt his unstoppable enthusiasm for the next shift would be higher than ever, but he had to remember this sort of thing did not happen every day. He remembered his tutor saying, "You have to make your own luck Treavey. It doesn't just happen."

It was so true and usually those who hadn't taken the chances or put the work in felt rather jealous and would dismiss others' results as simply good luck, but his tutor had been right even though it hadn't really been Treavey's success. Yes, his name was on the statement at least, but someone on their first day in the job could have found those drugs. He considered it to be Micky's success this time. He had won the respect of everyone, just by thinking outside the box a little. Treavey would remember that. He wanted to be the best copper he could, and he was determined to be so.

Chapter 16

Crash, crash, crash

It was two days on, and Treavey was starting a night shift. He was on his own as Bomber, who would have been on nights with him, had been pulled onto a day shift to help with the drugs bust investigations. He entered the parade room and saw a collection of CID and other colleagues sitting there. The Bradford brothers had stuck to their 'no comment' replies in the interview so had been charged and remanded as the intelligence from various areas had been sufficient to do so. The primary part of that was the obvious find in their house which would keep them in custody until the case started in several weeks. There wasn't sufficient evidence on their mother, so she had been bailed out from the station. Nobody believed she had been directly involved anyway, but it had to be covered. She just was not that type, and if all of them had been jailed the police station would have had to permanently adopt Wolfy the cat. How ironic.

With the enthusiasm still surging around his veins, Treavey took a car out on patrol, looking for just as high-profile drug suppliers, although he knew it just was not going to happen. This was Perranporth after all. The first call he received was to a house in Perrancoombe where there had been a report of a woman being attacked and the caller was from a very nice house indeed. It was always a pleasure to go to these jobs as it was highly likely to be a fox screaming, not in fright or pain, but they have a terrible blood-curdling scream which sounded like a woman being attacked. There were a couple of reasons why this was a good job to go to. Firstly, the middle-aged caller had probably just been spooked by noises and shadows and now the scream, of course, made worse because she was alone, and secondly, it usually resulted in a nice cup of tea or coffee in a rather grand house, the woman happy to have the security of the brave young officer to comfort her for a while.

He was invited into the house and spoke to the lone rather concerned-looking woman, whose husband was, indeed, away on business. She was in her late forties and looking very attractive for it, even though she was almost double his age. Treavey could tell she could afford to look after herself in the best ways possible, possibly with a personal trainer too. The house was meticulously set out, spotlessly clean with high ceilings and some expensive antiques on display.

She walked him through the house towards the kitchen.

"Thank you, officer, oh, are you on your own? Goodness, okay, I hope I haven't wasted your time, but I'll take you through."

He was led through to the back of the house into a huge kitchen which looked more like a showroom with a huge Aga oven and an island breakfast table in the centre. He was led in through the conservatory and into the back garden.

He listened in silence for a moment before turning his torch on and scanning it around the immaculate lawn and well-cared for bushes.

"What did you see exactly, Mrs. Carter?" Treavey asked with some empathy.

"Oh, I didn't actually see anything, but I heard the noise here in the back. It was screaming, an awful noise like a woman was being attacked. It couldn't have been anything else."

Treavey shone his torch into the trees. "You get foxes here don't you, Mrs. Carter?"

"Yes, I do, but they don't make that noise, do they? I mean this was as if the poor woman was terrified."

Treavey walked to the end of the garden as far as he could and listened. There was dense woodland at the rear, and he knew all the signs were there to confirm a fox, but he had to pacify the woman.

He returned to her and said, "How long have you lived here, Mrs. Carter?"

"Oh, about five weeks now. We've moved down from London."

"Right okay, if it sounds anything like this, now are you ready for it?"

Treavey filled his lungs and screamed as loudly as he could dragging the screeching tone to a high note before pulling it down to a low scream fading away to nothing.

The woman stared at him in somewhat disbelief. "Er, yes, a bit like that."

Treavey explained, "It's usually in the mating season, but foxes also scream like that to mark their territory, and also for communicating, Mrs. Carter. They sound terrifying the first time you hear them. You'll hear them a lot more in January when it's most common."

"Oh, my goodness, thank you, I feel such a fool."

"Oh, don't feel like that. We quite often get calls about them. I would rather you call the police if you think something has happened. I was only just about to make a cup of tea, so no problems."

Treavey hoped she would take him up on the hint.

"Oh, well I can let you get back to it then officer, thank you so much."

He left the house without having had a cup of tea and returned to his car chuckling to himself. He must be losing his touch. He turned the ignition and made his way out of the driveway.

"Golf 31," Came to the rather low-key sounding call. Treavey wasn't going to get too excited about this one.

There was no urgent tone in the voice. Treavey answered the radio and awaited the job details.

"Golf 31, if you could attend the fields in and around Zealah, there's an anonymous call that there are some gunshots up there. They suspect poachers. We can't give you any further details I'm afraid as the caller left no details."

Treavey already knew this was a waste of his time although he wasn't doing very much. This was a common call from members of the public not used to rural life and yet no one wanted to ignore the call, in case it was the one occasion when something sinister was happening, and the police hadn't bothered to turn up. The area was massive too, and he was not going to start wandering into dark fields on his own in case he was mistaken for a rather large rabbit. He would do a drive though in a moment, but for now, he wanted to check something else out now he was at this end of town.

He decided to turn right towards the airfield. He fancied a drive to clear his head over the events which had happened in the last few days, or months even. Being stationed in Perran had not been the quiet posting he had been expecting. It was quite a pleasant evening so he decided to drive south along the coast for a bit which would kill a bit of time too. These night shifts could be quite long if there weren't many jobs, and you did not plan your night out.

The panda car pottered along the country lanes momentarily stopping where there was any sort of view to enjoy. It should be too early to get a tired pang, but he was already, and he was concerned about how he would make it through the night without desperately needing to have a power nap. He hadn't slept much the previous couple of days mainly because of the excitement from the events which had happened, so he was struggling to stay alert. Only rarely would he try to find a spot he could tuck the panda car in to get a few z's in. It always made him feel so much worse anyway, especially if he was thrown out of his slumber with the radio calling him to go to a job. Far better to try to stimulate himself and keep himself alert. But the night was quiet. The bad guys had been caught, and nothing was moving.

He pulled the car over near the top of the cliffs just to the south of the runway. That infamous airfield used to be a Spitfire Airfield during the second world war. Treavey stepped out of the car and gazed across the airfield and out to sea to fill his lungs with cool fresh air. He imagined the ghosts of the past coming into land with bullet hole-ridden aircraft. Those young men who taxied onto that very same runway powered up and whose wheels lifted from this Cornish land, but never to return. Gone forever. He pondered how each one of them was probably convinced they would come back, which was probably the only reason they took off in the first place. How they must have thought in the back of their minds about their lost colleagues they had been losing at alarming rates, and that one day it would indeed be themselves.

Treavey felt the hairs prick up on his forearms. It felt creepy now in the darkness, with only the moonlight to light up the hedges and the runway. It was eerie to see this industrial slab with outbuildings leading off into nothingness; nothing but the sea and the skies beyond. The stories those ghosts could tell.

A set of headlights came into view. Treavey lifted himself on his tiptoes to take a better look over the hedge. Yes, definitely headlights and they were coming into the airfield. "How strange," Treavey thought to himself. He continued to watch, and the lights came to a stop. "Poachers? Maybe, but only for rabbits, surely." He continued to watch them, and the lights switched off. Silence and darkness again. "How very strange" he muttered to himself under his breath. Suddenly he was wide awake. What he was seeing was very out of character for this place at this time of night. He looked at his watch.

"3.00 am, what on earth are they doing at 3.00 am? A courting couple maybe?"

The silence broken by nothing but the occasional long grasses moving in the breeze was disturbed further by a distant hum. It was not clear where it was coming from. It sounded like a lawnmower, or maybe a motorbike.

The throbbing of the rhythmic engine became more noticeable and Treavey soon realised, "It's a plane. A light aircraft. What the hell is that doing coming here again?"

He ensured his lights on his panda were switched off and stood on the sill of the car, using it as a step to reach higher to get a better view over the hedge. He could now judge the direction it was coming from. It was really low and not deviating from its heading, from the west, and directly towards the runway. Treavey thought about coming in on the radio but stopped himself. Maybe he was getting too jumpy because of all the excitement over the past 24 hours. It could be a wealthy plane owner landing. Maybe they've got a private hanger there having flown back from the Channel Islands.

The plane was in full view, reducing its height, shining its dim white front light onto the runway as it approached. It reduced speed and height and at the last moment opened up the throttle a little before touching down and rolling along the runway. He could smell the fumes from its exhausts as it taxied off the main runway, and back on itself coming to a stop. "It must be getting ready to take off again," Treavey thought.

He noticed the small car was heading towards the plane at speed turning in a horseshoe around the aircraft and coming to an abrupt halt. One person got out of the car and opened the boot of the car. One other person exited the plane, jumping down onto the runway, before pulling a large heavy item off the plane and finding some difficulty in walking it over to the car. The car occupant was helping with the lifting of another large object from the plane. They looked to be in a rush, and it was now

266

looking incredibly suspicious. Just as one of the people returned to the plane, Treavey heard it rev and begin to move forward.

He had seen enough and was jumping into his car and driving as fast as he could towards the exit of the airfield to cut the car off from leaving. By the time he got to it, the car was darting out of the airfield and into the darkness of the lanes in front. Treavey was after it like a fox after the scent of a rabbit. There was one thing he knew, and that was, there was no way he could afford to let this car disappear now.

He planted the accelerator and used the experiences he'd gained in driving these lanes in the best way he could to keep up. He closed in on it as it darted from one side to another. Treavey looked in astonishment as he recognised the car. "It was Bradford's car. It was only the bloody red XR2." He was confused for a moment. "Surely it can't be, have they got bail? Did no one tell us? Is the registration number correct?"

Treavey teased it a bit, letting it pull ahead a little to encourage it before dashing the driver's hope again by pulling right up to the rear end of it once more to bring their morale right down. If they met any traffic in these lanes, it was game over. At least it confirmed his suspicions, the car wouldn't have made off from him like this if the driver had been innocent. It was time to call this in and to find out what the hell was going on. "Why was this car not parked outside Bradford's house down the lane and how come they got hold of the ignition key? They must have got bail and had a spare key."

The car doubled back on itself, making its way back out from the direction of Perran, and headed south, past the airfield location once more and repeatedly turning downside lanes trying to shake him off the pursuit, but not having much luck with it. The driver looked as though they were getting more confident now, realising there wasn't help anywhere near for Treavey. Their driving was

267

improving and Treavey was having difficulty keeping up with such a powerful small car, compared to his panda car.

"Victor from Golf 31," Treavey shouted down the radio of his Ford Escort panda Car handset.

A soft calming voice replied, "Go ahead Golf 31"

"I'm pursuing a Ford XR2, registration is Echo seven three two Yankee Alfa Oscar, I'm currently…"

Treavey suddenly realised he had no idea where he was. The country lane he was whipping along was so narrow with passing areas only and yes, he knew the XR2 driver would be able to see oncoming headlights, but he was still driving into the unknown to a certain extent. The only variation to the road was the occasional grass growing in the centre, protected from passing tractor tyres. These roads were certainly rural.

"…I'm not sure exactly where I am," continued Treavey hesitantly, "I've come from Perranporth town centre and I'm heading up towards St Agnes. Towards the A30 I think."

"Roger," the reply came, "We'll get some more units towards you."

"Is Oscar 99 available, Victor?" Treavey requested, hoping the police helicopter could pinpoint his position and be able to talk in other units, and only if Treavey could keep up with this more powerful car, of course.

"Yes, Golf 31, requesting now, but will be some time, coming from Exeter."

The XR2 flicked to the left without warning. Treavey was twenty metres behind it, so reacted by dabbing his brakes, then stamping on them when he saw it drive up the Cornish hedge, and the back end kick out but there was no room to spin so the little red car bounced its rear end of the opposite hedge rebounding again where the metal box started to disappear in a cloud of earth and grass from the hedge. The whirling spinning beast was now vertical, pirouetting like a drunken ballerina, the

268

lights flashing through the earth cloud as if it were a lighthouse searching through a thick fog.

Treavey managed to skid the car to a halt. He felt stunned as he watched the dust begin to settle in front of him. A part of the exhaust lay on the road immediately in front of him. He surveyed the scene through his headlights and after what seemed like an eternity, reached for his door handle, and opened it slowly. He grabbed his heavy Maglite torch purposefully, wedged between the passenger seat and the centre console, and pulled himself out of the car. He paused and listened in the silence, the dust in the light cast from his headlights thinning quickly and he could see the skeleton of what was a Ford XR2 car on its roof. It had come down hard and had partially collapsed at the front leaving shattered glass glistening in the headlights scattered across the road.

He briskly walked forward to assess the injuries of those inside, or indeed, if there was any life at all. He noticed a sweet smell. He knew what it was as he had smelt it several times before at fatal road traffic accidents. Differential oil was very distinctive in its sweetness and came from the axle of the car. He realised if he could smell it, it had been a massive impact and had never filled his nostrils in the past without it signifying death.

He walked down the passenger side of the car, and knelt beside the front window, scooping some broken glass aside in the middle of the road. He shined his torch in through the shattered and deformed window in front of him. There was a haze of dust still circulating and contents of the car were now littering the roof lining. His torchlight searched through the deformed structure and settled on the face of a body.

In amongst the body, was a large number of packages. It looked like drugs, but it was hard to confirm, but it really could not be anything else. It looked a whitish brown, so probably heroin. There was a lot of it, and he could see some had ruptured so Treavey did not want to go climbing in there.

The body shuffled slowly, and a weak groaning could be heard. Treavey could see there was no way he could free them as the car was so twisted but fortunately it did not look as though it was on fire, for now at least.

He got on to the radio, "Victor, urgent, I need fire and ambulance here. The car has crashed, and the single occupant is injured. I need urgent assistance."

A voice came from the car, "Treavey... is that you?"

Treavey froze. He realised immediately who it was.

"Fuck, Micky, what the fuck, Micky? What are you doing here?"

"I thought you were attending some anonymous poachers far away from here Treavey."

"That was you, was it? You wanted me out of here. Sorry to disappoint you, Micky."

"Well, that's me done. If I get out of this, they will get me anyway. I owe so much cash I had to do something."

He paused to deal with the pain which had just shot through his body, and continued, "It all ran away really. It was nearly so good too." He laughed to himself, but

Treavey could see he was in severe pain. "Don't worry, I have help coming, they'll get you out of there mate. You'll be safe soon."

Treavey could see blood flowing steadily from under Micky's body and begin to pool on the roof lining. It was flowing quite fast, was sticky and thick, and he knew Micky was in trouble. He couldn't get in there with him to stem the blood, even with the bandages he had in his first aid kit, there was simply no point in grabbing it out of the car.

"I feel a bit dizzy, old boy," he said more quietly. "Get hold of Mary, Treavey, tell her she doesn't owe a penny. Tell her the debt died with me. They don't even know about her. I set her up. I needed to make the losses up."

"What do you mean Micky?" Treavey asked with some urgency in his voice.

He knew this was important information from a dying man. He did not want to lose Micky without some more answers. He now knew he was a drug dealer, someone who had played him, played them all and he'd fallen for it. He needed information now.

"How come you are driving this car, Micky?" There was another pause before he answered.

"The plane. It would not have stopped unless the pilot saw this car. They were expecting the Bradfords to deliver to. I had to make sure they were out of the way, you see, the Bradfords didn't know I was involved, and they were becoming a liability. They had already paid me for the seized drugs anyway. They thought they were dealing with Stewart and then Mary when Stewart killed himself. They thought the Londoners were the muscle behind them, but it was me. The consignment this evening was going to balance the books, for the lost drugs in the plane and the yacht that got wrecked."

"That plane that crashed, were there drugs in it?" Treavey quickly asked as he could not quite believe what he was hearing.

He laughed, "No, well there had been, but the idiots threw it out over the airfield, or it must have ended up in the sea in that storm. So, a whole consignment went missing and had to be paid for."

"But the dog signalled drugs were in the wreckage." Treavey pressed,

"It had been moments before. They'd got rid of it mate, those two corpses in the wreckage."

Treavey was trying to process all the information. "I'm not your mate, Micky, you've double-crossed me. You have destroyed people's lives and you lived a total lie as a police officer. You are going to jail you know, don't you?"

There was a delay. Treavey thought he had slipped away, but then, "I don't think I'll make it to jail."

271

Treavey was thinking just that but tried to keep him awake. "What does Mary have to do with it?"

"Tell her, her debts gone. No one is coming after her. That's all she needs to know, that's all you need to know."

Treavey could see the blood pooling even more now. There was no chance he was going to survive even if the emergency services could cut him free. Treavey could not even hear their sirens yet.

Treavey stood up to stretch his cramped legs and could hear the faint sounds of sirens in the distance. They would not be long now. He had also called for a supervisor who was coming from Truro, CID needed to attend, and eventually the police complaints, because of the involvement of the drugs. This was massive. Treavey's head was swirling, it felt so confusing he did not know what to do first. He knew he urgently needed to go to Mary, however.

An ambulance and fire engine arrived on the scene and the crews from both were busy doing what they needed to do. Treavey was surprised how little he cared for Micky now. He was dying amongst the heroin he had peddled with the Bradfords, to pass on to naive, stupid people who were bored or feeling down. He had killed many people and destroyed many others in what he had done. He took one more look at him. There was no movement from his body, and the blood had started to form a skin in the pool.

He waited a little longer looking for any sign of life. The paramedics arrived and were in as far as they could but were equally cautious of the heroin in the car as Treavey had been. They just had to wait for the car to be cut open by the firefighters who wore face masks to avoid inhalation of the drugs. Stepping back and gazing at the scene, he knew the end had come. Micky was dead and it was probably for the best.

He knew he should stay at the scene, but he remembered how insistent Micky had been that he should go to Mary and tell her what he had said, so he asked one of the firemen to move the truck to the side a little, telling him he was going to shut the road off the further back. He reversed down the lane into a gateway which was when he saw the traffic car turning up across his bow. It stopped in front of him, and he could see it had a loan driver in it, and the driver's door opened. Treavey could not see who it was until he stood up and faced him.

"Shit," he thought. It was the same sergeant he'd met at the fatal in Perranporth. Sgt Olly Tayler.

He slowly walked over to Treavey's driver-side window and bent down to speak to him. Treavey opened the window and Sgt Tayler spoke in a very controlled but stern manner.

"And where do you think you are going?"

Treavey didn't know where to start, but he knew he had to convince the sergeant to get out of his way and it was going to be difficult.

"Sergeant, it's me, I was with you in Perran earlier in the summer..."

"I know who you are, Treavey, my question is, however, where exactly do you think you are going? Shouldn't you have learned enough to know you should stay on the scene if you have been in a police accident where someone has been injured? Are you driving my evidence away now, young man?"

"He's not injured, sergeant" Treavey responded trying to minimise the seriousness of the situation before realising he had just made it worse.

"That's good then, but why did you call an ambulance?" Sgt Tayler queried.

"When I say there is no one injured, I mean they've... died already."

Treavey had finished his sentence very hesitantly, so it could almost not be heard.

Sgt Tayler was getting redder by the second and Treavey could see he was not going to give an inch on letting him go so he decided he just had to tell him what he knew.

He breathed in deeply and then... "Sergeant, you are just going to have to believe me, the driver is Micky, a copper, it seems he's been supplying drugs to the area completely flooding it causing all the deaths around here. He lost a couple of consignments recently, which meant he had to make this one work as he owed so much money to the London gang. Well, I killed him... wait, I mean I pursued him after the pickup, and he crashed and... well I would be surprised if he's alive still, anyway he's given me some vital information which I need to deal with now as someone else is in trouble, and they need my help, right now. I mean, right now. I've got a bad feeling."

The sergeant stared at him through the window. He attempted to speak but hesitated. He looked like he was going to say something but stopped to think again as he could sense Treavey had something important to do first.

Sergeant Tayler straightened himself up and said, "Right, if anyone asks, you were gone before I got here, is that understood?"

Within a minute Treavey was heading for Perranporth and towards Mary's flat. He knew he had gambled with what he'd told the sergeant and maybe this would ruin any future attachment with Traffic forever. What if this was all a pile of rubbish Micky had given him. He could not be trusted and would say anything to improve his cause, but it felt like Micky had given a dying confession. It sounded like he did not expect to survive and was telling him everything.

He pulled up at the flat he felt he knew quite well by now. He walked up to the door and banged on it with his fist. He pressed the doorbell but there was no response. He thought perhaps she was asleep. He continued for a bit longer, listening for any forms of life within. He ran over what Micky had said to him in his mind. It did not make sense, but why would he say to get to Mary in his dying last words?

He did not remember coming to a conscious decision, but he found himself kicking the flimsy door in, and it bounced off the wall causing the glass panel to crack down the middle and slip down onto the floor smashing into large shards and making a horrendous noise which set a neighbour's dog barking. He pressed the light switch which flooded the stairway with light, and made his way up, half expecting Mary to appear at the top looking sleepy and confused, but no one appeared.

"Maybe she's not even here?" he thought as he walked into the lounge but found nobody there, so he quickly returned to the room where he had found her dead boyfriend those few weeks before.

As he opened the door and reached around for the light, he saw a mound under the filthy duvet exactly where her boyfriend had died, and on the very same side, he had been. With seeing some drugs paraphernalia on the side cabinet as had been there on the previous occasion, Treavey knew exactly what she had done so rushed over to pull the duvet back and revealed the pale face of Mary staring directly at him. She looked very dead, and he felt it was probably too late to help her, but he felt sure there was a flicker of movement in her eyes. He was on the radio in a flash; "Victor, from Golf 31, I need an ambulance here immediately; I've got an overdose and I don't think we have very long."

He spurted out the address to the controller who sounded rather confused.

"Okay Victor 31, you need to return to the police accident as this has been confirmed as fatal, so the sergeant wants you there immediately."

Treavey had no time for the procedure right now; "Victor, this is a life-or-death situation here, I need that ambulance here immediately if there is nothing, they can do for... for the driver of that car. I had to come down here to save a life. I will update you fully later, but for now, just bloody well do what I ask, please."

The comms operator immediately got on with the task she needed to do, and a couple of minutes later, confirmed an ambulance was on its way. Treavey monitored Mary whilst waiting for the ambulance. He didn't know whether she was breathing enough to sustain her life and considered mouth to mouth. As much as he liked Mary, he knew this was not the time to risk it with the lifestyle she had led.

Ten minutes later and he saw the same crew had turned up who had been at the collision. "Hey, thanks for coming guys, I take it there was no chance for the other driver?"

The female ambulance technician led her male colleague up the stairs. "No, I'm afraid not," she replied taking deep breaths as she carried her heavy medical bag up the stairs, "...we just couldn't get to him and he had no vital signs anyway."

"In here," Treavey said with some urgency. Both paramedics hurried their pace and pushed their way into the bedroom. There was some shuffling through the bag and the male technician hurriedly handed over a vial to his colleague.

"What's that?" Treavey enquired, trying not to interfere but desperately wishing to know if Mary was going to survive.

She took the vial off her colleague and filled a syringe.

"This..." she tapped the syringe ensuring the bubbles were pushed out of the needle, "...this is Naloxone. It will hopefully bring her around. She may be extremely angry having wasted her hit, she had been trying to have, or she could be absolutely fine. Time will tell."

"How long will it be before we know?"

"Oh, I've got a vein, so a couple of minutes. About five if I had had to put it in the muscle, but we've been lucky."

Three minutes went by, and she injected slightly more Naloxone into Mary, and some more a little later still.

"Why don't you put more in earlier?" Treavey asked her, now sounding rather frustrated.

She glanced over at him and did not look best pleased.

"Slowly does it, bit by bit. She has obviously taken a whack of the stuff. I'm wondering if this was a suicide..."

She paused and then, "...attempted suicide I should say, there, here she comes, back into the land of the living; Hello Mary!"

Treavey could not believe his eyes. "Christ, she's almost normal."

He watched Mary push herself up to lean back on the headboard, looking confused, and asking some questions, "What the hell... what are you all doing here?"

She paused, not really taking in her surroundings at first, but as if slowly focusing on reality.

She looked at Treavey and said, "No, no, I don't want to be here, I can't be here. Why did you do this?"

Treavey moved closer, squeezing himself around the ambulance woman to get in closer to her.

"Hey Mary, I've just spoken to Micky. He told me to tell you something urgently. He said something like, 'the debt is clear, he takes the debt with him and I can tell you he says he set you up to think it was your debt, but it was his all the time. He's died in a car crash now, but before he died, Mary, he was adamant I tell you; they don't even know about you. Does that make any sense at all?"

Mary was sitting still trying to take things in.

"The London gang said it was Stuart's debt, that's why I think he couldn't take it, and why he killed himself. Why should Micky take that debt off Stuart, and therefore me?"

She looked around her at the bed.

"That's why he killed himself here, because he knew he could never pay it off and they'd come and get him, the Londoners. He had got into selling drugs, you see, but the plane crashed, and the drugs disappeared along with the drugs in the boat, and the debt was his, or that's what the Londoners had told him, and then, when Stuart killed himself, they said it had passed on to me."

Treavey replied, "It seems that Micky had organised that plane shipment, and Stuart was only the middleman, so it was Micky's debt. Thank goodness you survived the jump off the cliff, Mary, and this overdose. It would have been for nothing."

Treavey could see the weight being lifted from Mary's shoulders as she slowly realised that she was free. He reflected on the moment. He and Micky both had known he had to get here as fast as possible, because they knew the pressure would be too much for Mary to take. She had already gone through with jumping off a cliff, and yet Micky wouldn't have stopped her attempting suicide again if he had not been caught by Treavey. What a low life that man had been.

"Yes," she replied, "I miss Stuart, but I can live without him. He only brought me trouble, but the Londoners were coming to get their money from me, or so I thought. They said I had to pay it back one way or another. I couldn't even contemplate that amount of money. So, it was Micky all the time."

Everything fitted into place for Treavey.

"I know what Micky meant by the debt dying with him. He 'is' the Londoners, Mary. You thought Stewart, your boyfriend, was dealing with Londoners, but he was dealing with Micky, but he didn't know it. Micky needed a few people between him and the street dealers to keep his cover. That is why the Bradfords were dealing with you, and not Micky. The clever sod. All was going well until he lost the drugs with the plane crash and then the boat sinking."

Mary was visibly relaxing as the stress fell away. "So, I don't have to pay Stewart's debt now, to anyone?"

Treavey walked towards the bedroom door leaving the ambulance crew to get her ready for the trip to the hospital. He stopped and looked back, watching the scene as Mary was ushered off the bed with a blanket wrapped around her.

"Hey, Mary!" Treavey exclaimed. She looked at him with a smile he had not noticed on her before.

"Hey, Mary. New start hey, new start, you have a clean slate, don't waste it."

Before heading back to the scene to liaise with the Traffic sergeant, he had to do one more thing. He drove his panda car to the quiet and very dark beach car park which he often found himself heading for when he needed some peaceful contemplation. He stepped out of his car, and began walking towards the beach, hearing the giggling memory of Felicity in that yellow bikini, her body looking stunning, her smile, and then feeling her lips on his as she teased him later at the station. He realised he needed to talk to someone. He wanted to get closer to Felicity and he was going to stop messing about. Life was too short. He breathed the mild air deep into his lungs, glancing around him into the darkness.

It was hard to imagine the next land over the ocean would be America, but here he was, standing on the edge of the car park looking out to sea. The tide was out, and he could faintly hear the gentle white noise of the surf in the distance. It felt so calm and peaceful standing there, feeling fortunate that his city colleagues would not ever have the pleasure of doing what he was doing right now. He looked at the white specs of the herring gulls sheltering amongst the cavities in the cliff, tucked in for the night before continuing their rather chaotic lives the following day hunting for unnatural human food sources. The days of their forefathers catching herrings were long gone now. Now, these fine beasts should most probably be named Wimpy Gulls, or Burger Gulls. His thoughts were becoming more random when,

"Hello Treavey, what are you doing here?"

He spun around to see Grace standing there a few metres away. She walked up to him and joined him looking out into the darkness.

"It has been a night Grace, but I reckon the drugs supply has been well and truly stopped now."

"Oh really? Do tell," she inquired with genuine interest, leaning towards him slightly as if to ensure no one could overhear.

"It was Micky, Grace, he was up to his armpits in it, and you were right on so many fronts. I reckon I can get you some money for your information Grace."

"Oh no, I'm not interested in that. What would I do with money, for goodness' sake?"

Treavey continued trying to explain things as quickly as he could.

"Mary is fine too. Oh, there is so much to tell you, it's where to start."

They both stood together gazing into the darkness when a thought came into Treavey's mind.

"The canoe. It didn't turn up when the boat did. He warned the canoe off but why not the boat?"

"That one's easy," Grace said, "He warned whoever was in the canoe off, or it may have even been himself. But the boat, maybe he didn't expect you to paddle out that night and he may have been trying to get it landed further along the coast later on when it wrecked itself."

Treavey nodded in agreement. He turned and slowly walked back towards his car.

"They'll wonder where I've gone. I have a scene and an angry Traffic sergeant to attend. Things are going to be a lot quieter around here with Micky gone, the Bradfords gone, and who knows what Dawson has to do with it all. Not a lot by all accounts. Yes, things are going to get a lot quieter around here now."

Grace turned away and waddled off towards the road which led up to her bench looking over the bay.

"It'll never be quiet around here, Treavey, it'll never be quiet around here."

The End

Printed in Great Britain
by Amazon

14863839R00161